He was a professional therapist—he could handle this

As Dan waited for Kathleen to finish her shower, he tried to ignore how much this seemed like old times. *Waiting heightens the intensity,* she used to say about sex. She would slow down, pull away, make him wait until he was nothing but pounding lust, his focus narrowed to her breasts, her mouth, her moans, her softness, being inside her...all the way.

Relax. Settle down, he coached himself, squeezing his eyes shut tightly. This tour wasn't about their secret past. It was about promoting his book, showing the world that moderation and balance worked.

"Dan!"

He jerked open his eyes and saw Kathleen. Naked. Dripping wet.

Heat and ice washed over him at the sight of her body, just as she had appeared in so many guilty dreams. He turned away quickly, but he'd caught it all...every sexy inch of her. Desire spiked in him, and the only thought running through his head was how much he wanted her.

There was no way he could handle this!

Blaze™

Dear Reader,

Have you ever been so in love you scared yourself? That happened to the people in this book, and the experience sent them careening onto opposite paths—Kathleen to ever more intense sensual experiences and Dan to a life of careful restraint and self-discipline.

The last thing they expected was to meet again and, worse, to feel exactly the same after ten years. They'd grown up, gotten wise, right? Surprise! I love it when love opens up people's possibilities and changes their views of themselves.

Both Dan and Kathleen share a focus on living an aware life. This is something I strive for. In fact, the research for this book helped me live each day more deliberately. Now I try to squeeze the juice out of every berry, or, as Kathleen would say, use the guest towels, the antique teapot and the real silver (okay, so that means regular polishing, but so what?). I hope Dan and Kathleen inspire you to enjoy every moment of *your* life.

Happy reading and my best to you,

Dawn Atkins

P.S. Let me know what you think of the story at dawn@dawnatkins.com. Please stop by my Web site, www.dawnatkins.com.

Books by Dawn Atkins

GOING TO EXTREMES

Dawn Atkins

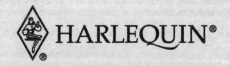

HARLEQUIN®

TORONTO • NEW YORK • LONDON
AMSTERDAM • PARIS • SYDNEY • HAMBURG
STOCKHOLM • ATHENS • TOKYO • MILAN • MADRID
PRAGUE • WARSAW • BUDAPEST • AUCKLAND

To David for helping me remember that a balanced
life is different from a balancing act

ISBN 0-373-79180-1

GOING TO EXTREMES

1

"WHY WOULD I go on a book tour when my book's not even written yet?" Kathleen Valentine asked her agent, JJ Norris, who was puffing away on her usual coffin nails. They were in JJ's Manhattan office surrounded by her curvy wood-and-black-leather furniture, African tribal art, spindly tensor lamps and three walls of shelves jammed floor-to-ceiling with books.

"That's the beauty of it," JJ said, leaning against the sofa arm—that had to be painful. Kathleen sat on the softer middle cushion, though she didn't like leather sofas. She preferred her leather in jackets, bustiers and miniskirts, not furniture, which was supposed to hug and comfort you. Leather was too cool and smooth. *Mental note: Bring brocade pillows for poor JJ's S and M sofa when next in New York.*

"The other publisher wants you because you're famous," JJ continued. "They want you for sparkle, for contrast with their author and because the media love you."

"They want me because misery loves company." Kathleen leaned forward to straighten the blooms she'd brought—cut flowers were her calling card. "Book tours are brutal. Insane pace. Crack-of-dawn talk shows. Toxic airplane food and air. Uncertain mattress quality. Pure torture."

"Torture, Kath?" JJ scraped a fleck of tobacco from her lip with a French-tipped nail and shifted her position—to ease the pain, no doubt—making the leather squeak. Now the *sound* of leather Kathleen loved. It sounded...promising.

"Maybe not torture, but punishment. *Severe* punishment. Speaking of which, I'll bring pillows for this sofa so you won't cripple the other clients you seat here to browbeat."

JJ rolled her eyes. "Please. The cool deal is that because it's Cunningham Publishing's author's launch, they're paying the tab."

"Look, I'll be glad to help the author with tips, even a perfect neck pillow for the plane, but I'm not, *not* going on book tour. Especially not someone else's book tour. That is not the kind of excess I'm known to be queen of."

"It'll be a breeze. Ten days and five cities. You can do it in your sleep."

"I'll have to, since I won't be getting any at night."

JJ ignored the jab. "It's the usual—signings, readings, a couple of college appearances, a media satellite tour or two and some radio and TV talk shows in New York, Chicago, Phoenix and L.A. The extra dollop is a pop-psych jamboree in San Francisco at the end. Talk about a visibility boost. High-end crowd of book buyers. I mean these people have to buy shelves to go with all the books they buy at these conferences."

"It sounds exhausting."

"You need this, hon." JJ tapped Kathleen's knee with a sharp nail to emphasize her point. "The Princess of Pleasure needs this. *Sensual Living III* tanked."

"Don't say *tanked*. It slouched a little is all. There

was that political tell-all out at the same time. And I'm busy on the next one," she said, feigning more confidence than she felt.

"Sorry to be an ice bucket, hon, but how's that going?"

"It's incubating."

JJ rolled her eyes, sucked on the cigarette, then snorted out twin streams of smoke like a cartoon bull.

JJ wasn't the only one blowing smoke. Kathleen's current book wasn't incubating, it was at a dead stop. Temporarily. Which was scary, since her first two books, *Sensual Living* and *Sensual Living: The Daily Pleasures,* had flowed like music. The first had been a how-to, exploring Kathleen's philosophy of sensual awareness, which she called Healthy Hedonism. It gave list after list of ways to enhance appreciation for the gifts of the body.

Her second book contained a workbook and a calendar with practical exercises and monthly to-do lists, along with the most popular section—success stories of converted readers…weary souls reborn to life through Kathleen's ideas.

Sensual Living III, an update of the first book, had felt as flat to Kathleen when she wrote it as its subsequent sales chart. The problem had been her life at the time—so full of speaking engagements, interviews and, yes, book tours, she'd neglected to refresh her own personal well of sensory appreciation. And it had showed.

This fourth book had to reverse the trend of dwindling sales. Tentatively called *Sensual Living: Roots and Rhetoric,* it would explore the underpinnings of her theories. But it had stalled. Kathleen had stalled. Fear jabbed her soul with an insistent finger.

She wasn't used to feeling afraid. Whenever she got scared, she just pushed through, brazened it out. Nothing kept her down for long. Until now. Now she felt...shaky.

An ache swelled behind Kathleen's eyes. She'd slap on a wintergreen eye-pack tonight for sure. Otherwise she'd end up with black sausages under her eyes. Unacceptable. *Buck up, girl. Shine it on, keep moving.*

"The tour will get you back in the groove, warm your backlist and boost your buzz," JJ said, using her silkiest coax. That meant that even her hard-bitten agent was worried.

Kathleen had hired JJ for her instincts—nearly as good as her own—so she knew the woman was dead-on. Which made Kathleen cranky. "So whose book tour are you trying to drag me onto anyway?"

JJ's eyes lit with triumph. "I'll show you his book." She did a suck-whoosh on her cig, put it out against one of the serenity candles, then sprang for her desk.

Kathleen closed her eyes against the travesty of tobacco touching the Peaceful Breeze pillar, which she'd brought on her last visit as the perfect counterbalance to JJ's frenetic style. She sighed. You could lead a harried soul to sensual pleasure, but you couldn't make her drink it in.

Now JJ was mauling one of the trio of book towers that littered her gigantic desk. "I had it right here," she muttered, while the stack wobbled...leaned...tilted... At the last instant, JJ righted it and started on another. She had uncanny instincts.

JJ's secretary, Moira, ensconced in an alcove across the open space of the office, waved away JJ's smoke with an exaggerated gesture. Years before the smoke-free workplace act was passed, JJ had declared her office no-smoking, even though she was the only one with a habit and now she risked a $200 fine for breaking the law. Maybe more, since Kathleen thought she'd gotten caught once already.

"You have to stop smoking," Kathleen said. "If not for Moira or your flash-fried lungs, for your poor skin. You want to turn into Leather Face? I've got the name of a hypnotist who's magic with smokers." She reached into the roomy satchel she used as a purse for her contact notebook, fat with business cards, price lists and scribbled tips on personal care, health and entertainment.

"Ah-ha!" JJ said, whipping a book from the bottom of a stack like a magician yanking a tablecloth from under plates. She returned to Kathleen and thrust the book at her. On a teal background the title appeared in huge gold letters: *The Magic of Moderation,* by—

Oh, God, no. "Dr. Daniel McAlister?" Kathleen said, raising shocked eyes to JJ.

"You know him?"

Know him? Ten years ago she'd been madly in love with him. But she wasn't about to tell JJ that. "I've, um, heard of him." To buy herself some calming heartbeats, she busied herself fishing the cigarette butt out of the melted candle wax. "This is unsavory, JJ." She held up the wax-coated butt, then placed it on a coaster.

JJ shrugged off her concern, but at least she'd forgotten Kathleen's reaction. "They call him Dr. Moderate and he's very hot right now."

He'd been hot back then, too, but not the way JJ meant. Back in college she'd been Kathleen Dubinofsky, journalism major, not Kathleen Valentine, celebrated arbiter of taste, variously known as the Princess of Pleasure, the Queen of Excess and the Pied Piper of Hedonism. So many lovely names, so little time to prove them all true.

How could it be Dan? Of all the people in the world. The man who'd broken her heart and temporarily torpedoed her confidence. Her lungs squeezed so she couldn't take in a full load of air.

"He's a therapist specializing in behavioral issues," JJ went on. "And he stands for everything you oppose— self-discipline, restraint, the absolute flatline of experience." She handed Kathleen the book.

It didn't surprise her that Dan had retreated into restraint. At times, she'd called him Ice Man—partly because of his icy blue eyes, but also for his too-cool-for-school affect. Her intensity had shaken him up.

Now he was Dr. Moderate? He'd been studying clinical psychology when they'd met as seniors and now he was a Ph.D. She'd changed her name and he'd earned a doctorate. Figured.

Had he suffered over the breakup? Doubtful. He'd dumped her, after all. He'd probably shrugged her off like an ill-fitting jacket and moved on.

"There was a puff piece about him in *Publisher's Weekly,* I think," JJ said, lighting another cigarette. "Hang on." She bounced up and over to Moira's desk. "Have you seen the last *PW?*"

"In the pile." Moira faked a cough. "And that's the fourth cig in twenty minutes. Watch out. I'll call an inspector in here."

"We're having a crisis."

No kidding, Kathleen thought.

JJ launched a search for the magazine, leaving Kathleen with Dan, who stared up at her from his photo, wearing an outdated turtleneck, his face hardly marred by the coffee ring JJ had branded him with.

There was the same intellectual's high forehead, the same crackling blue eyes. Chilly and serene as an arctic lake. But no glasses now. Nothing to lessen the impact of those icy blues. How she'd loved to tug off his glasses and kiss away the pink dents they'd made on his straight, straight nose. Those tender marks made him seem more human somehow, more open to her.

His brows were fierce and his jaw strong, but his lips were soft and full. The contrast of severe features and sensual lips had made her system hum. Especially when he talked. The luxurious excess of his lips contradicted his spare words—the sexy little secret that only she knew.

He'd been irresistible to her. Uncovering his wild side had thrilled her. She got a little quiver remembering that she'd reached him, gotten through, made the Ice Man tremble with desire.

"Dr. McAlister lives in Vermont," she read below his photo, "where he maintains a private psychology practice and enjoys quiet contemplation, peaceful sails and moderation in all things."

No wife. No kids. Not even a dog? Is that what moderation did for you? He didn't look lonely. He wore the wry expression she'd disliked—as if he found the world amusing, but not quite worthy of his involvement.

She'd conquered that look for a while. *Dig in to life, wallow in the lovely mess.* That had been her message to him.

And he'd gone along with her. It had been a rush like

the best drugs were supposed to deliver. Until he'd lost his nerve and left, conking her over the head with her own vulnerability.

She should have known better. Her mother's mantra had always been to count on herself, to be her own best friend, not to expect anyone else to make her happy. She'd operated that way until Dan. And after him, too. Somehow, he'd swooped in under her radar—so steady, so stable, so rock solid that she went for it, fell in love. Counted on him. On them.

Just thinking about it brought back the empty feeling that had scared her so much—the hollow numbness that was way too much like how she'd felt after the childhood accident. It was as if someone had shut off the lights inside. Pure dark. Echoing and empty.

Way too scary.

And now JJ was asking her to spend ten days with the man who'd pushed her into that humiliating crash-and-burn? No way. Kathleen had to get out of the tour. She'd built a wall around those memories and had no interest in putting in a window.

"Here it is!" JJ waved a magazine in the air.

"Watch it!" Moira shoved a foam cup under the ash flaking from JJ's swooping cigarette.

JJ madly flipped pages, found what she wanted and marched it over to Kathleen. Beside another photo of Dan looking smug was a short article Kathleen pretended to read, then handed back with a dismissive sound, her fingers trembling only a little. "A tour with this guy would be a waste of my time. He's obviously a wrongheaded jerk." She kept her voice steady, but her knees quivered, so she smashed them together, determined not to give herself away to JJ.

"All the better to take him down a notch. Or is that a peg?"

"Notch, peg or even iota, no thanks."

"He's cute for a wrongheaded jerk, though," JJ mused, studying the face Kathleen couldn't forget. "I sure wouldn't kick him off my tatami mat, or whatever the hell he sleeps on—a bed of nails?"

"Not my type."

JJ considered his picture. "I bet he seethes with inner heat."

"I doubt it. Can't you see? He's so cut off from his emotions he wouldn't know lust if it gave him a lap dance."

"You have quite the opinion there." JJ gave her a speculative look and tapped a nail on her bottom lip.

Kathleen had overstated the case. "The point is that I'm not interested in him—as a man or as a mate on the Good Ship Book Tour."

JJ and her instincts honed in on Kathleen's face.

To avoid detection, she pretended to sniff the flowers, inhaling the cool green of the carnations, the thick syrup of the sweet peas, the dense musk of the roses. Flowers packed a lovely sensory wallop.

"What's up?" JJ said. "Do you see him as a threat?"

"How could I? He's completely wrong."

"So, show him the error of his ways. It'll be an experience. Experience is your whole modus operandi."

"Now you're giving me Latin?" she said, though JJ was right about her focus on experience. Her column in *PulsePoint* magazine, which had launched her career, had been called "Experience It!"

In it, she shared her views and adventures with all things sensual—food, music, art, fashion, recreation and sex. If it felt good, she'd done it…and written about it in dripping detail.

In love with the column, JJ had sought her out as a client. With JJ's bulldog support Kathleen had zoomed to the top of the bestseller lists with her first book. Also the second. The third had wilted. And the fourth, unwritten, was in limbo. Was she bored? Burned out? Had she exhausted her topic? Her life? She refused to believe that.

"The point is that he's a streaming comet, book-wise, Kath. Hook your cart to his tail and tag along for the sky ride."

"Does he know about this?" Kathleen said, seizing on the hope that Dan would nix the plan from his end. She'd been the dumpee, so he'd be more embarrassed than freaked about seeing her again. He hated interpersonal tension, though, so he would surely dread the reunion. "I can't imagine he'd want me to steal his thunder."

"His agent said he was hesitant at first, but, being new, he didn't understand how important a tour is in terms of publisher support."

Hesitant, huh? She wished she'd seen his face when he heard the news. Even the Ice Man must have gasped. He obviously hadn't revealed their past or JJ would have said something. What would people think if they knew Dr. Moderate had had an earth-scorching affair with the Queen of Excess?

For that matter, what would Dan have to say for himself after all these years? She was curious, now that she thought about it.

Then she caught herself. This was Dan. She didn't want to face him again. "I can't do it, JJ. Dr. McAlister and I are anathema to each other."

"Anathema? You mean where Disneyland is? I can't believe you'd make fun of my Latin, little miss word-a-day. Your anathema-ism is the very reason they want you. Reporters love conflict. Two appealing experts at polar extremes? What could be more delicious?"

"A million things. Can't happen. No way."

But JJ didn't flinch, didn't even shake the lengthy ash from her cigarette, and her eyes said, *Yes, way.* "After the lag, this is a gift, Kath. You need this."

"What I need is a writing retreat. No phone, no Internet. Just a laptop and the beach house at Gualala." But the idea gave her a desolate feeling, as if her writer's heart had been swept as clear of ideas as a beach at low tide.

"You've been there, done that and come up with bupkis."

"So, I need a little more time," she bluffed.

"No point arguing." JJ finally tapped the snake of ash into her palm and leveled Kathleen a look. "It's happening."

"It is?"

"It is." JJ sucked in smoke, blew it out. That meant Herman Maxwell, her publisher, had spoken.

She swallowed hard. "I'm sunk?"

"Sinking. But we'll turn this around." JJ picked up her gold cigarette case, opened it and tilted it at Kathleen, as if for sustenance.

Kathleen waved it away. Things were really bad if JJ was offering her a smoke—like a prisoner before a firing squad. Which didn't feel that far wrong.

"You need to shake things up, Kathleen. This will do that."

Oh, yes. Dan McAlister could shake her up, all right. She took a deep breath, gathering her strength, her determination, her sense of humor. If she had to do this tour, and it looked as though she did, then she'd make it work. Meet Dan head-on and not miss a step.

That would not be easy, since she was no poker player when it came to emotions, but she'd manage. She had too much pride to do otherwise.

At least she knew she wouldn't be attracted to him. She'd learned her lesson. Repressed guys were way too much work when there were so many available sensualists in the world. She had a lovely romantic life. Well, except for the odd emptiness that had crept into her lately. But she wouldn't think about that now.

She had enough on her mind, what with her blocked writing, her possibly sinking career and being forced to spend ten days in close quarters with the man who'd delivered her one and only broken heart.

Dr. Anathema himself.

2

His AGENT had declared it a coup, but Dan McAlister wasn't happy about this book tour with Kathleen Dubinofsky. Make that *Valentine*. She'd changed her name. Probably for her career, but maybe just for fun, knowing Kathleen. Kathleen had fun built into her soul. And whimsy. For Kathleen, anything worth doing was worth overdoing.

But *Valentine?* That was kind of silly. When he'd known her, she'd wrung every ounce of delight out of every moment, but she'd never been silly.

He checked out the view from the window of his New York hotel room. This place, world-famous for its luxury, had no doubt been selected with Kathleen in mind, since she'd built a career out of her passion for extravagance. Smart of her, really, to turn her inclinations into a source of income. He'd always admired her savvy, her directness, her purposefulness, even when she was making him nuts.

And now she was famous enough that his publisher wanted her on his book tour.

He became aware that his heart was racing again. Every time he thought about her, his system flooded with adrenaline. Being with Kathleen had brought him face-to-face with a side of his character he disliked—

his wild side—and which he'd successfully wrestled to the ground. Just thinking her name brought it all back.

They were to meet their agents and his publisher's publicist for dinner in two hours, but he wanted to speak to her privately first, confirm what they'd agreed upon via an e-mail—that they'd keep their past a secret.

She'd sent a quick reply. "The irony of our relationship would certainly detract from our credibility." The oddly dispassionate words made him wonder if she'd changed from when he knew her. She'd always been fiery and outspoken. The *irony* of their relationship? Even he, whom she'd called Ice Man, wouldn't use that word to describe their affair. Wrenching and life-altering maybe, but never ironic.

He hadn't been crazy about the book tour even before he'd heard Kathleen would be with him—too much fuss and hassle—but his agent insisted it would build "buzz," whatever that was. So, he'd agreed. If he gained more readers, reached more people with the ideas that had saved him and helped so many of his clients, then it was worth every bit of awkward embarrassment.

In his practice, he specialized in overcoming self-defeating patterns, and he found it extremely rewarding. He'd developed checklists that allowed his clients to analyze the sources of immoderation in their lives, along with willpower boosters and self-control builders—tools with which to reshape their behavior in more positive directions.

Grateful clients had urged him to write a book, and over the past two years he'd done so. He'd been honored when first an agent, then a top publisher had seen the value of his work. Publishing *The Magic of Moderation* was an opportunity to reach more people with his ideas. Fame made him uncomfortable, but it was a means to an important end.

Then he'd learned about Kathleen and the world had shuddered to a stop for a while. He knew about her work, had even bought her first book, but seeing her was the last thing he'd expected. Or wanted.

The e-mail exchange had been too impersonal and brief. He had to see her, get the first meeting over without witnesses. They were adults, of course, and college was a decade ago, but their relationship had reverberated through his life and he wasn't sure how normally he could act around her.

Again his heart sped up and his breathing went shallow. *Get a grip.* There was no reason to expect the worst. In fact, the trip might be healing for them both. He could apologize for his immature behavior, how out of control he'd been and the abrupt way he'd broken it off. They could acknowledge the power of what they'd shared, experience closure and, perhaps, end up friends.

He straightened his tie, ran his fingers through his hair—God, he was primping—and stepped out into the hall.

Her room—a named suite, actually—was unnervingly next door. He saw that a waiter was attempting to drag a cart with an ice bucket of champagne into the room. Champagne had been her favorite liquor, he recalled—not easy to afford on a student budget, but she'd managed. *Some things are worth the sacrifice,* she'd say. He smiled at the memory. To this day, the bubbly liquid made him think of her.

These days, he rarely drank, and never champagne, which gave him an instant headache. Or it had since Kathleen—a psychosomatic reaction no doubt.

Dan held the door for the waiter, stepped in after him and found himself in a large sitting room, dotted with huge arrangements of exotic flowers. He could hear water running. Kathleen was in the shower. She loved water.

"It's Dan," he called out, not wanting to startle her.

"Be right out," she called back, not sounding surprised. Maybe she'd expected him to drop in.

The waiter handed him the bill, which he signed, distracted by the complex scents that filled the room—creams, perfumes, powders, candles and mists. So Kathleen. He searched for her smell underneath all the commercial fragrances. He'd liked that scent best.

The waiter departed and he waited for Kathleen by the champagne. Condensation dribbled down the silver bucket like the sweat sliding down his body inside his shirt.

This was a familiar situation. In the old days, he'd spent lots of time waiting for Kathleen.

Waiting heightens the intensity, she used to say about sex. All true, of course. She would slow down, pull away, make him wait until he was nothing but pounding lust, his focus narrowed to her breasts, her mouth, her moans, her softness, being inside her…all the way. Around her, he was as shaky and enthralled as a kid on his first time.

An erection threatened. Over a memory, for God's sake! *Relax. Settle down,* he coached himself, squeezing his eyes tight. *Focus on what matters.*

Which was his book—and figuring out how he and Kathleen would approach this tour. He was a professional therapist, dammit, but he felt like Tom Hanks in *Big*—a thirteen-year-old abruptly swimming in an adult's baggy suit and grown-up life.

"Dan!"

He jerked open his eyes and saw Kathleen—naked, dripping and shocked. Embarrassment shot across her face, but she banished that with a sharp smile. She'd always pushed through awkward moments with bravado. She gave a light laugh that squeaked at the end, betraying her distress.

Heat and ice washed through him at the sight of her body, just as she'd appeared in so many guilty dreams. He turned away quickly, but he'd caught it all—her round, high breasts, pink nipples and that triangle of hair, golden against her pale skin. At least his mortification had iced down his erection. With his back turned, he explained himself. "I came in with the waiter. I called, but you must not have heard me. I'll let you get dressed." He started for the door.

"Don't go. It's fine." She had the same husky voice— a whiskey voice in the vernacular of detective novels— and it warmed him like a quick shot. "I thought you were my agent JJ. I just popped out for my robe."

He stayed with his back to her while a suitcase zipper scraped, a clasp rattled and fabric rustled.

"There. All covered, Dan," she said, sounding amused.

He turned and found her wrapped in a black silk robe that clung to her breasts and ended high on her thighs. She was a voluptuous woman with a figure that rivaled Marilyn Monroe's, except she was taller. She was a presence, a gathering of female energy that drew male eyes wherever she went.

He had the familiar impulse to touch—her skin, her silk-covered breasts, her shiny golden hair, loosely swept up on her head. Completely insane, of course. But the way he felt about Kathleen had never made much sense.

"I just wanted to touch…base…before we officially got together." He felt himself redden.

"Good idea," she said, her eyes restless on his face, then gone. That wasn't like her. She'd always contemplated him carefully, soaking up every detail, every reaction.

He held out his hand to shake—as stupid as that seemed.

"Oh, please." She lunged forward and threw her arms around him. But she held her body away from his and kissed the air beside his cheek—a gesture for show.

He was relieved. And stupidly disappointed.

She moved to a sofa thick with overstuffed pillows and patted a spot beside her. "Let's talk. We've got time before JJ gets here. She's always late. Just like me." She laughed nervously again, which made him want to say something reassuring.

"You look the same. Beautiful as ever."

"You look good, too. Losing the glasses was a good decision."

"Thanks. They got in my way." He was preoccupied with trying not to look at the curve of one breast visible through a gap in her robe. She had great breasts. A firm handful with nipples that had tightened into plump knots whenever he touched them. She'd loved him to spend time there. He'd loved it, too. What was not to love?

He moved his gaze, only to have it sink to the dark space between her legs, where the hem of her robe separated. *Control yourself, man.* "Why don't you get dressed? I can wait."

"No, no. I've got time," she said, "Unless I'm making you uncomfortable…?" She was acting cool, sliding a red-painted nail along the edge of her robe, but the finger trembled and her breath was shaky and she still wouldn't quite meet his gaze.

"If you're fine, I'm fine," he said, determined to manage his reactions. Her toenails matched her fingernails, he noted inanely, watching as she curled her toes around the edge of the table's glass.

"How about some champagne? I was going to drink it with JJ, but she won't mind if we get started. This is a kind of celebration, after all. The first time we've seen each other in, what, ten years?" She jerked the champagne bottle brusquely from the bucket, spilling ice on the floor, betraying her nervousness. This was new, too. Above all else, Kathleen had always been confident.

With her so jittery, he couldn't refuse the drink. "Sure. For old time's sake." He leaned forward to help her hold the bottle that was now shaking in her hands.

"This is so symbolic," she said. "We've taken different paths and now, ten years later, they've converged." She popped the cork and her green eyes jumped at the sound. "Seems like kismet."

He smiled. *Or karma.* A chance to make up for hurting her. He watched her pour the liquid into two tall, elaborate glasses.

"Don't you just love these flutes? Hotels use those terrible saucers that allow the bubbles to zip away. I travel with these." She was obviously chattering out of that nervousness.

"Very beautiful," he said, feeling protective of her.

"Aren't they?" She admired her brimming glass. "Made from a single piece of blown glass in a little shop in Italy. Perfect weight and balance. Just holding one of these makes me feel better." She did seem calmer and she gave him the glory of one of her open smiles. This one almost lit her eyes, but not quite.

"To us," she said, extending her glass. "To the past…which shall remain our dark secret." She regarded him over the bubbles that misted above the rim. What did she want? She used to grab him with a look. He should be beyond that now, but he felt the tug like pain in a phantom limb.

I've missed you. The words formed in his head, but there was no point in saying them. It would just make things more awkward. "To the next two weeks." He intended to tap her glass with his, but instead their fingers bumped.

Her eyes widened, and he felt a surge of heat, which he attempted to douse with a quick swallow of champagne. The stuff tasted almost otherworldly. Kathleen had that power over things. When they were at Arizona State together, she used to make every moment a celebration. Mimosas for the first sweet blast of citrus blossoms in March, a desert walk after every rain, marshmallows toasted in a chimnea for the first winter chill, the entire apartment filled with candles for something called Candlemas, homemade brownies—complete with a whipped-cream fight—for the end of finals.

She arranged every detail to intensify the moment, to make everything seem more significant than it was. He'd asked her about the source of that inclination— were her parents so celebratory? *It's just me* was all she would say. But there was more to the story, he knew. With Kathleen, there always was.

"So, what do you think?" she asked him, playful now.

"I think it's great you've done so well."

"I meant the champagne. But thanks. I've been lucky."

"It's very nice. Very pink."

"Exceptional, really. The tiny bubbles are the mark of a fine champagne. This one's been fermented slowly in wood for a fuller bouquet, allowing the pinot to turn it rosé. It's a myth that rosé champagne is sweet. This is a brut, which I prefer. You?"

"Champagne's your drink, Kathleen. What did you used to say? 'I am drinking stars'?"

"Actually, that was Dom Perignon. I just happen to agree."

"I hope this isn't as expensive as it tastes. I have plebeian preferences, you remember. An occasional beer does me fine."

"It's never too late to refine your palate." Some devilment flashed in her eyes. "Actually, what would people think of the Master of Moderation swilling champagne before five? *Très extravagant.*"

"No doubt." He'd only been in the room with her for ten minutes and he was acting out of character. He put the glass on the table.

"Come on, enjoy it, Dan. I'll never tell." She touched his hand, just a brush of fingers, but a feeling shimmied through him like tires on ice.

"So," she said, "you wanted to get together to get our stories straight?" She raised brows as delicate as Japanese calligraphy. "That we met for the first time here? That we know each other's work…not each other's…everything?"

He grimaced at the deception. "I know that sounds bad, but I thought it would be best."

"You're right." She gave him a steady look. "If people knew about us, the focus would shift to us as a couple, not us as authors, which is what matters on this tour."

He'd always liked the way Kathleen cut to the chase.

The mischief returned to her green eyes. "I mean, we wouldn't want anyone to know that Dr. McAlister once spent an entire weekend in bed, only going to the door for pizza, right?"

"Lord, no."

"Or that he once had sex in an apartment hot tub?"

"That either," he said, wincing at the memory.

"No one would believe it if I told them."

"I hardly believe it myself."

"Exactly." She paused, unfathomable emotion in her silence. "Talking about what happened wouldn't help my credibility, either." She snatched her lip between her teeth—a sign of hurt—and guilt seized him.

"I'm sorry, Kathleen, about how it ended. I was abrupt and I know that I hurt you."

She held up her hand. "Don't apologize, Dan. It was time. We were done." She stuck her chin up, pride bright in her eyes. "I know I was too intense for you."

"We were young."

"And clueless." She managed a choked laugh. He tried to read her expression, but she wouldn't hold his gaze. She tipped the delicate glass to her lips and swallowed fast—also not like her. Kathleen took her time with champagne.

He watched her pretty throat undulate, felt the old desire rise in him. Ten years had passed, but he felt the same.

They'd brought out the worst in each other, gotten completely swept away. The whole world shrank down to the size of the two of them and their bodies. Toward the end, Kathleen had gotten irritable and elusive, which had made him even more single-minded in pursuing her. He'd failed classes, let his practicum patients down, couldn't think of anything but being with her. Not even academic probation had scared him. In the end it had been an inappropriate jealousy that made him realize that he'd let his life spin out of control.

He remembered it all, sitting here, watching her put down her empty glass, lick her soft lips and give him that look—the one that held both challenge and promise, the one he'd sunk into, lost himself in.

He yanked away his gaze and drained the glass as if it held beer on a sunny day. He extended it for a refill. He shouldn't be drinking so much—and certainly not champagne—but this was a special occasion, right? He'd cut himself some slack this once.

She poured champagne into both their glasses, lifted hers and looked him straight in the eye. "To being older and wiser." She ticked her glass against his, the delicate ring a warning bell in his head. "And to keeping our secret."

As the champagne headache kicked in, he wasn't sure the first was true or the second would be easy.

JUST DESSERT to go, Kathleen thought, gritting her teeth as the dinner with Dan, their agents and Rhonda Lockhart, the publicist from Dan's house, eased to a close. She'd achieved her goal—behaved with her usual flair and kept JJ off the trail of any dynamic between her and Dan. Dan had managed just fine—cool as gazpacho fresh from the fridge. Sometimes she'd kill for some of his restraint. Her skin itched, her stomach jumped and her heart skittered in her chest like a hockey puck.

At least she didn't have that hollow feeling that had started that night with Troy, the last man she'd been with. Something was definitely amok with her, which added another knot to the string of knots she'd been tying in her stomach since she'd agreed to this book tour.

Rhonda—their scheduler, media hound and general gofer for the tour—had chattered nonstop, which helped Kathleen hide her feelings. Rhonda reminded Kathleen of Reese Witherspoon—all perky and bouncy and blond, a regular publishing cheerleader. Kathleen could practically hear her pom-poms swish. *Go, book tour, go. Win, book sales, win.*

Rhonda had gushed over their books, passed out the tour itinerary and asked Kathleen to choose, then sample, her entrée as well as make dessert selections for the entire table.

Which Kathleen was happy to do, since it reminded her of all the joys in the world she loved. Once the desserts were ordered, she excused herself for the ladies' room for some recuperation time.

Inside the flower-filled, mirrored anteroom, she flopped onto an elegant chaise. Just a few moments all alone was all she needed.

As if on cue, JJ strode in.

Damn.

"Oh, my God, that man has such a thing for you." JJ plopped into the facing chaise and lit a cigarette, its end glittering like her eyes, hot with her scoop.

"Dan's agent? Not my type," Kathleen said, attempting a feint.

"Please." JJ snorted smoke and flicked the mouth-end of her cigarette with her thumb.

"You mean the waiter?" Kathleen tried, all innocence.

"Don't insult my vibe meter. I'm talking about you and Dan McAlister. Sparks were flying both ways, hon. I may be a narcissistic workaholic, but I'm not blind. Besides, the waiter was gay and Dan's agent is dullsville."

"We were just being polite to each other."

"When you passed the rolls to him, your fingers touched and you practically dropped the basket."

"I was weak from hunger."

"And when you were tasting everyone's food—"

"That was Rhonda's idea, not mine."

"Whatever. The point is that while you were doing it and moaning, he stared at you like you were having a climax."

That made her breath hitch. JJ had hit on something. She did make similar sounds when she came. And, of course, Dan knew that. Which explained that extra gleam in his eyes.

"Speaking of that, does Dr. Moderate approve of recreational sex? Oh, who cares? Just sleep with the man. I don't buy all that serenity bullshit."

"JJ! Are you crazy? Why would I want to sleep with him?" She sat on her hands to hide the way they'd begun to shake.

"To show him he's human. On general principles. Though…you know…what a book that would make. Kathleen Valentine, Pied Piper of Hedonism, converts Dr. Moderate to her religion of the senses. Herman would be ecstatic."

"You're insane, JJ." Her heart tripped into double time.

JJ took a deep puff of her cigarette and blew it out through her smile. "Come on. You have to admit he's hot."

"If you go for that type."

"The handsome, brilliant, sensitive type? What's the prob?"

"JJ…we're supposed to be opponents, polar opposites, remember?"

"Where there's friction, there's fire."

"Even if I were interested, which I'm not, he would never do it." Her heart started a rolling rumba.

"He's a man. What man can resist Kathleen Valentine?"

"You're flattering me."

JJ shrugged.

"If you're so hot for him, JJ, come on the tour and *you* sleep with him."

"If only…"

"Come on. You hate tours as much as I do." Kathleen would never sleep with Dan, but she was annoyed to notice that the rumba her heart was doing had added a maraca rhythm.

"You're thinking about it," JJ said, a dog with a bone. "You're all pink."

"That's the wine. Wine stimulates circulation. You're flushed, too. Just look at yourself."

JJ stared into the mirror, then ran her fingers roughly through her bobbed hair. "God, I look like an ancient diner waitress. I should start calling everyone 'hon.'"

"You already do." Kathleen leaned in to study her agent's face. "There are incipient wrinkles developing. Let me give you my cell-plumping cream." She extracted the excruciatingly expensive tube from her satchel and handed it over to JJ. "The Web site's on the label to order more."

Wrinkles weren't JJ's only problem, she saw. "You need more vitamins." She picked up a strand of her hair and rubbed it between her fingers. "Not enough protein. Are you eating?"

"Not so much. Barry and I are on the outs."

"Barry the Brooder? No wonder. You have to take care of yourself, JJ. You're in charge of your own happiness." That was one truth she knew from the inside out.

She took out her business-card holder and extracted a card she gave to JJ. "This is a food delivery service—homemade stuff, all fresh and vitamin-rich. Set yourself up for a month to see how you like it."

"I'm fine. Really."

"Then consider it an early birthday gift from me."

"I just had my birthday. You're making me feel guilty. Here I send you on this book tour and you're giving me gifts."

"Just take care of yourself and forget the guilt. Guilt is unhealthy. Talk about producing wrinkles. Oh, and here's that hypnotherapist's card. For the smoking."

"You're too good to me," JJ said, taking the card, her face warm with an affection that made Kathleen feel uncomfortable.

She liked JJ a lot, but it was best to keep things professional. "I'm buttering you up so you'll get me an even better deal on my next book."

"Easy breezy if you do a Converting Dr. Moderate book. Let's get back to the table before somebody scarfs up my bananas Foster. Bananas have calcium, right?"

"Potassium. But that's good, too."

"What's with you, Kathleen?" JJ said. "You look funny." She stubbed her cigarette in one of the pots of cut flowers. Kathleen grimaced.

"Just feeling the pain of those poor blooms. Let's go."

She went for the door before JJ saw right through her.

3

THE NEXT NIGHT, Dan held the door so Kathleen could climb into the back seat of the car-service limo. They'd just finished the launch party at the Barnes and Noble on Fifth Avenue, which Rhonda had informed them was "the best, most star-studded bookstore in Manhattan."

Kathleen's smile as she slid into the seat sent heat through him. He was so easy. He joined her, cramming himself against the far door to nix the urge to bury his nose in her thick hair, which she'd worn his favorite way—loose and wavy.

How could he advise his patients to control their urges, when he was ready to jump the woman? Damn this book tour. Damn the way her skirt rode high on her thigh. Damn him for noticing.

Kathleen drummed her fingers on the book in her lap—his book, back cover up, showing his photo with that chilly, superior expression on his face Kathleen used to criticize in their quarrels. *Like you're above us mere mortals.*

That wasn't fair. Sure, he reflected at length on problems and assessed all factors before making a decision. Did that make him dispassionate? Hardly. But he wasn't surprised Kathleen hadn't understood that. She was all impulse and urge.

And heat. Lots and lots of heat.

She'd been generous, too, and kind. Like tonight when she'd bought his book and stood in line for him to sign it—a gracious gesture he'd been too dazed to duplicate. Book-signings and their attendant rituals were a new and mortifying experience.

Kathleen sighed a rich sigh and wiggled into the seat, as if to get comfortable, then turned her head on the headrest and looked at him. "I love fabric seats, don't you? I have black velvet in my car. Pimpish, I know, but it feels so good against bare skin."

Bare. He didn't want to think of that word around Kathleen, let alone hear it come out of her silky lips. Her wiggling around had shifted her skirt up a bit. Nothing obvious and she was clearly unaware of it. He wondered if she was wearing panties.

Ouch. "I never really thought of it that way." The over-warm car seethed with her perfume. He watched her pulse throb softly in her neck, wanted to press his lips there, taste her skin with his tongue. "Stuffy in here," he mumbled and rolled down his window.

Rhonda barreled into the front seat beside the driver, slammed her door and looked at them over the seat. "That was fabulous. Great turnout. You two were a hit. *Every*one was there." She rattled off the news outlets in attendance, practically bouncing in her seat.

"Sounds good," Dan said. He was used to speaking at small workshops, so he'd been rigid with tension at the crowd.

"We sold tons of books," Kathleen said. "Good job, Rhonda."

"Thank you, Kathleen. You were a joy to work with." Rhonda beamed at her. "You, too, Dan. Absolutely."

She cleared her throat. He'd been tongue-tied and sluggish, he knew.

Kathleen had gleamed like a jewel as she bantered with reporters and with him when they were formally announced and invited to speak. She'd been lively and engaging and he'd been awed by her performance.

My advice is to buy both our books and decide which makes you feel better, she'd said. *Of course, my books come with a coupon for a sample of imported chocolates.* She'd turned to him then. *I don't suppose you supply any coupons, Dan? That would be too indulgent, correct?* She'd offered him a bonbon, eyes twinkling with mischief and delight.

He'd declined, awkward as a kid at his first dance…which pretty much nailed his whole performance. He'd sold far more books than Kathleen—hers had been out for a while, after all—but she'd ruled the event, start to finish. Somehow, that seemed right.

"You need to loosen up, Dan," she said to him now. "Next time, take the chocolate I offer you and say something about falling off the wagon." She leaned into his shoulder, then pulled away. The tiny moment of pressure lingered on his skin. He was such a fool.

"If you'd like, I can do some prep with you, Dan," Rhonda said. "Some Q and A rehearsal for media? If that would help?"

"Sure. That would be fine," he said, though he instantly had second thoughts, knowing Rhonda's penchant for chatter.

"So, Dan, can I ask you a question?" Rhonda said.

"Sure." He was grateful for the distraction from the claustrophobia he felt sitting so near Kathleen.

"In your book, there's a self-control checklist. What

if a person scores high except when they're in a relationship? What would you say to that person?"

"I'd say that's good self-awareness," he said, glancing at Kathleen, who wore a half smile. *Make it good, Dan.*

"The person would need to determine whether the immoderation came from within—fear or insecurity—or without—the partner's behavior or attitude."

"Oh, yeah. Use that Insecurity Meter in your book?"

"Yes. But if the immoderation is external, a discussion would be needed with the partner, who'd have to change."

"But what if the, um, partner, won't change?"

"Some relationships are emotional landmines and must be sidestepped."

"Oh." Rhonda was not happy with the answer. No one ever was. Love was the biggest danger zone for most of his clients.

"Or," Kathleen said sharply, "you could go with your feelings, Rhonda, and not catastrophize. Worrying doesn't fix tomorrow's problems. It only zaps today's joy. The point of life is to live it. And where can you feel more alive than in the arms of someone you love?"

"Good point," Rhonda said with a heavy sigh.

I feel alive in your arms. Kathleen had used those exact words on the afternoon he realized he was losing control of his life. He'd blown off an important meeting with his advisor, frantic to see Kathleen, waited for her to emerge from a news-writing class, then pulled her into a nearby soda-machine alcove and kissed her until he was blind with the need to be inside her.

I love when you want me so much, she'd said, tugging him with her into the narrow space between the machine and the side wall, where anyone close enough to buy a Coke would hear, if not see, them. The machine had been new, the space clean—perfect for two people desperate to make love *now*—and when she'd unzipped him and offered her warmth, he'd slipped inside before he knew it, helpless with lust and lost to her. He'd gripped her thighs as she rode him, her eyes flashing with need and demand, and they'd both moaned with pleasure.

Footsteps approached, but she held on. *We're almost there.*

He'd lunged into her faster, as hard as she could take, caring only about her sounds, her needs, her climax and his release. They'd shuddered to an orgasm seconds before the person dropped coins into the slot. They'd grinned at each other, listening to the tinkle of quarters, the clunk of the soda, the snap and fizz of the can being opened, then feet shuffling away.

I love you like this, Dan, she'd said, while they leaned against the warm machine catching their breath. *I love that you lose control with me.* Her eyes were tender and he'd let that be enough. He'd refused to see that he'd lost all sense, narrowed his life to Kathleen alone.

Abruptly, Rhonda thrust her arm over the seat between them. "Will one of you please pinch me?"

"Excuse me?" Dan said.

"So I know this isn't a dream. I can't believe I get to hear your ideas up close and personal."

"This isn't a dream," Dan said. This was real, all right. Too real. Kathleen was really beside him, her heat and scent and voice and body all he could think about.

Kathleen, on the other hand, seemed completely self-possessed tonight. Last night she'd been nervous. That didn't surprise him. She'd been far less bulldozed by their affair than he. Too restless to stay with anything long, she would have ended it soon, if he hadn't acted when he did.

Right now, he wished he could end this tour, fly home to Vermont for some peace and quiet on the lake, take whatever professional fallout came of it. Just get away from her.

He was a man of his word, though, and he could surely master this. If he couldn't, what did that say about his theory that practice and focus could conquer extreme appetites?

When the driver stopped in the hotel portico, Rhonda suggested a nightcap, but they both declined.

"Oh." Rhonda's smile dimmed for an instant, then clicked back into high beam. "No problem. We'll have lots of drinks over the next ten days. I have such a good feeling about this tour."

"It'll be great," Kathleen said, sounding as weary as he felt.

He climbed out of the car and helped Kathleen out, liking the feel of her hand in his—warm and strong, but soft, too. Like the woman.

"I asked them to put the tea you like in your room," Rhonda said to him, leaning out the front window of the car.

"Please don't bother on my account."

"And the double pillow top for you, Kathleen."

"You're spoiling us," Kathleen said.

"If you need anything or have any questions, call me any time, I mean it," Rhonda said. "And charge everything to your rooms—breakfast, late-night snacks, in-room massages, movies, whatever. And use the minibar. That's what it's for."

"We'll be fine, Rhonda, thank you," Dan said.

"I'll be here with the car for the airport at nine," she called to them, waving out the window as the driver pulled away.

"She wears me out," Dan said, sagging with relief.

"Oh, me, too," Kathleen said. "She's like a class-three rapids when you want a bubbling stream." She shot him a rueful smile that he returned. "We're just lucky she has a cat waiting at home, or we'd be playing pinochle here with her tonight. Good luck with that media training she's going to give you, Dan."

"Lord."

Her expression warmed with honest pleasure and kind commiseration. He liked this smile much better than the theatrical one she'd worn at the signing. This smile was direct, energetic, mischievous and a little shy, too.

This was the smile that had drawn him the day they met. Along with the fact she was about to be smashed to the ground by the gigantic mattress she was jamming through her apartment door. He'd just moved into the same complex and had rushed to help her get the thing into her bedroom.

I can't afford this bed, she'd said in her whiskey voice, looking down at the mattress, which filled the small bedroom wall-to-wall. *But once I lay down on it, oh, my good glory, I was done for. It said, 'Sleep on me, enjoy me, use me 'til I sag.' What could I do? I'd been had.*

Before long, he'd been had, too. By Kathleen and how she swept away his defenses, his restraint, his carefully structured days and comfortable routines. She awakened an impulsive intensity in him he preferred dormant. Or dead. He'd lived a quiet, studious life until he'd stumbled upon Kathleen and her bed.

"You okay?" Kathleen said now, as they headed across the lobby for the elevator.

"Me? Fine. Just thinking."

"How can you? I'm completely wiped. The mattress last night was…bumpy." The excuse sounded hasty, as if to cover the real reason for her exhaustion.

"You were pretty perky at the signing."

"All an act, Dan." Her heavy tone told him there was more acting going on than she intended to reveal.

He understood. He was acting, too—just not very convincingly. She'd surely picked up on his tension, though she was classy enough not to mention it.

They rode the elevator to their floor and headed down the hall, managing small talk about the signing and the tour and laughing companionably. Anyone seeing them would assume they were long-time lovers headed for bed. But it was all an act, as Kathleen had observed.

A moment later, they stood before the doors to their adjoining rooms. "So this is good night then," he said.

"Yep. I've got new bedside reading." She raised his book, back cover facing him, but upside down, so that he appeared to be standing on his head. How appropriate.

"Thanks for buying that. I should have bought one of yours, but I was…I already had one, so I didn't—"

"Really? You have one of my books?"

"Of course. I have it with me. In fact, will you sign it?"

"That's not necessary."

"No. I insist. I'll bring it right over."

She started to object, but he cut her off. "Kathleen, I want to."

"Okay, then. Suit yourself." She slid her key card into the slot and breezed inside, but not before he caught the wisp of a smile that told him she was delighted.

Which made him far too happy.

He would breeze into her room, sign the book, say good night and be back in his room in an easy ten minutes.

SHE COULD have signed the book tomorrow, for heaven's sake, but the delight that Dan had read it had overridden Kathleen's good sense. Now she was stuck. One more minute of acting witty and cool when she felt shaky and confused and her over-wound nerves would snap through her skin.

She needed a long, hot bath to soothe herself. Her reaction to Dan alarmed her. The animal in her had nosed out the positive changes in his physique. He was stronger, broader, more physically confident than he'd been in college. He used to envelop her so tightly that she felt wrapped up in a big Dan blanket. How would he feel now? Even more secure, no doubt. More masterful and carnal.

Cut it out. She didn't want the man anymore. How tiresome his life must be, with all the rules and repression he swore by. Her reaction was pure biology. An example of the female's genetic drive to connect with a virile male to propagate the species with sturdy offspring. That was how she would explain the importance of male physical prowess to female arousal in the sexuality chapter in *Roots and Rhetoric.* When she wrote it, that is.

But she was uneasily sure that genetic drives didn't completely account for her reaction to Dan. Physical stuff had gotten weird on her lately. Take what had happened with Troy just three weeks ago.

She'd met him at a wine tasting and he was exactly her type: classy, sensual, funny, smart, sexually confident and not the least intimidated by her reputation.

They'd returned to her place after an exquisite dinner. Soon they were in her bedroom, where the air was aromatic with cinnamon candles and a hint of the lusty Bordeaux she'd opened, the light golden and dim. There was Troy in her bed, covered to the waist in her black satin sheets, his bare chest promising, his look predatory...everything just the way she liked it.

She'd stepped toward him, but was swept by a wave of exhaustion so overwhelming she'd stopped moving. Her whole being felt the way skin feels when it's been stroked too long on the same spot—chafed, burned and aching.

She'd forced herself to sit on the bed beside Troy and put her hands on his chest, hoping the contact would banish the peculiar sensation.

But it hadn't. Troy moved to kiss her, but she stopped him. Her lips had gone numb and rubbery—the way they'd felt after the accident. She'd pulled away, apologizing like mad.

Troy had been disappointed, of course. And puzzled.

She was, too. Especially by how happy she was to have sent him away. The minute he left, she'd cheerfully wrapped herself in a microfiber throw and gotten absorbed in a black-and-white historical movie, where the brush of a man's lips on the back of a woman's hand practically produced a climax. She'd felt like a guilty child allowed to stay up past her bedtime.

Now she slid off her shoes, undid her garters and peeled off her stockings, digging her toes into the lush sponge of the dense carpet.

She didn't feel numb now. She felt fully alive, zings and pings firing joyously all up and down her body—a stalled engine finally coming to life.

Not good. Not good at all. She was done with Dan. Except while she waited for him, she tugged at her ear and breathed in hungry little pants—signs of sexual anticipation. She hadn't felt like this in a long time.

Dan knocked at her door with crisp, evenly spaced raps as rational and matter-of-fact as the man. He was so different from her that she wondered what she'd seen in him.

She opened the door and remembered. His kind eyes, sensuous mouth, the intelligence in his face and that smile—knowing and mysterious—that promised more. Much more.

He held her book in his hand and tilted it at her.

"Come in." She led him to the couch and he sat beside her, placing her book on her lap.

It was her first. Many times she'd wondered if he'd read her magazine column or any of her books. It was childish vanity, but she wanted him to see what she'd gone on to accomplish…and what he'd given up.

She looked into his blue eyes. They held an emotion that she, as usual, couldn't read. Curiosity? Sadness? Regret? Desire?

Did you miss me? Did you suffer without me? Those were the mucky, wounded-ego questions she wanted to ask. If their time together had been important to him, if the breakup had been difficult for him, too, then she wouldn't feel like such a weak fool. Maybe if she asked, she'd stop feeling so strange.

"Can I ask you something?"

He nodded.

She opened her mouth, but the words wouldn't come. What if his answer made her feel worse? "Do you have a pen?"

He looked at her quizzically.

"Because if you don't, I do. I have a special signing pen that I love. It has a tip so smooth it makes the words come out like liquid thought," she babbled. "You'll want something like that…a special pen, I mean…"

Dan ended her torment by whipping a pen from his suit-coat pocket and handing it to her, still warm from his body.

"Great." She clicked it on, then set to her task. When she lifted the pristine cover of her book, the binding crackled and the first few sheets were attached at the edges. "Have you even read a page?" she asked, trying to sound amused, not hurt.

He reddened. "I bought it to support you, Kathleen. It wasn't my thing."

"How do you know if you haven't looked past the cover?"

He shrugged. "I just know."

"You used to at least try things," she said. He used to say that she was a bad influence on him, but she'd assumed he was joking, been certain he enjoyed the pleasures she exposed him to. "Remember karaoke night?"

He groaned and shook his head. "Lord. What a mistake."

"Come on. You had fun. And 'Born to be Wild' was the perfect song for you to sing."

"I sounded like an idiot—an off-key idiot. I don't know how you talked me into that."

"I had legendary persuasive powers," she teased.

"True." He shot her a smile. "And I'd never met anyone like you."

"You lived like a monk in that sad little apartment. And your roommate. Religious studies, right? Such a somber dude. He always looked like he was writing a funeral sermon."

"Oh, he usually was."

"I was good for you. Admit it." She used a teasing tone, but she was deadly serious.

Dan stayed silent. He thought she was bad for him? Really? She felt obliged to defend herself. "You had three different kinds of antacids in your medicine cabinet when we met. You never touched them after we got together. Plus you had insomnia before me. I helped you sleep."

"You wore me out," he said dryly.

At least that. "Not to mention how I fixed up your apartment. Or should I say prison cell. Bare cupboards, no dishes, not even a shower curtain. Nothing pleasant or comfortable or soft."

"I was poor, you may recall." His voice had been warmed by the memories.

"So was I, but I had my priorities."

"You bought me silverware and plates." He smiled. "Even sheets."

"I had to. You were desperate. And they were on sale."

"And then you had to borrow money for textbooks."

She shrugged. "It was a short-term cash-flow problem."

"And I wasn't desperate. You were. To change me."

"It was better, don't you think?"

"It was different." Then he seemed to soften. "It made you happy and that's all I cared about at the time."

"I remember." An odd warmth seeped up from her toes at his words. She hated that. It confused her. She broke off her gaze and balanced his pen on her finger. "Evenly weighted. Good grip. You have taste in writing implements."

"At least that." He smiled.

"One little thing we still have in common." She sighed, then opened to the title page and wrote in bold letters the first words that came to her: "To past pleasures. Read and reconsider, Dan. Ever yours, K." *Ever yours?* What the hell did that mean? Impulse was not her friend tonight.

Dan leaned close to read over her shoulder, his breath tickling the tiny hairs on her neck. She fought a shiver, closed the book with his pen on top and handed it to him.

He took it, but held her gaze, wondering, no doubt, what she'd meant by the inscription.

She shrugged. "What? It's better than what you wrote in mine—'Everything in moderation...Dan McAlister.' Pretty impersonal, don't you think?"

"I was caught off guard. I was a little stunned."

"I know. I'm teasing. Everybody has that deer-in-headlights reaction to their first signing."

"I could have written more, you know, in the book. Lots more."

"I know." Their eyes met and she felt that rush of being recognized, that joy of mattering so much to one man that the whole world shrank down to the size of his smile.

"We were something else, huh?" she said without thinking.

"Oh, yeah."

"Sparks and fireworks." Which were starting up again in her stomach and all parts below.

"More like scorching flame."

"We were intense."

"You were intense. I was...bewildered."

"We had good times, Dan." Maybe they weren't right for each other, but their affair had been powerful and vivid and remarkable.

"Yes, we did," he said, his tone reassuring her that she wasn't alone. "And I'm glad to see you again. I thought of you. A lot."

"I thought of you, too." Entirely too much, replaying every moment in her mind. She hated remembering how insecure she'd been after he left—a blob of needy jelly instead of the strong, independent woman she was proud to be.

"If I had to go on a book tour, I'm glad it's with you."

She smiled. Was this okay? Could they be friends again? No hard feelings and all that jazz?

Something, some undercurrent of distress, told her it shouldn't be that simple. And how come he was so damned comfortable letting go of the past?

"Take a peek at my book," she said, tapping it. "It could change your whole perspective."

"But I've staked my career on my perspective."

"Mmm. Then this is too dangerous for you." She took the edges of her book and tugged gently.

"I can handle it." He tugged back, letting her feel his strength, the stretch and recoil of his muscles.

Holding his gaze for one more teasing moment, she let go. "Okay…I only hope you know what you're doing."

"So do I, Kathleen." He gave her a lovely, self-mocking smile that made her melt.

To hide that fact, she led him to the door.

In the doorway, he seemed reluctant to leave. "So, tomorrow we head to Chicago?"

"Yep. Cheerleader Rhonda and the car will be here at nine. Wonder when she'll give you that media training session."

He gave an exaggerated shudder. "I'm not sure I'm

up for that." An idea seemed to dawn on him. "Couldn't you do it? You were good with the reporters."

"Me?"

"You've had more experience than Rhonda."

"I suppose I could give you some tips…sure. Maybe we should plan how to handle the upcoming appearances. Why not?" *Because this is Dan, you dope.* And because the possibility put a hitch in her heart rate.

"I'd like that. I'll tell Rhonda I don't need the prep session, after all." He kept standing in the doorway, looking at her. "Shall I wait for you in the morning?"

"If you'd like."

He didn't move and his gaze was restless on her face, circling her features, hovering at her eyes, nose, chin, finally settling on her mouth.

"Is there something else?" *You missed me desperately? You thought you'd die without me? You want to kiss me senseless?*

"I don't want you to think I didn't learn from our time together," he said, his cool blues maddeningly earnest. "Because I did. I learned what I needed in my life. Our affair was…pivotal."

Pivotal? What the hell did that mean? "That's supposed to be a good thing?"

"Of course."

What, he expected her to be pleased? *Oh, Dan, thank you. As long as I was pivotal, then it was all worth it.* She managed a smile. "Good night, Dan."

"Good night." He shifted ever so slightly, leaned an inch or two closer so that she knew he intended to kiss her. But his face was tense and she knew it would be the kiss equivalent of the awful hug she'd given him when they first met—a tight peck she never, ever wanted to get from Dan——so she wiggled her fingers in farewell. "Get some sleep. Tomorrow's a big day."

"Sure. You, too." He looked both disappointed and relieved when she slowly closed the door.

She stared into space, musing, fuming. She was irritated, resentful, sad and hot for him, damn it all to hell.

Pivotal, my little pink behind. So their relationship had provided a philosophical catharsis for him? A *learning* experience?

It had been more than that to her. They'd been dragging themselves up a dangerous emotional cliff together, hanging on to the rope for dear life. Then, abruptly, Dan had let go, just let her tumble to the canyon floor, while he dusted himself off and hiked happily onward without a backward glance.

Get over it, she told herself, crossing her sitting room, distracted for a second by the squish of the thickly padded carpet beneath her bare feet. *He can't apologize for what you never told him he did.* The last thing she wanted him to know was how badly he'd hurt her.

Grow up. Be grateful. After all, the shock of the breakup had jolted her into much-needed changes. She'd left ASU, transferred to a small college in California, shifting her major from journalism to liberal arts and while still in school, started writing the freelance entertainment pieces that led to her column at *Pulse-Point* magazine, which led to her book career.

So Dan had been *pivotal* for her, too.

And she'd been careful with men ever since, kept things friendly and sexual, and that had been plenty satisfying. Much better than an unhealthy bonding and the agony that went with its inevitable end.

She'd been stupid and naive with Dan. Ten years later, she was savvy and successful, confident and self-assured.

And Dan was still an uptight guy. She'd pushed him out of his comfort zone, but he'd raced right back to it and then some, going for hyper-restraint and extreme control. He was the last guy she'd ever want.

Get over it, Kath. Close the book, brick the wall. She blew out a breath. *Make the most of every moment.* That was her creed. She would live it on this tour, too, despite Dan's presence. She would experience the best of the tour and ignore the worst.

Maybe Dan would be pivotal again—jolt her into action on the new book. So far, she'd been bored by the research and frightened by her computer cursor blinking like a heartbeat on the blank screen.

For now, she'd get some sleep. She put on her slipperiest nightgown, relishing its cool slide over her skin, grabbed the lilac linen spray from her comfort suitcase, which held her lotions, special pillows, aromatic oils and other necessities, and misted her sheets.

Opening one of the small champagne bottles she brought on trips for nightcaps, she curled into bed with Dan's book. She'd see what the buzz was about and remind herself why the breakup had been the best thing that had happened to her.

She scanned the chapter titles until one caught her eye. "The Excesses of Youth" started out in italics:

A young man of my acquaintance fell head over heels with a woman who considered sensual pleasure her religion.

Hmm, that sounded familiar.

*Being young and naive and uncertain of himself,
he was soon drowning in the whirlpool of her passion. He couldn't be away from her, began failing
classes, avoiding his friends, until he had nothing
else but her. In short, he completely lost sight of
his identity, his needs and his life goals.*

This was about Dan and her, no question. Electric-
ity rushed through Kathleen. She skimmed ahead.

*Of course, inexperienced as he was, the young
man was unable to recognize the psychological
problems with which his lover struggled. Her obsession with pleasure kept her from recognizing
real emotion. Sex was like a drug to her. The
young man's intense reaction—she'd forced him
into her world of excess and extremes—affirmed
her sense of herself and her importance in the
world. Her narcissism made it hard for her to see
the damage she was doing to the man she believed
she loved.*

  *Luckily, the young man had enough self-knowl-
edge to realize what was happening before it was
too late. After a terrible incident of anger and
jealousy, he broke away from the woman before
her emotional recklessness destroyed him.*

Oh. My. God. So much for Dan's "We were
young...I was bewildered" bullshit. He thought she was
narcissistic, unbalanced, immature and emotionally
reckless?

She'd accept *immature* and *unbalanced*. Maybe even
reckless. But she'd been crazy over him, too. A little

scared, but mostly because of how jealous and possessive he'd acted at the end. In his book, he sounded noble
and brave, standing up for himself against the depraved
nymphomaniac.

Oh, this was outrageous. Anger pulsed through her
in thick clots, thudded against her skull, pounded at her
temples. She would talk to him right now. Straighten
him out, once and for all. She launched herself out of
the bed and marched across her suite, her feet barely
touching the carpet.

At her door, she stopped. If she burst into his room
and yelled at him, she'd look like an emotional maniac.
Any person would be upset—no, enraged—at being
maligned, even anonymously, in a book to be read by
thousands. Tens of thousands if their promotional tour
had its intended impact.

But she would not give Dan the satisfaction of seeing her yell or cry. She would calm down first and rationally explain how dead wrong he was.

She took a deep breath and blew it out slowly, dizzy
with fury. She clenched her fists, then forced herself to
release them. *Calm, calm, calm. You can handle this.*
But her anger wouldn't go away that fast. She began to
pace, stopping each time just as she reached for the
door to go to him, spinning on her heel and marching
the length of the suite again, like a caged leopard—a
caged, furious leopard…the source of her fury just outside the bars.

Dan McAlister was not above the sexual fray. Maybe
he could fool his readers, his clients, the Rhondas of the
world, but he couldn't fool Kathleen. She knew him.
That way.

For some reason, JJ's words came to her: *So sleep*

with him. Show him the error of his ways. No. Absolutely not. Sex was a beautiful physical connection between two caring people, dammit. It should never be an act of revenge or anger.

Besides, how could she sleep with a guy she wanted to deck?

No, she would talk to him. Gently explain in her most sensible voice what a wrongheaded, self-centered dick he was.

4

THEY'D BARELY checked in to the hotel in Chicago, when someone banged on Dan's door. He had a whole hour before dinner with Kathleen and Rhonda, and he needed every second to recoup, relax, meditate and do some writing.

Through the peephole, he saw it was Rhonda. Better than Kathleen, at least, who'd been oddly irritable all day—in the car to the airport, on the plane and at the book-signing, shooting him angry glances and eye rolls and delivering unnecessary jabs about his work. He expected their after-dinner media training to be similarly unpleasant.

What the hell had happened overnight? He'd thought they'd had a nice closure moment, agreeing that they were both better off after the affair. She'd given him an odd look with a spark of resentment, and she'd waved away his good-night kiss as though he had bad breath. Maybe he'd sounded smug. He tended to do that when he was self-conscious. And around Kathleen, he was nothing but self-conscious.

Maybe she'd slept poorly on the hotel bed, even with the extra padding Rhonda had arranged for her. She was the princess and the pea when it came to beds. He knew that from college.

Meanwhile, here was Rhonda. On the plane she'd asked his advice for a "friend who might be seeing an old boyfriend." Evidently, Rhonda had an ex in Chicago.

With a sigh, he opened the door and Rhonda breezed in, looking earnest and upset, holding a foam cup, a bakery sack and a small tin box. "Can we talk?"

"Of course."

"I hope you can help me." She handed him the cup. "It's a chamomile-lemon blend. Not your favorite, but variety is good, too, right? No, wait, that's Kathleen with the variety stuff. You're with ritual and habit."

"I'm sure it's fine."

"Taste it before you thank me."

He took a sip, feeling her eyes on him. The tea had a medicinal lemon and herb flavor. "I like it."

"Great. Here's more." She handed him the tin, then swept past him to fling open his curtains, washing the room in late-afternoon light. She sank into a chair at the table under the window and dug into the pastry bag for two large muffins, extending one to him. "They're healthy, don't worry. Bran and oatmeal." She took a huge bite of her muffin. "I only eat when I'm anxious."

Dan put the tea tin and the cup she'd brought him on the table and sat across from her.

"Dry as dust." She made a face, then glanced at his tea. "Mind if I make myself some tea?"

"No, no. Make yourself at home."

She busied herself at the refreshment area and, while the water percolated through, talked about room service and how stale the in-room tea usually was. "Practically fossilized. I use raw sugar in mine. Sure you don't want some more?"

"No, no. I'm fine."

"I always add cream. It cancels the tannic acid, which can be a carcinogen. Did you know that?"

"I didn't."

"It's in Kathleen's book. Kathleen knows so many fascinating things." She returned and sat, dunking her tea bag methodically in the mug while she talked. "So, anyway, what I wanted to talk about... Aren't you going to eat your muffin?"

"I'd rather wait for dinner." He rarely ate between meals, preferring a gentle hunger that made him appreciate each bite of food.

"I wish I had more self-control. I'm weak with food and love." She sighed. "I have to tell you that the *friend* with issues is really me."

"I kind of got that idea."

She smiled sheepishly. "I'm obvious, huh?" She tucked her hair behind both ears and folded her arms across her body, holding in both anxiety and excitement, he could tell. "Anyway, the guy's name is Dylan and he lives in Chicago. I did, too, two years ago. We were in love. At least I thought we were. But then Dylan started disappearing on me."

She gulped more tea, ate more muffin and kept talking. "He claimed he was just out with his friends, but then he got a message on his answering machine from a woman."

"And you overheard it?"

She blushed. "I figured out his check-messages code, so I'd been anticipating a problem. You know, to brace myself? Checking now and then. Well, every day. Sometimes twice."

He just looked at her.

"I know. Unhealthy sign, but my instincts were dead-on. There *was* a woman. I confronted Dylan, but he said I was trying to put him on a choke chain like a dog. I told him he *was* a dog—a bad, bad dog—but he said I should enjoy the time we had, we only have the present moment and other existential blah-blah."

"So, what did you do after that?"

"I couldn't hack it. Smelling another woman's perfume in his place or finding a forgotten hair band on the sink just brutalized me. So I broke up with him. There was this amazing job in New York, so I went."

"So, you made a decision to take care of yourself."

"What else could I do? I was miserable, eating my roommates out of house and home. I would tell them to hide the good stuff, but I'd hunt it down and eat it anyway. Totally out of control." She finished her muffin, then glanced at his.

"Help yourself," he said.

"If you're sure."

He nodded. "So, you moved on…" he prodded her.

"Yes. To New York. And that's been awesome. I love my job. I have friends. And I'm dating this guy Mark. He's not exactly my type, but he's always buying me gifts and flowers. And he listens to me. Dylan never listened. I think Mark wants to get serious. Which is all good…" She made another face. "This muffin is even drier than mine." She tossed it into the trash basket.

"Mind if I check out your minibar?" she asked.

"By all means. Like you said, that's what it's there for."

She shuffled through the contents of the small refrigerator and emerged with a packet of Lorna Doone cookies and a bag of Raisinettes. How did she keep her weight under control? Maybe she didn't do anxious eating often.

She ripped open the candy bag and offered him some. "No, thanks."

"Oh, right. Waiting for dinner." She put a few raisins on the cookie and wolfed it down. "Where was I?"

"It was all good?"

"Yes. But just before we left New York, I called Dylan to tell him I was coming. And he was so happy about it. And I do want to see him again. So much. I'm afraid that going to New York was just running away from our problems. But maybe that's fooling myself and I should let it go."

"That's a serious dilemma that many people—"

"It's like sticking your tongue in a sore place on your cheek, you know? How you can't leave it alone?"

"In my experience, after a breakup, there is a tendency to want a chance to revisit the relationship."

"That's from the 'Love…the Ultimate Imbalance' chapter in your book, isn't it?"

"Yes, and—"

"But maybe until I say goodbye to Dylan, I can't say hello to Mark. Does that make any sense?"

"That's a possibility, but—"

"But I could be rationalizing. Except Dylan sounds so different. People can change, can't they?"

He opened his mouth, but she kept going.

"I know. People are basically who they are. If Dylan is toxic to me, I'll get my heart broken again."

While she paused to prepare another raisin-topped cookie, he managed to say, "So, you're concerned about how it will be to see him again?"

"Yeah and I know you'll tell me not to sleep with him." She took the cookie in one bite and washed it down with tea.

"If it distorts your sense of self and direction, then—"

"Don't do it. Right." She spilled the last of the cookies from their package onto the table and dunked one in the tea. "Except our best times were in bed, Dan. How will I know we're over if I don't sleep with him?"

He didn't speak. What was the point? His role seemed to be sounding board and refreshment source.

"So I should use the willpower mantra from your book—'Stop, challenge and decide'—when I'm with him, huh?"

He waited to be sure she actually wanted him to answer, then said, "And take your emotional pulse from time to time."

"So I'll get some self-control practice at least."

"Sounds like it." He resisted the urge to say more. She'd clearly decided what to do.

"Thanks, Dr. McAlister," she said, emotion shining in her eyes. "I know, call you *Dan*, but this has been therapy, so I owe you a *doctor* or two, don't you think?" She dunked the last cookie into the tea and inhaled it, then looked at her watch. "Sheesh. It's dinnertime and I'm full." She shook her head, then looked at him, sheepish now. "Do you mind if we do the media prep session in the morning? I kind of told Dylan we'd get together after dinner. If it's all right with you and Kathleen."

"Not a problem. I don't think I'll need help."

"Are you sure?"

"Absolutely." Though right now, he'd prefer Rhonda's chit-chat to another cranky encounter with Kathleen. Too bad *she* didn't have an old boyfriend in Chicago to visit. Besides him.

THIS WAS RIDICULOUS, Kathleen thought, rushing around her suite after dinner refreshing the flowers and lighting new candles for Dan's arrival. She was acting as though this was a date, not a disagreement.

But bustling kept her from stewing, which she did every time she thought about the section she'd practically memorized in Dan's book.

She regretted being testy with Dan today. She needed to behave rationally if she expected to convince him that he was as much responsible for how crazy things got as she was. No matter what, she would not yell or make snide remarks...

Or threaten him with nail scissors.

Her heart thudded against her ribs as though it was doing the bunny hop on speed. What was going on here? Her desire for Dan and her anger at him were mixing dangerously, like the two parts of nitroglycerin—separately serene, but explosive together.

To enhance the moment and reduce her distress, she'd ordered a selection of desserts from room service, chilled drinks—champagne for her and flavored mineral water for him—put a soothing instrumental on her CD player and misted the room with lavender-rosemary for its calming effect.

For comfort, she wore her stretchiest T-shirt and a pair of jersey shorts so soft they felt like a second skin. How things felt—and smelled and tasted and sounded—meant everything to her. She'd been that way since childhood. Mostly since the accident. A memory she usually avoided. Being around Dan brought up lots of disturbing memories.

She'd been ten and her father had allowed her to ride her bike on the big street—usually against the rules, but he had a client coming and wanted a quiet house. She'd had a blast and felt so grown-up and adventurous riding over to her friend's. On the way back, she'd misjudged a corner and been hit by a car.

Spinal damage caused much of her body to go numb. Her limbs felt the way an arm does when you sleep on it. Except without the tingles that promised life would return to the bloodless limb.

She would tell herself to lift her arm and watch it rise, but it didn't feel like part of her. It was strange and surreal and terrifying. Especially because, at first, the doctors weren't sure she would get the sensations back.

After three weeks, though, tingling started here and there—wisping along her nerves like an ice cube down the back. Her first real awareness was of the weight of a book her mother had braced on her stomach with a pillow. Kathleen had grabbed its edges, squeezed its corners, rubbed its smooth surface and burst into tears of relief.

She'd appreciated every moment of her recovery. It was as if someone had opened her up and poured new life into her.

After that, all sensations took on an unexpected vividness—the nothingness had made her appreciate every bodily reaction. Not just touch, but also taste and smell and sight and sound. In a way, the accident had set her on her life course.

It had done other things that weren't so good—like led to her parents' divorce—but she preferred to focus on the positives.

She hadn't written about the accident in her column or any of her books. Unlike Dan, she didn't feel compelled to confess painful seminal moments—not even disguised as a "young woman of my acquaintance." Her philosophy stood strong and fine without explanation. Besides, the story was far too intimate.

She pushed away the memories and focused on displaying the desserts to their best advantage...much more satisfying than a walk down a mucky memory lane.

Dan arrived right on time carrying a small hotel notepad and pencil, wearing the same clothes he'd worn for their travel day—khakis and a golf shirt—an ensemble that on most men wouldn't draw a second glance, but made him look hotter than ever. Worse, the pants hugged his buns the way her hands itched to and that made her cranky.

"Aren't those pants uncomfortable?"

He looked down. "What's wrong with them?"

"They're too tight." And in front, she caught the outline of...oh, dear. Her sex pinged.

"They feel fine."

"You're probably so used to discomfort you don't even notice it any more. But let's not start arguing already."

"Arguing?"

"I mean discussing." She turned to the table where she'd laid out the desserts. "I ordered some food. Crème brûlée is your favorite, right?" There were also fancy truffles streaked with raspberry sauce, and a traditional favorite—strawberries to be dipped in a gravy boat of chocolate sauce.

"There's enough here for four people," Dan said.

"We'll just graze. I got you raspberry mineral water, since I know you're not wild about champagne." She tapped the bottle. "Effervescence and aroma. Raspberry is a natural appetite enhancer. Did you know that?"

"No, I didn't." He sat on the sofa beside her.

"I went heavy on the chocolate for the endorphins. Do you know they still don't understand what makes chocolate so addictive?" She was showing off out of nervousness, but it couldn't be helped. "They think it might be theobromine, which gives a caffeinelike boost of serotonin, the pleasure hormone."

"Interesting."

Stop, stop, stop. But she was riding a runaway info train and she couldn't seem to put on the brakes. "You'll want to have facts and figures about moderation to give to reporters, Dan."

"Sure," he said, raising a brow in zing-inspiring amusement. How dare he be charming when she was pissed at him? "You went to a lot of trouble for me." He shifted his body so he could smile at her, sending her a whiff of hotel soap—too drying for his skin. She'd have to give him some moisturizer… "Huh? Oh, no trouble. Just wanted sustenance."

"You always did elaborate dinners. I remember for St. Patrick's Day you made soda bread, wasn't it, and corned beef and cabbage?"

"A traditional Irish meal. Right. And don't forget the lime body scrub. Green in honor of the day?" The friction had been delicious in the tub later… *Forget that, block it out.*

"Yes. Green. Little green grains *every*where." He cleared his throat.

Those tiny nuggets of friction had reached every crevice, and the two of them had had so much fun getting it all off…

"And there was hand-cranked ice cream for the Fourth of July," Dan managed to say in an overly cheery voice.

"And we went to the roof and watched the fireworks." And made some of their own. *Stop. You're only making it worse.*

"You cooked special foods to help us study—brain food, you said it was." He was obviously jabbering to hide a turmoil similar to her own.

"Salmon and broccoli. Yeah. For enhanced mental performance. I can't believe you remembered that."

"I remember everything, Kath," he said, low and slow.

She remembered everything, too. "You liked when I cooked naked," she whispered, unable to stop herself.

"You were so beautiful. You still are."

Silence swelled between them in rolling waves, making them both sway. Then Dan cleared his throat, a hard, sharp sound that cut the moment like doors yanked open on illicit lovers. "We'd better get started. Let me get this for you." He lifted the champagne from the bucket, rattling the ice. She helped him, holding the bottle while he worked the wire cap.

This was the second bottle of champagne they'd opened together in as many days. This time Dan was doing the work. The flex and release of his forearms mesmerized her, along with the biceps swelling under the short sleeves. The visible parts of his arms were tan. Probably from some healthy activity, not sunbathing, though she'd love to see him stretched out on a white-sand beach, gleaming with sweat, chest muscles rippling…

The cork popped and foam shot out of the bottle and down the sides—she'd been too distracted to make certain the bottle was angled correctly—so she leaned forward to lick the precious effervescence from the back of her hand. Her tongue brushed Dan's fingers, too.

He pulled away abruptly, and she heard the rasp of his breath and caught the quake of his body.

The accidental contact aroused her, too. When everything was taboo, a mere tongue flick was cataclysmic. "Sorry," she said. "Didn't want to waste liquid gold."

Dan's hands shook as he poured champagne for her. At least this reminder of the old heat would help Dan recognize that it took two to tango where sexual fixation was concerned. She'd be sure to point that out when the time came.

For now, she busied herself pouring Dan's mineral water, then clicked her glass against his. "To the lesson," she said, weighting *lesson* because she intended to teach him more than how to handle media.

Dan looked at her, wondering at her tone, no doubt. She merely smiled. "What would you like to try first?"

"Maybe a mock interview?"

"I mean what dessert?"

"Why don't we reward ourselves afterward?"

"How can you resist?" She picked up a cocoa-dusted hazelnut truffle and nibbled off a piece. Dark chocolate laced with hazelnut and a teasing zing of vanilla exploded in her mouth. She pressed the bite to her palate and let the flavor cascade. "Oh, God. Oh," she moaned. "You have to try this." She extended the rest of the candy.

He hesitated, not wanting to eat from her hand, she figured, but finally nabbed a quick bite, holding his lips away from her fingers. "It's good," he said through the mouthful.

"Good? It's practically orgasmic."

A smile lifted his lip. "Only you would put it that way."

"Great desserts should be eaten as appetizers, I believe, so that you relish their subtleties. It's all in my book, but you haven't read any of it, right?"

"Not yet, no."

"I read some of yours."

"What did you think?"

"Oh, we'll get to that soon enough." She picked up a plump strawberry and dragged it through the chocolate sauce. "Chocolate had religious significance to the Aztecs, who first grew cacao, you know."

"Is that so?" Again with the sexy brow lift.

"It was considered a gift from Quetzalcoatl, the god of wisdom and knowledge. Only rulers and soldiers were trusted with the power it conveyed. The court consumed two thousand pitchers of it a day."

"You're nervous, aren't you?"

Yes, desperately. "Why would you think that?"

"Because you're talking nonstop." Another grin.

"I'm sharing factual tidbits as an example of what you'll want to prepare. And reporters are always fascinated when I point out that Moctezuma chugged an extra goblet of chocolate before visiting his women at night."

"Did he now?"

"For strength in the sack." She took a slow bite of the chocolate-drenched strawberry to emphasize her point. "You *have* to try this. Nature and decadence in one tart and musky morsel." She dipped a fresh berry in the chocolate and aimed it at his mouth.

He gripped her wrist and plucked the fruit from her fingers. "I can feed myself, Kathleen. And it's chocolate and fruit, not nirvana, no matter what the Aztecs thought." He snapped off a bite and swallowed.

"You hardly tasted that. You have to give your olfactory system a chance to do its work. The subtleties of taste come from smell."

She paused, caught by the scents she picked up from him—chocolate, strawberry, plus the soap on his skin and his own delicious musk. She loved how he smelled.

"Smell is the most primitive sense," she managed to say. "Aroma goes straight to the brain, without interpretation, which is why scent memories are so strong." Her voice got fainter as she spoke, and she felt herself tilt toward him. "Smell is very basic to our beings. In fact, a quarter of the people who lose their sense of smell lose their sex drive altogether."

"How strange." Dan swallowed hard, tilting, too. Then he frowned. "Can we just work?"

His exasperated tone brought her back to herself. "We *are* working, Dan. Everything I said gives you insight into my theories and you'll want to do the same with yours for reporters and for book-signings."

"So, all that with the chocolate and the strawberries was a media tip?"

"Exactly." That was her story and she'd stick with it. "So, surely there's something interesting about restraint you can share."

"I'll see what I can come up with," he said dryly.

"You should also prepare quotes. Here's a favorite of mine from Epicurus, the original voluptuary— 'Is man then meant to spurn the gifts of nature? Has he been born but to pluck the bitterest fruits? For whom do those flowers grow that the gods make flourish at mere mortals' feet?'"

"Okay. I get it." Dan opened his notepad and began to write. "Find facts, memorize quotes." He looked at her. "Next?"

"Next, take a bite of crème brûlée. But savor it this time."

He did what she'd asked, looking so hot doing it she could hardly stand it. "You happy?" he demanded.

"Getting there."

He drank a swallow of mineral water, his Adam's apple doing a muscular glide and bounce. Sheesh. The man made the simple act of drinking sexy. She liked the rounded pads of his fingers on the glass. So competent-looking, as if anything they touched would go *ah*. She used to go *ah*, she well recalled, and *ooh*, and *yes* and *don't ever, ever stop*.

"Should I read excerpts from my book?" he asked.

"Huh?" She'd been distracted by his finger pads.

He repeated the question.

"At signings maybe—short excerpts—but not for reporters. Reporters want snappy, pithy, sharp." She snapped her fingers.

"That's one of my points. In today's culture, we're always rushing, looking to fill our emptiness, wanting more and more—"

"Too leisurely." She held up her hand, paused and thought a moment. "Try this instead. 'These days, we run on speed, need and greed.'"

"That's too simplistic."

"Maybe, but Chicago's a tough town." She patted his hand, teasing, but the sensation was surprisingly intimate and his eyes gave off a silver heat. That was the magic of being with Dan, she realized. Heating up Dr. Cool. And the dynamic had not lessened with time.

Back to business. "You need sound bites that contrast with my views. Also prepare a condensed version of your professional history. Rhonda's got something in our press kit, but you need to make it more personal and fresh."

She made a fist, tilted it at him as if it held a microphone and spoke in a rich broadcast voice. "Dr. McAlister, how did you come up with your theories about moderation?"

"Right… Okay… Let's see… As an undergraduate student of psychology, I took a practicum in addiction."

"Practicum is too technical. Say, 'I studied addiction.' And I didn't know that. You were in clinical psych when I knew you."

"After I left ASU, I found an addiction project that attracted me."

"And why was that? Was addiction an issue for you?" She used her reporter voice, but she was dying to hear the answer.

"An issue? Not really. Addiction is pervasive in society…" He was fumbling, she could tell, and she thought she knew why.

"Wishy-washy. Guaranteed to raise reporter antennae. You need to use the technique called bridging. Give a quick answer to the question you don't like, then shift to one you do."

"Bridging, huh?"

"Yes. You could have said, 'No, but what is important is what I learned about human behavior while there.'" Or, *yes, I was addicted to a woman and wanted a cure.* But she wouldn't bait him. She would be calm and collected. She could always bait him later.

"I see."

"And by saying 'what's important,' I used a technique called *pointing.* Give reporters an organizing cue—the three rules…the best thing…the four key elements. Suggest a list and reporters start scribbling."

"Very good." He took more notes.

She put the mike under her own chin. "So, you studied addiction? What kind of addiction? Sex? Alcohol? Drugs?"

"And gambling, eating, spending. All addictions. In the course of that experience, I saw firsthand the crippling effects of overindulgence—the damage to self, family and friends."

He held her gaze as he spoke. Here was the same smug attitude that was in his book, which had kept her up twitching with anger half the night. She maintained a neutral face. "So, that would mean, Dr. McAlister, that, in your eyes, Kathleen Valentine pushes people into addiction?"

"People who aren't vulnerable to addiction can keep Ms. Valentine's views in perspective, I imagine, but for some people, yes, her advice could be harmful."

"Not bad," she said, irked as hell. "More or less rational. Reporters love conflict, so I would respond with something provocative, like, 'Dr. McAlister robs people of joy. He makes them feel guilty for enjoying the pleasures of the world. My work is aimed at non-addicts. Addiction is another issue."

"Okay," he said, pulling her mike hand to his chin. "Just as the tobacco companies seduce people into using their product despite its addictive properties, the allure of Ms. Valentine's approach could draw vulnerable people into financial or emotional crises they might otherwise avoid."

"You're being paternalistic," she said, irritation making her tone rise. "Your problem is that you think people are basically weak and evil. I believe that when left to their own devices, human beings will choose what's good for them. I merely empower them to protect and enhance their sensibilities. I urge them to find their joy."

"People are easily seduced into things that aren't good for them," he said. "Madison Avenue makes them think they must have the latest gadget, the newest clothes, the most expensive vacation. Overindulgence in eating is rampant. The child obesity stats are chilling and—"

She cut him off. "Too shrill. You sound like a kook. You're not a kook, are you?" It was hard to smile when she was pissed.

"No. And what I said was true."

His superior tone was killing her. "So, basically, Dan, you want me to issue a disclaimer. Warning: This book may be hazardous to your health?"

She grabbed one of the truffles and took a big bite, forgetting to savor the complex notes of the ball of cocoa delight. Moctezuma would be so disappointed in her.

"Not a bad idea," Dan said. "However, that would probably make the books irresistible, human nature being what it is when it comes to the forbidden." He gave her another wry smile she couldn't help but return.

Don't let him get to you.

His gaze dropped to her chest.

She glanced down and saw that in her agitation, she'd shifted so that he could catch significant cleavage. At least she was getting to him in some way.

When he looked up, she told him with her eyes that she'd seen.

He blinked away his daze. "As I was saying, I studied addiction and the therapies used to control it. Of course moderation is no answer for true addiction. But for non-addicts it is an effective way to manage appetites and live happier, healthier lives."

Time to dig in. "Let's get back to your interest in addiction, Dr. McAlister. Have you ever been tempted into excess?" She shifted slightly closer to him.

"Reporters won't ask that, Kathleen."

"They most certainly will. Especially if you act nervous like you did just now. Reporters are like sharks around a paper cut—hesitate and you're chum."

"You know what happened," he said softly. "I met you."

Right. A nympho narcissist who used sex to avoid real feelings. That thought sent a spike of anger through her. How could she calmly lay out her case, when she wanted to punch him?

"My experience is irrelevant to my point, which is that addiction is the dark side of indulgence," he said, using bridging and pointing, dammit. He gave her that I-know-better smile she hated.

"And what about the dark side of moderation?" she snapped. "Emotional starvation, masochism and misery. Where's your disclaimer? Warning—If you follow my advice, you'll never have another freely joyous moment in your life." Her voice went high. There were times when she envied Dan's self-control.

"We don't want to argue with the reporters, do we?" Dan said, maddeningly calm. He evidently thought this was a mock argument. "We don't want to be defensive or shrill, right?"

"No, we don't want to be defensive or shrill," she said, exasperated. She had to settle down. She was sounding like the kook she'd accused him of being.

"What's wrong, Kathleen? What are you angry about?"

"I'm not angry. I'm…just…disappointed in you. You're much more closed off than you used to be."

"Because I don't moan over chocolate on a piece of fruit?"

"No. Because you think enjoying yourself is some kind of crime. Because you think you're better than the rest of us, because you think that having needs and wants is somehow weak or wicked… And because you think I'm a possessive, sex-obsessed egomaniac."

"What?"

"Oh, don't pretend you don't know what I'm talking about." She grabbed his book from the table, flipped it to the section she'd peppered with exclamation points and stuck it under his nose. She was so upset, she was shaking.

She was supposed to gently but firmly point out how unfair he'd been, and suggest that he rethink his position. But instead, she was staring at him, steaming and trembling, while he read.

He looked up from the book. "This is what has you upset?"

"Upset? I'm furious. How could you be so self-righteous? So judgmental? So blind to your own role in what happened?" She grabbed the book and read the part about her emotional recklessness nearly destroying him. She put a finger down her throat and pretended to gag.

"You were there, too, Dan McAlister. For every reckless, obsessive, narcissistic moment. What happened took both of us. I didn't almost ruin you. Take that back right now."

"I wrote it the way I saw it. Clearly, I participated in the affair and I was vulnerable to you, but—"

"Vulnerable to me? You were a possessive maniac. You practically stalked me. Admit it."

"You have a point. But you enjoyed keeping me off balance, making me chase after you."

"At least then I knew you felt something. You weren't above it all, distant and cool and untouchable."

"Exactly my point. You were like a child who wanted attention at any price. We shouldn't fight about this."

"Why not?" She was almost yelling now. "It's emotional. It's honest. It's real. And that scares you."

And what was happening between them right now was scaring her. They were flushed, breathing hard, leaning closer. Dan's gaze dipped to her breasts, then to her thighs. He would love the panties she had on under these easy-to-remove shorts. Black lace. They would rip so easily. She'd love for him to tear them off and make her come in a few strokes.

She watched his face. His eyes were sending up flares of desperate desire she was sure matched her own. She could practically see the sparks in the air between them.

She should be yelling at him—he still hadn't admitted his role in their disaster—but she was liquid with want.

Since when had anger been a turn-on? Maybe from him, any passion would do. She watched a shudder move through his body. His hand lifted, as if to touch her, but then he forced it to the sofa.

"Of course you don't want to fight about this," she said, trying to stay mad. "You don't want to have any strong feeling. Your blood might flow in your veins. You might do something dangerous and impulsive like…"

And then she kissed him. And it was like two forest fires colliding, hot and sharp. Dan crushed her against him and they kissed hard, frantically, mouths smearing against each other, messy, missing, then hitting, as if they couldn't get enough, couldn't get it all.

His hands held her protectively, but pressed her ever closer, showing her how much he wanted her. His erection pushed insistently against her belly.

After a long, delicious time, he broke away with a moan.

"Why are you stopping?" she practically sobbed. She sagged like a released rubber band, grabbing his upper arms to steady herself.

"Because this is insane."

"Maybe it's what we need."

But he was right. She knew it even as she slid her fingers up his sleeves and inside to stroke his chest under his shirt. More than once, this very act had led them to get sexual in semi-public places. She loved his skin…its texture so elastic and smooth…and his muscles…strong, not showy.

"Don't." He gripped her wrists and firmly removed her hands from his shirt. "We can't do this. We don't want this."

"Sure we do. We want it like crazy."

"We agreed to forget the past. We can't just push aside the rules because we feel an urge."

"An urge? That's what you're calling this?" Wanting dessert on a diet or a Kate Spade bag on a budget was an urge.

"What else is it?"

An unquenchable passion, an overpowering drive. Except maybe not to Dan or else he was stronger than she was. She sure as hell wasn't going to show her weakness to him any more than her body had already broadcast it in 3-D neon. "Okay, it's an urge."

"I should leave," Dan said. She had the satisfaction of noting that he was looking at her mouth like a kid outside a candy store, panting steamy circles onto the glass.

"Suit yourself." She managed to sound reasonably cool.

"You act like you just won something."

"Maybe I did." She looked directly at his lap. At least she'd gotten a human reaction out of him.

"Because I got aroused? There's no shame in that. You're an attractive woman and we have a sexual history. But we are more than our desires. We can shape our lives, stay in balance, stabilize ourselves against the winds of want."

"The winds of want? Please. I know I said you need sound bites, but lose that one. Reporters will laugh you off the dais."

"It's what I believe."

"What happened to you?" she asked softly, not exactly angry, more curious and a little sad. "At least back in college you were willing to explore."

"You, Kathleen. You happened to me. And being with you brings it all back." He sounded so lost and vulnerable that her resentment melted.

Until he said, "Let's forget this happened and start fresh in the morning." So cool, so confident, so quickly in control.

He was right, though. She certainly wasn't going to sleep with him. Why had she even considered it? Out of curiosity? For old time's sake? To prove that she was still irresistible to him?

That would make her as messed up as he'd declared her in the book. And she wasn't. Well, maybe a little. But she could be just as mature and sensible as Dan could, dammit.

She walked him to the door and said good-night, not remembering until he'd gone, that she hadn't gotten him to apologize for the book or acknowledge he'd been at fault, too.

Dammit. She marched to the table of desserts and inhaled a truffle without tasting a gram.

The man had made her too upset to enjoy chocolate. Un-flippin'-forgivable.

5

BACK IN his room, Dan found himself unable to meditate or read or even think. He lay on his bed, Kathleen's kiss still electric on his lips, his pulse beating under his skin as though it wanted out.

What the hell had just happened? Had she been playing him with all those reminders of sex, licking champagne from his fingers, feeding him chocolate? No, that was just Kathleen being herself. She'd been nervous, jabbering on about Moctezuma, acting the expert just to avoid the tension between them.

She'd been stewing about the chapter from his book, of course, which explained her hostility. But the sexual flash fire their argument had sparked had surprised her as much as him.

Their history loomed over them like a lightning storm over the primal ooze, ready to spark into life at any moment. There was so much chemistry between them it felt unstoppable.

Damn.

He'd almost left that anecdote out of the book, but in the end, he needed to see it in print. Did disguising himself as an "acquaintance" make him a coward? Possibly. But clients did not want to know their therapists' human failings. No reader wanted to know he'd once bathed

nude in an outdoor hot tub, ditched class to spend endless days in bed with Kathleen, developed a jealous fixation that scared him. No, he was right to leave that out.

Kathleen's anger about the anecdote made sense. It
was painful information and he'd been blunt. Maybe
he'd framed her too negatively, but the point had been
his need to establish boundaries and identify his best in-
terests—the theme of his book.

Meanwhile, he was alarmed by his response to Kathleen's kiss. He'd been ready to take her right there on
that sofa. He'd risen above self-destructive behavior,
hadn't he?

Evidently not.

And for all Kathleen's claims that heedless passion
was good, he'd seen fear in her face. She was like a
rough-and-tumble kid goading a friend to make the
skateboard jump first to cover her own terror. The difference between Dan and her was that in the end Kathleen would go for it, terrified or not, while he knew
better.

Self-control was the key to his success. He knew
that. And he believed his approach might help Kathleen,
too, though she'd strangle him for saying so. Clearly, her
lifestyle wasn't doing her any good. She seemed frantic and edgy. And not just because of seeing him. Something else, something bigger, was going on. Her
radiance had dimmed. She seemed insecure, subdued,
dissatisfied.

If he could help her, he wanted to. To make up for
hurting her. And because he still cared.

You still want her, you horn dog. Just admit it.

Damn, he was weak. How could he help her if he kept
stripping her naked and pinning her to the wall with his

eyes? He had to exercise the restraint he'd built over the years. He would do it, too. What did it say about him if he couldn't?

Filled with new determination and sweating with anxiety, he went to the wet bar to make himself some tea—the lemon-chamomile blend Rhonda had given him. The act of pouring the water, listening to it hum and hiss into the pot was soothing. He wasn't immune to sensation. Kathleen made him sound like some cold, repressed machine. An *ice* machine.

He had to guard himself against her and his feelings for her. Everybody had a crucial relationship—one that taught them what they needed to know about themselves and happiness. His relationship with Kathleen had been that for him.

For her, too, perhaps, though she would never tell him. She had too much pride. For all her pretense at openness, she was emotionally guarded. He wouldn't be surprised if instead of being hurt by the breakup, she'd been angry that he'd beat her to it. *Hold it, buster. I'm the one who leaves.* He smiled, imagining her saying that.

Being around her put him in deep turmoil. No surprise, considering how much emotional baggage they carried—hell, it was a moving van's worth. He poured the hot water over the tea, breathing in the soothing medicine of it.

So, how could he get through the remaining time without another incident? He sipped the barely steeped tea, enjoying its warm glide down his throat.

What did Kathleen want from the tour? She'd said what was important was their books, their status as authors. What specifically did she hope to achieve? If he made sure she got it, the other stuff—the Bekins van of

their past—might fade in importance. He didn't dare ask
her straight-out. If one paternal or condescending syl-
lable slipped out, she'd deck him.

He had to handle her with kid gloves.

Handle her. He thought about that shiny black robe
she'd worn the first night in New York. He'd ached to
strip her of it and stroke her until she moaned the way
she had when she'd eaten that damnable chocolate tonight. The woman was sensuality incarnate. A husky-
voiced, swollen-lipped, sweetly curved Venus. *For
whom do those flowers grow?* Indeed.

The tea wasn't enough to calm him, so he strode to
his bathroom and splashed cold water on his face. In the
mirror, he saw that he looked haggard and haunted.
Hell, he *was* haunted.

Standing there, he heard the rush of water in the pipes
in the wall. *She's taking a bath.* Kathleen had practically
lived in hot water when he knew her, bathing when she
was stressed or happy or playful or aroused…any excuse would do. They'd had numerous episodes of slippery sex in her roomy tub, overflowing with expensive
suds. In fact, she'd told him she'd chosen her apartment
for its sunny kitchen nook and its big tub.

Some of his most erotic mental pictures were of
Kathleen in a tub heaped with foam, hair up, leaning forward to shave her legs, the line of her shin catching the
light. No one enjoyed a bath as much as Kathleen. She
inhabited every second of every drip, slide and splash.

The rushing sound stopped. He heard the squeak of
a body moving against porcelain. She was in the water
now. Naked. He thought about her body…her long
legs…the curve of her torso…the way she would lean
back and run a big bar of soap over the slick rise of her

breasts, stroking her swollen nipples—small, ripe fruit waiting to be teased and tasted.

The air was always sweet with vanilla. The suds and soap were made with real vanilla beans. She'd told him about the rare and exotic vanilla orchid, all the while soaping his cock with her clever fingers.

No domestically grown food in the world requires more labor than vanilla. Did you know that?

No, he didn't, he'd managed to say, massaging her breasts with his soap-coated hands while she worked his shaft with hers.

Mmm, yes, it's true. A little lower…just like that… The white flower blooms for a single day and must be hand-pollinated exactly on time.

Oh, yeah? He'd been hypnotized, transfixed by her touch and her whiskey words.

When the bean is perfectly ripe, it's plunged in boiling water to stop its growth, then cured for months and months…nearly a year.

A year?

Nearly. Eventually, they harvest the vanillin crystals that form on the pod. And that's how we get vanilla—a true treasure of nature.

Then he'd touched her sex under the bubbles. Her eyes had widened and deepened in color. She'd trembled, moaned, pulled him close. So he'd entered her, thrust deep again and again until the waves of pleasure blended with the waves of water and they rocked to an orgasm that flooded the bathroom.

She was in there now, soaping up, with that look on her face, no doubt, maybe touching herself. God. He could practically smell the vanilla musk and her special scent.

Slow your breath, he told himself now. *Feel, then be*

*the air in your lungs. Breathe in...two, three, four...
out...two, three, four.*

Screw that. He rested his forehead against the mirror. The smooth coolness did nothing to distract him
from the fact that he was fully awake, painfully erect and
aching with lust.

He went to bed to satisfy himself swiftly, permitting
a fleeting fantasy of joining Kathleen in the tub. When
his release came, it brought no relief. If he went to her
right now, would she welcome him into her sweet vanilla arms?

Why torture himself? Punching his pillow, he rolled
over, determined to sleep. He would find out what Kathleen wanted from the tour and make sure she got it.

As long as what she wanted wasn't him.

"I WOULDN'T SAY that Dr. McAlister is repressed," Kathleen said, giving the University of Chicago audience a
broad wink. "I'll leave that to his therapist."

The crowd laughed. Despite her exhaustion, she was
managing to amuse. This was their last event of the day,
thank God. They'd already endured an early-morning
television show, a radio talk show, radio-feed interviews
and a book-signing—so it was reasonable to feel a little lost, a little woozy, a little flat.

There was more going on, though, than interview
burnout.

She couldn't stop thinking about how she'd blown it
last night with Dan—undercut her own strength in both
their eyes by kissing him and suggesting more. She felt
stupid and weak.

She was counting the minutes until she could make
it back to a hot bath, though last night she'd had to re-

sort to a sleeping pill on top of an extra-long soak to get to sleep.

She hated that Dan had been the one with sense enough to stop them. Sleeping with him would have been weird and sad and confusing. And wrong.

She had to control this urge. Focus on the book tour, on the boost it could give her career. Forget Dan and their past—her own personal Waterloo. Who needed another taste of that?

Even for old time's sake? For healing?

Forget it. It was just that after Troy she'd felt that scary weariness and with Dan she'd felt so alive…every cell screaming with vibrancy. Her stomach shimmied at the thought, but she ignored it to focus on Dan's response to her latest jab.

"As a therapist myself," Dan said, "I must point out that many of my clients have benefited from my approach. The wisdom is not new. Consider Cicero's words from centuries ago. 'Never go to excess, but let moderation be your guide.'"

Very good. He'd used bridging and a quote. Quick learner.

"Ah, but I prefer W. Somerset Maugham," she countered, "'Excess on occasion is exhilarating. It prevents moderation from acquiring the deadening effect of a habit.'"

"Healthy habits are life-affirming, not deadening."

"We are biologically designed to seek pleasure," she argued, fighting to keep her words from feeling as dull and flat as day-old brut. "The search for joy is wound in the lattice of our DNA like climbing honeysuckle. We have an entire center in our brain whose only purpose is to experience joy. We're hardwired for it."

"But the search for pleasure can be destructive," Dan said in stern tones, a perfect setup for her rebuttal.

"What's destructive is the puritanical guilt on which you capitalize, Dan. You encourage people to suffer. You make self-denial a holy act. You boil life's sweet peas to mush."

"People already suffer, Kathleen, but not from the lack of pleasure, from a surfeit of it. Just as music played too loudly becomes noise, our super-size, super-sweetened, super-sexed culture has numbed us so that we no longer feel or taste or hear anything but the loudest, harshest, most bitter things."

Not bad. He'd adapted her idea and created a nice quip. The students in the audience seemed enthralled and many were taking notes. Rhonda had said a magazine writer was here, too.

"Enjoyment is a celebration of our humanity. Both the Talmud and the Koran—books filled with behavioral rules and regs—promise punishment to those who refuse to enjoy the approved-of pleasures."

He blinked at her, opened his mouth to respond, but then closed it. Sometimes he seemed transfixed when he was listening to her. He'd been like that in the old days and that gave her a lovely rush of power.

"Humans are pleasure-seeking, true," Dan finally asserted. "But they are also goal-driven. Working with a purpose gives us peace and direction, and allows us to put pleasure in its proper place."

"Pleasure's proper place is every place." The audience applauded and she continued, "Pleasure is vital to good health. Unhappiness has been linked with increased illness."

"I'm not suggesting that people should suffer," Dan

said. "The mind is happy and content by nature. Consider the Zen poem—'Sitting quietly…doing nothing…spring comes…and the grass grows…by itself.'"

Good one, Dan.

The audience applauded gently. Dan was no media star, but he was holding his own. They were becoming a book-tour team, which was good…because the only reason they were together was to build book sales and earn fans. She had to focus on that.

With that in mind, she dragged up as much fire as she could and said, "We're only here for one life so far as any of us knows. Revel in it, see the sights, smell the smells, listen, taste, rub up against it. Use the guest towels, the fancy china, the heirloom teapot. What are you waiting for? Life's here, so live it."

Applause exploded, echoed and bounced against the high ceiling and far walls. This was very good. Almost enough to restore her flagging spirits.

Dan leaned close. "Uncle," he murmured. "You're good. Can we quit?" When she nodded, he leaned into the mike. "It's time we let our work speak for us. We can answer a few questions and then we'll be happy to sign our books for you at the back of the hall."

His words were gracious, but Kathleen heard exhaustion in his voice. His eyes held an uncharacteristic fog and were underlined by gray bags. He must have slept poorly, too. They were both a mess. Something had to give.

They handled questions, the audience issued its final approving applause, then rustled to its feet, conversation swelling and echoing. Rhonda scampered over to them, grinning. "That was terrific! Did you guys practice?"

"In a way." Kathleen gave Dan a faint smile.

He returned it. They were coconspirators now. They'd agreed not to say anything to Rhonda about their media-training session. They didn't dare risk her reading between the lines.

"After you sign books, I need you for a photograph," Rhonda said. "I scored the cover of *Midwest Life*. Isn't that great?"

"Terrific," Kathleen said. Rhonda had an extra bounce in her step and more sparkle in her smile, if that were possible. She'd mentioned going to see her old boyfriend at dinner last night. It must have gone well. Kathleen would ask Rhonda about it when they had a free moment.

When the books were all signed, Kathleen and Dan followed Rhonda to a backstage corner where two people stood near a silver lighting umbrella and a sky-blue backdrop, along with a camera on a tripod.

The reporter introduced herself and her photographer and the two consulted about the shot, then posed Kathleen and Dan back-to-back, arms crossed, holding their books so the titles were visible.

The photographer retreated to her camera.

"Wait a sec," the reporter said. "Your books are wrong."

Kathleen looked down and saw she held Dan's book. She exchanged it with the one he held.

"That would have been awful," the reporter said, "Though it would be interesting if you switched, huh? Tested each other's theories?"

"It would be," Kathleen said, the idea catching her fancy.

"Give us 'determined and triumphant,'" the photographer called out. "Like you just won the battle of the books."

"Oh, but I did win," Kathleen said.

"I think I held my own," Dan said, his chuckle rumbling against her spine.

What if they did test each other's ideas? Talk about interesting...

"Ms. Valentine?" the photographer called to her. "You're giving me 'speculative.' I want 'competitive.'"

"Sure, sure, sorry." She composed her face. She could do competitive. Or something even better...

A few hours later, Kathleen sat with Dan in the dimly lit hotel coffee shop to talk about it. They'd shooed Rhonda off to see her ex-boyfriend and the restaurant was virtually empty.

"So, what is this idea you have for making the tour go better?" Dan asked her, sounding uneasy.

"Relax. You'll like it." She patted his cheek, relishing the bristles in his jaw and his taut skin and muscular cheek. Stolen pleasures were the best.

"Why do I doubt that?"

"Because you have no faith in me. Not that you don't have reason to doubt me, but this is different." She sipped her mocha latte with cinnamon and leaned onto her arms, folded on the cool marble of a table so small their knees bumped under it.

Dan's eyes shot to her chest, then up to her face. She liked how attuned he was to her, tracking the merest weight shift, breast swell, knee brush or hip wiggle. He was far more lusciously and responsively human than he wanted to be.

But we are more than our desires. Why would we want to be?

She felt a special smile tease her lips. One of her old troublemaking smiles. She'd missed making trouble.

"I'm sure I'll regret this, but go ahead and tell me."

"Experience is the best teacher, right?"

"Right…" he said slowly.

"And we both need to learn from each other?"

"More or less."

"So, how about instead of reading each other's books, we live them?"

"Live them? How?" He leaned closer. He had the most gorgeous eyes. Navy flecks swam in pale blue seas that went deep into some beautiful beyond.

"The reporter gave me the idea when she suggested we test each other's theories. So let's do it. I'll take some time—part of a day—to teach you and you do the same for me. I'll show you sensory fun. You show me moderation and balance."

"I don't know…" His eyes narrowed, pondering the concept.

"It'll be research. An experiment." That ought to get him. He had a background in clinical research, after all.

"An experiment, huh?" His eyes followed her as she sat back in her chair to let the idea percolate. "We'd have to set some parameters."

"Parameters? You mean about sex?"

He glanced around as if she'd suggested a drug deal and someone might have heard.

"Relax. Sex is completely off the table, Dan. Or the bed…or the floor." She grinned. "Sex is too easy."

"You're saying I'm easy?"

"Hey, a joke! You're loosening up already. The point is that I don't need sex to prove I'm right about pleasure."

"And when it's my turn, you'll do whatever I ask?"

"Short of walking on coals or a high colonic, yeah. But you want to convert me, not torture me, right?"

"This isn't a religion, Kathleen. I don't want converts. I want you to be happy. And I do believe I can help you."

There was that paternal tone again. For the sake of her plan, she bit back a smart-ass rejoinder. "I'd like to help you, too, Dan." Maybe help them both. At the very least, they'd understand each other better.

Would she win the battle of the books? Convert Dan? Well, there was that. She could be competitive at times. And she did want Dan to admit he didn't have all the answers.

"What about Rhonda?" Dan asked.

"We'll be discreet. Her boyfriend will distract her tomorrow, which is pretty open. And the first day in Phoenix is light, too. We'll just tell her we're separately busy."

"Still, it's risky. Maybe we just agree to disagree."

"After all we've been through? We owe it to ourselves to understand each other better." She paused, letting her words sink in. Muzak drifted through the coffee shop, that Paul Simon song about all the ways to leave a lover. Occasional clangs from the kitchen spiked the quiet.

"Things between us are…complicated," Dan said, looking down, running a finger through a water ring on the table.

"You're not afraid, are you? Scared I'll shake your theories?"

His eyes snapped to hers. "Of course not."

Don't underestimate me, darlin', she wanted to say, but she bit her tongue. Again. It was getting bruised from all the restraint she had to exercise around Dan. He'd taken the hook, anyway, so there was no reason to yank on the line. "I'll be first. *You* need to *relax*. How can you even hear with your shoulders up around your ears like that?"

He smiled that wry smile she loved.

"Massage will definitely be on the schedule."

"Massage?" He quirked a brow.

"Therapeutic massage. I always get massages when I'm on book tours. Keeps the muscles loose, the blood flowing, the lactic acid expelled."

He just looked at her, still doubtful.

"I promise no funny business."

"I'm not sure that's a promise you can keep."

"You'll just have to trust me. I have as much invested in this as you do. I can promise you'll learn something."

"You think so?"

"I know so." She'd show him that reveling in pleasure had value. That it made life memorable and meaningful.

He drank his coffee with another erotic little swallow, then set down the cup with two sets of careful fingers. "I don't really see it, but if it helps you…"

"If it helps *me*…?" She bit her lip this time, since her tongue was too sore. She'd won her chance to convince him, no sense bristling. Tomorrow, they'd see who helped whom.

6

DAN WOKE EARLY, anxious about the upcoming hours he'd promised Kathleen. He'd come far too close to lapsing into dangerous behavior alone with her in her room and he was voluntarily heading there again. But if exposing himself to her theories for a few hours meant a chance to help her with his, then it was worth it.

He didn't like the weariness in her face he saw when she didn't think anyone was watching her. Or the frantic sparkle in her eyes, as if she conjured her energy out of thin air and despair. That wasn't like the old Kathleen. That Kathleen had eyes that gleamed with the fun she spent her life hunting down and squeezing the life out of. The old Kathleen had so much energy it bubbled over like champagne opened wrong and intoxicated anyone who got within a splash.

Especially introverted loners like Dan. She'd made him feel alive and part of things. But she was different now. Troubled.

He'd seen the same look on some of his clients' faces—an accumulated weariness like soot in a chimney or sludge in an engine. Like frogs in steadily warming water, they kept paddling, adapting and adjusting to the rising heat until they went emotionally belly-up, had a breakdown, lost a job, destroyed a marriage.

Kathleen was right that after everything they'd shared, they owed each other. He owed her the help she needed. Not in a paternalistic or arrogant way, but simply as a friend with a gift to give.

To get there, he had to handle whatever sensual adventure she'd cooked up. Massage would probably be the easy part.

To gear up, he doubled his meditation time and swam laps after his usual run. Refreshed and energized, he headed for the elevator. Inside, he pushed the button for his floor.

"Dan!"

He looked out and saw Rhonda rushing toward him. He pushed the open-door button and she stopped in the doorway to glance down at herself, then up at him. "You caught me. Last night's clothes. I just had to throw out the checklist, Dan."

The elevator buzzed its objection to her standing on the threshold too long. She stepped inside, the doors shuddered closed and they zoomed upward.

"But Dylan said all the right things. He's changed. He has." Her eyes gleamed in a way that told him her self-protective instincts were out of commission. Once the desire switch got tripped, self-control—notoriously fragile in matters of the heart—dissolved like a sugar cube in coffee.

"What do you think? Am I deluding myself?" At their floor, Rhonda banged the close-door button with her palm, waiting for his answer.

They sailed upward and Dan sighed. "Well, I would say—"

"Be careful, right? Take a deep breath and go slow. Don't start planning who's going to move. I mean I love my job. He did say he was interested in living in New York, which is so cool…"

At the top floor, the elevator opened, closed, then headed downward. Dan gave their floor button three quick jabs.

"So, you're right," Rhonda continued. "That's jumping way up the ladder of assumptions. We haven't established shared meanings yet… Wait, that's not your book. That's *My Way or the Highway: Winning in Relationship.* Sorry."

"Not a problem," he said, banging the button again for good measure. "Just don't do anything—"

"Hasty. Right. I hope you don't think I'm a loser for sleeping with him. You don't, do you? Oh, and telling him I love him. Was that insane?"

"I think you're human and that your feelings are—"

"Strong. Very. What can you do? What do *you* do, anyway? How did you train yourself to control your emotions?"

"Well, I—" The door opened on their floor, and he practically leaped out. "What I do isn't really relevant, Rhonda, I don't think." He walked backward down the hall.

She walked toward him. "But I might learn from your experiences."

"Oh, I doubt that." The allegory in his book was as close as he ever wanted to come to sharing his affair with Kathleen.

"So, listen, I talked with the concierge about a museum-slash-architecture tour," Rhonda said, still approaching. "Sound good?"

He realized he could save Kathleen a phone call and stopped walking away. "Actually, Kathleen mentioned she had plans and I could use the downtime. Why don't you catch up on your sleep, do some work, see Dylan, whatever."

"Are you sure? All I need is a power nap and I'll be ready to groove. We could hit the Art Institute maybe?"

"We'll be fine. You take the day for yourself."

"I could arrange for you to sign books at a distributor's warehouse."

"No, no. We're worn out. Really." He began backing away.

She kept advancing. "I don't want you to think Dylan is interfering with my work, because I'm completely dedicated."

"Oh, we know that." Just when he was sure she was coming straight into his room for tea or something, she stopped. "This is me," she said, pointing her key card at the door.

"Great. Rest up. Enjoy." He practically ran the rest of the way to his room.

Once there, he showered and dressed, then booted his laptop to write until the time Kathleen had declared "decent" enough to start his foray into her world—eleven.

He meant to work on the outline for his second book or at least formalize the new chart he'd sketched for measuring serenity, but after Rhonda's rant, he decided to write about the hazards of romantic obsession.

He'd been far too vague on the subject in his first book. In the second, he wanted to devote a whole section to it. Spending ten days with Kathleen would give him an up-close reminder. And a chance to practice what he preached.

Just the thought of her made his pulse zoom and his breathing go shallow—miles away from his diaphragm, the source of stability. He'd built his inner strength over the years, but around Kathleen, he felt as if he stood naked under a punishing sun—as if his philosophy were an outfit he wore, instead of deeply held beliefs that ruled his life.

Maybe it was their past. The deep pain, the original influence, did have power. He knew that from his own childhood. His parents were both artists—his mother a painter, his father a writer—and both temperamental. They'd fought. A lot.

They'd loved him, of course, but he'd been peripheral to their day-to-day drama. Tempers flared, doors slammed, dishes crashed to the floor or were loosely aimed at the other's head.

He'd spent his childhood shutting out the smashing china, the harsh words, the threats of divorce, his mother accusing his father of locking her away from her friends, his father claiming she was cheating on him, didn't love him, loved only her work.

As a therapist, he'd studied the various effects emotional chaos had on children. His parents had been heedless of the fallout of their passion. Once, in a blind fury, his mother had smashed the clay paintbrush holder Dan had made for her in his eighth-grade art class. He'd spent hours getting the shape just right, painted it with care and given it to her with pride. She'd made him blush with praise and awarded it a prime spot on her work table.

Then in a moment of rage she'd mindlessly tossed it at his father.

She'd begged Dan's forgiveness afterward, tears in her eyes. No problem, he'd said, scoffing at her attempt to glue together the shards that survived. It was just a dumb pot.

But he still felt the shock of seeing his precious gift lose all value in the face of his mother's momentary fury.

He preferred to focus on the good times. There were plenty—trips to the beach, where his mother painted and his father wrote in longhand, while Dan chased waves and built structures in the sand.

Joyous Sunday breakfasts where his mother experimented with extravagant blintzes, crêpes, or French toast, the stereo blasting out her wild rock or his father's Mozart, the dreamy looks his parents exchanged as the meal wound down, their disappearance into the bedroom for a nap.

Once he was old enough to figure out that his parents didn't spend those lazy Sunday afternoons asleep, he'd cringed with mortification, but had been reassured, too. Love endured.

He'd had good times with each parent, too. Hung out in his mother's studio, where she chattered to him as if they were peers. She was alive with joy when she painted. His father demanded pin-drop silence in his study while he wrote, but he encouraged Dan to read on the sofa and would look up from his computer from time to time and smile at him.

Still, the passion, the fits, the instability had led Dan to crave serenity. A serenity that his bizarre affair with Kathleen had shattered.

That relationship had imprinted his soul, too. That must be what was going on. Just as when you visited home, you reverted to childhood behaviors, being with Kathleen transformed him into the man he'd been with her.

And made him say smug things to push her away and distract himself from the steady drum of desire—as if his heart's rhythm beat to the syllables of her name. Kath-leen, Kath-leen, lub-lub, lub-lub.

He became so engrossed in what he was writing that when he looked up he realized he barely had time to brush his teeth and run a comb through his hair before heading to her room.

Dress comfortably, she'd told him, he remembered. *Comfortably* to her probably meant stark naked. Just thinking about that made him button his sport shirt to the very top.

He peeked out the door into the hall to be sure Rhonda wasn't in sight, then slid down the hall and around the corner to Kathleen's suite like a criminal. Not an auspicious sign.

He'd barely tapped on the door when it jerked inward. "Come in," Kathleen said. "We're waiting for you."

We? Caught by the sight of her, he stilled. Her face was fresh with light cosmetics and she wore clingy black pants and a red top that exposed her stomach. Her hair was in a thick braid that rested on one breast.

"Don't just stand there." She pulled him inside.

We, he saw, consisted of Kathleen and three musicians—a stand-up bass player, a guitarist and a guy with a keyboard.

"Dan, meet James, Raider and Cole," Kathleen said, gesturing at the group. "They got up early to play for us."

The three musicians, whose names he recognized from the marquee outside the hotel's bar, nodded at him.

"You hired a band?" he said, stunned.

As if on cue, the keyboardist muttered something, started a count, and they launched into "It Had to be You."

"Live music is so much more vivid than recorded." Her eyes shone with the excitement of a child presenting a gift. "Have a seat." She'd placed two upholstered chairs facing the musicians.

He sat and Kathleen joined him, immediately swaying in her chair to the beat, both feet tapping different rhythms. How did she manage that? "Isn't this great?" she said.

"Sure. It's nice."

She watched him for a moment. "You're not even moving."

"I'm moving inside?" he tried.

"Maybe we should dance."

"You want to dance?"

"No, you *need* to dance." She leaped to her feet and tugged him up with her.

He moved automatically to take her in his arms—one hand on the curve of her hip, the other gripping her small hand.

She seemed startled by the sudden intimacy. So was he.

"Whew. Think we can handle this?" she asked, trying for a light laugh. "Dancing is sexual, but it doesn't have to be." She bit her lip.

"Sure we can." He wasn't about to admit he already had a painful hard-on. He took a quick turn to demonstrate his focus was on dancing, not holding her close, not breathing in her scent, not looking into her green eyes. "So, what else do you have in mind…besides music and massage?" He'd actually managed to sound businesslike.

"I thought we would focus on the senses."

"What does that mean?" It sounded innocent enough, but knowing Kathleen, it could go wicked at any moment.

"I want you to be the sensuist—a person who focuses

on the senses. Valuing sensory experience is not decadent. It's rejuvenating. There's self-discipline in my world, too."

"Okay." But he couldn't concentrate, because as she talked, she leaned into him, so that he felt her thigh muscles against his own. He shifted away from her.

"You're a little stiff," she said, tugging at his hands to loosen his posture.

You have no idea. He tried to relax his hips and legs, while managing his erection—no easy feat. "How's that?"

"Better. How about if you close your eyes and let the music inside? Maybe that will help you relax into your body." She sounded so earnest. She must really believe this stuff. She wasn't being the least bit seductive. Or no more than her every glance, wiggle or word already was.

Which was no help. Kathleen not trying to seduce him was even more appealing than Kathleen trying to.

He closed his eyes as she'd instructed, but instead of getting into the music, he got into Kathleen—the sweet puff of her breath on his face, her wiry muscles beneath his fingers, the sinuous sway of her hips. Mortified by the tyranny of his erection, he was careful to keep his distance.

The trio moved into a new song—this one in a minor key that was poignant and had an unusual rhythm.

"Thelonious Monk," she breathed with a sigh of pleasure. "The song is 'Ruby, My Dear.' Doesn't it just make your brain lift in your skull?"

He opened his eyes and smiled at her. "Only you would put it that way."

"How would you put it?"

"Not like that."

"But isn't this relaxing?"

"Sure," he said, knotted in every place that could tighten. How could he relax with his hands on her incredible body, her green eyes on his face, not letting him escape at all?

"You don't act very relaxed and your palms are sweating."

He sighed. "I'm doing my best."

"I hope so. Today, you're mine," she said, teasing him, he could tell.

"So it seems." Their gazes locked for a hot instant, then they looked away fast. "So, I'm supposed to appreciate my senses, huh? Get into the music?" He might as well concentrate on what she wanted to teach him. The sooner he got it, the sooner he could escape her whiskey voice and tempting body. "What else?"

"While you're here, just delve into everything you hear, touch, see, smell and taste. I have lunch coming, too, by the way. Try to peel back the layers of every sensation like a sweet onion. Notice everything."

Her husky voice held him hypnotized. "Whatever you say, Kathleen."

She narrowed her gaze, evidently misreading his daze as uncertainty. "Don't tell me I'll need the blindfold?"

"The blindfold?"

"To cover your eyes while I give you things to feel or smell or taste. Without vision, your other senses become more alert."

"Sounds like a bad idea to me."

"Because you'd have to trust me, right? And you don't trust me."

"Not completely, no."

She paused, watching him. "Smart. I don't quite trust myself, either." He caught the flash of alarm and desire in her expression. Every feeling blazed across Kathleen's face like a comet marking the midnight sky.

She seemed to collect herself—and her sense of mischief. "So, cooperate with me and I won't drag out the blindfold. That's been done to death, anyway. So, what are you sensing right now?"

"The music's nice. You smell good. Your hand is warm." He squeezed it.

"Stretch your vocabulary. Let's have a little sensory inventory. Start with smell. You said I smell good, but break that down a little. What exactly do you detect?"

"Okay. Flowers. A spice of some kind. Not quite sweet. Reminds me of a Middle Eastern deli." Or an opium den. Intoxicating, overwhelming and possibly illegal.

"Yes. Much better. How about sound? Give me details."

"Your earrings clicking, our feet sliding on the rug. The music, of course."

"This song tickles my ears. Do you get that? It makes me feel so wiggly I have to do something—move or dance or sing."

"You're asking me if this music makes me wiggly?"

"Okay. You're not a wiggly kind of guy."

"But I do like jazz. I appreciate the patterns at play. It appears chaotic, but it's actually as orderly as math."

"Way to ruin the magic, Dan." She closed her eyes. "Listen to the way the notes strain up, twist and twine and trick you. You're riding along and then there's that stretchy high note…such a surprise, like a muscle pulled in a new direction. It almost hurts, but it's a sweet ache."

"Uh-huh." He wasn't really listening. With her eyes shut, he could freely study the dark curve of her lashes on her pale skin, and the way her eyebrows peaked and dipped when she concentrated or spoke. Her nose was not small—right size for her face—with a rounded tip and delicate nostrils. Her lips were perfect—soft and always moving—curved in a grin, pursed or scrunched in contemplation, getting licked or nibbled or bitten.

His cock surged again.

As if she sensed his reaction, Kathleen opened her eyes. "Hey, you weren't supposed to be looking." She smiled hesitantly, as if she wasn't having such an easy time of this close contact, either.

"Sight is a sense." He managed to sound innocent.

"I always loved how much attention you paid," she said softly. "Why do you fight your basic nature so hard?"

"I just don't see the need to get caught up in physicality." *Oh, please.* He prayed she'd buy his excuse.

She sighed. "It just means you miss out on so much…" She actually seemed sad for him. He was touched.

"It works for me, Kathleen." Especially around her. Being with her in the old days, he'd found it easy as breathing to become wild and reckless and out of control.

Take that last night.

She'd said she was meeting friends for drinks—celebrating somebody or other's birthday. She'd been escaping from him a lot at the time. He'd grown suspicious and followed her, blown off evening clients just to calm the fever in his head about what she was doing and with whom. When she'd stepped outside the bar with some people, including several men, jealousy had slugged him in the gut.

She'd smiled when she'd seen him heading across the street, but her smile had faltered when he got close enough that she could see the look in his eyes. The other people disappeared, and he pulled her into his arms and kissed her hard—almost angrily.

He'd had the fleeting urge to take her right there, against the back wall of the bar, but he'd fought it. Barely.

Filled with remorse, he'd later apologized for his ferocity. She'd laughed it off, but he'd seen her alarm, her sense of being trapped.

And he'd known then that he was out of control. Too much like his possessive father, who'd been ridiculously jealous of his mother. He'd been too caught up in being in love. Hell, he'd let himself drop into academic probation without a protest. So he'd ended it before it got worse.

"What's the matter?" she asked him now.

"Nothing. Can we move on?"

She studied him, as if trying to read his mind, then seemed to think better of it. "Okay. Next, how about touch? What are you aware of?"

Her body under her clothes...the way he wanted to brush her nipple through the thin silk...her fingers and what they could do to him...her braid tickling his arm, reminding him of her hair falling over his face when she was on top of him.

"The silk of your blouse," he choked out finally. "Your hands. On my back and in my palm. Our mingled sweat."

"Very nice. How about textures?" Was there a little tremble in her voice? "Like the pants you're wearing are corduroy." She moved their joined hands to his hip and slid his hand down the side of his leg. Her hand, pressing down on his, was a few inches from where he surged against his zipper.

"Compare this to the surface of my blouse, where your other hand is."

"Yeah," he said, sliding his hand across her back, feeling the silk, wanting to shove the cloth up and get at the warm cream of her skin. Now that was a texture he loved. "Bumpy versus smooth," he managed.

"How about this?" She took his hand and placed her braid across his palm. "A living texture."

"It feels soft," he said, swallowing across a bone-dry throat. His erection gave a hip-hop of hope being so near her breast. "Warm," he added, knowing she'd want detail. "Thick." He wanted to undo the braid and loosen the strands, slide his fingers there, guide her mouth to his and make her moan with pleasure.

"You always loved my hair," she said wistfully. Clearly she hadn't meant to say that. She trembled a little in his arms.

"Yeah." Especially when she collapsed on his chest, sweaty and sated, to smother him with its sweet-smelling weight.

The band started a fast song, thank God, and he dropped her braid to grab her hand and swing her out and spin her back.

She laughed, relieved, too. "Anyway, you get the idea of how texture, temperature and density can affect how something feels." She was trying to sound informative, but he knew she was as rattled as he was.

A knock at the door made them both start as if they'd been doing something wrong.

"That's lunch," Kathleen said, flushed and breathless. She hurried to the door, her butt tight, legs quick, braid bouncing on her back. Damn, she was beautiful.

He could only hope the band would stay through lunch and the massage because it looked as though Rhonda wasn't the only one in trouble in Chicago.

7

AT LEAST Dan was having a good time, Kathleen decided, as she watched him lick butterscotch milk-shake foam from his upper lip with that stupendous tongue of his.

Get a grip. "Delicious, huh?" she asked.

"Yeah. Very tasty. Everything has been."

"That was the plan." Lunch had been deliberately decadent with both subtle and sharply different tastes—potato waffles with smoked salmon, a Belgian endive and watercress salad with quail eggs, and a sample of honey-glazed duck confit. The milk shake served as both drink and dessert.

Dan smiled dreamily, floating on the sensory sea she'd plopped him into. She, meanwhile, was a mess of nerves. All the while she'd calmly urged Dan to catalogue his sensations, compare the textures of her silk blouse, his corduroy pants, her braided hair, she zinged and itched and ached like mad.

This is for Dan, she kept telling herself. To open him up to everything he'd shut out. And, of course, to prove she wasn't proposing some evil and addictive way of life.

If she jumped him now, she'd lose whatever credibility she'd retained after the other night's kiss. Today was about the sensuist in her, not the sensualist, who would mind her manners until Dan left.

"Deadly sludge for the arteries, though," Dan said wistfully, studying the creamy beige concoction.

"Oh forget that," she said, glad to have something to debate. "They don't even know the good from the bad anymore. *Stay away from fat,* the experts say. Then, *No, no, fat is good, carbs are bad. Alcohol's awful. Wait, a glass of red wine a day keeps the cardiologist away.*"

"You can't possibly believe this is good for you." He lifted his goblet and swirled its contents.

"I don't know, Dan. After an intensive study of longevity, a prominent research physiologist said the secret to a long, healthy life is modified hedonism. Which is my whole theory…with a few episodes of excess thrown in. So…" She clinked her glass against his. "Guilt is off the table today, Dan."

Along with sex, of course, which had sounded a lot easier when she'd so blithely declared it out of the question in the coffee shop. Thank goodness she'd arranged for an in-room massage instead of doing it herself, an idea she'd immediately dismissed.

"How are you feeling?" she asked. "Alive? Present? Aware?" The quicker he felt that way, the quicker she could hustle him out of here.

"Truthfully?" he said. "I feel full and overwhelmed."

"Maybe I've overloaded you. Too much too fast." She tried not to sound frustrated. "How about if I explain the scientific underpinnings of my philosophy?"

"There's a science to this?" He smiled just patronizingly enough to distract her from how cute he was.

"Yes, the new science of psychoimmunology. Based on the theory that your mental state affects your overall health."

"And there is research?"

"Tons. And the results of the studies coincide nicely with Polynesian medical theory. The Polynesians consider pleasure to be the seventh sense, ensuring balance and harmony within yourself and between you and the world."

"Okay…"

"*Aloha* means *the sharing of breath,* did you know that? And *haole*—what Hawaiians call white people—means *breathless.* That tells you everything you need to know about the differences between our cultures. Reveling in your senses, as the Hawaiian shamans advise, establishes your connection with everything on the planet."

She stopped talking, caught by the strange look on Dan's face. She waved her hand in front of him. "Hello?"

"Sorry." He blinked, collected himself. "It's your voice, Kathleen. It gets to me."

"Oh, yeah. You used to say it was…"

"Sex in sound. Yes. That."

"Maybe I should talk high and squeaky like Minnie Mouse?"

"I'll focus better."

"Maybe if you take notes…for the quiz later." She winked.

"I don't need to take notes. I remember—"

"Everything…I know." She took a shuddery breath. "Me, too." Tension stretched between them, tight as piano wire. She remembered his fingers on her skin, the glorious weight of his body, him inside her, helpless with lust.

His face was flushed now and his eyes gleamed with the same need she felt. Holding back was killing her.

Not to mention damaging her immune system. "Are you as aroused as I am?" she blurted.

"Hell, yes."

"I guess we'll just have to take care of things afterward." She wiggled in her chair to relieve a little of the pressure.

"Take care of things?"

"Surely masters of moderation masturbate?"

He shot a look at the band, but they were intent on their music—"Lush Life," a favorite of hers. "Of course. Just—"

"Not to excess?" She grinned, happy to tease him as a distraction. "We'll just retire to our separate spaces and relieve the tension. Non-excessively."

"I don't believe you've got me talking about *that*. And thinking about *you* doing *that*."

"Sorry. I gotta be me." She remembered the time she'd hounded him for a sexual fantasy and he'd finally admitted he fantasized about her touching herself. So she'd done that for him, described her sensations while he watched, shy and riveted, his breath rasping, eyes glittering.

When I barely touch my clit it feels like sparks are going off. And then I slip a finger inside me and imagine that it's you...

Before she reached climax, he'd entered her wet and ready body as smoothly and as welcome as a deep breath, and they'd come together.

She forced herself back to the present moment, but she couldn't help wondering if he'd shared that fantasy with another woman. "Is there a Ms. Moderate in your life?"

He blinked at the change of topic. "Not at the present time, no."

"Why not?" Why did she care? She did, though. A lot.

"There have been women, of course, but lately I've been focused on work. There's really been no time for a relationship."

"How about sex? There's always time for sex."

"I guess. But I want more than that, Kathleen."

"Somehow, I knew you'd say that." She was happy to note that he'd been breathing pretty heavily for a guy who wanted more than sex.

"What about you, Kathleen? Is there someone in your life?" His question seemed almost too concerned.

"Plenty of someones," she said lightly, not liking how he'd honed in on her like a therapist intending to interpret every word and gesture.

"But no one special?"

"Everyone's special when you get to know them."

"Surely you'll settle down one day? Get married?"

"I can't imagine anything duller."

"Oh."

The sympathy in that short word and his face jabbed her with irritation. "I'm happy with my life. I chose it." She thought about Troy and the weary feeling she'd had at the prospect of sleeping with another man she barely knew. Maybe she did want to rest in someone's familiar arms—a terrible thought to have with Dan looking at her as if he could read her mind.

"Myself, I want someone to get close with," he said. "Someone to share my life…be a partner in it."

"For me, that has all the appeal of a root canal." But that sounded too extreme. "Make that a bleach treatment. Annoying, boring and it takes too long."

He studied her, doubt in his eyes.

"I just can't imagine it," she explained, not joking

now. "How could you know how you'll feel forever? I guess maybe you, being so balanced and moderate and all, could know, but me? Can you imagine me with one person?"

He looked at her a long moment. "You're a remarkable woman and you deserve a man who will keep you interested for the rest of your life."

Her throat tightened and she found herself clutching her upper arms. She felt…lonely. For just those few seconds, while Dan wished her someone wonderful, she felt lost. "That's what you want, not me, Dan," she said, forcing away the feeling. "I couldn't stand that kind of life—the redwood deck, the beach time-share every August and meat loaf on Tuesdays."

He opened his mouth as if to argue, then stopped. She pictured him with some restrained, mature woman—a librarian or a scientist. At night, they'd sit by the fire reading something intellectual until precisely ten-thirty, when they'd make careful love, hardly wrinkling the sheets, turn back-to-back and drift off to boring dreams. How sad.

"If that's what you really wanted, wouldn't you have it already?" Her voice had risen as the words emerged. She didn't love Dan, but she sure as hell didn't want him to settle for some lukewarm excuse for a marriage. "What about passion? You need someone who makes you feel alive, Dan. Who makes you want more. Someone whose joy is your greatest pleasure."

She and Dan had had that…for a while, anyway. Or so she'd thought at the time. Young and clueless, she'd counted on what they had to last. Which was why it had hurt so much when he left.

"What about amazing sex?"

"Lush Life" ended so that her words rang out like a beer order across a noisy bar.

The musicians chuckled. "Sounds like our cue to vanish," Raider said, standing.

She blushed. "We're just having a discussion."

"That what they're calling it these days?" Raider said in his smoke-rough voice. "Set's up anyway."

Kathleen and Dan managed awkward small talk while the musicians packed up, accepted her check and left. Then she and Dan looked at each other in the silence.

"Sorry I got so fierce," she said. "Who and why you marry are none of my business." And starting such a debate was no way to get him to open himself to his true feelings.

"I hope you find what you're looking for, Kathleen." He didn't seem offended.

"You, too, Dan." She ducked his gaze. The idea of him with a perfect Ms. Moderate gave her a dull ache behind her eyes.

"So, what's next on the sensory itinerary?" Dan said, clearly trying to lighten the mood.

She looked at her watch. "The massage. Unless you're interested in a facial and a mud bath?"

"What?" His eyes widened and his brows darted upward, just as she'd intended. He was so fun to shock.

"Relax. I knew you'd freak, but you don't know what you're missing. A plethora of textures and smells, the slow sluicing of toxins from your tissues, graceful fingers applying creams and astringent and toner and exfoliant, stroking your cheeks and chin and nose and eyebrows. So rejuvenating."

"I think a massage will be plenty rejuvenating. I don't have to be naked, do I?"

"Please. A massage through fabric is like a hand job with a ski glove."

"But—"

"She's a professional, Dan, and she'll have you cover critical anatomy with a folded sheet."

He seemed to relax. "Okay. And after the massage?"

"A nice whirlpool bath with a scalp massage. The scalp is very sensitive and increased blood flow keeps your hair healthy and—"

"A bath? The masseuse is coming into the bathroom?"

"Actually, I'll be doing the scalp massage."

"You will?"

"You can wear your tighty whities in the tub and I won't look…or at least I won't *stare*. I'm kidding. I won't even peek."

He still looked uneasy.

"It will be okay," she said, determined it would be. "The idea is that pleasurably relaxing your body provides mental peace. You become more open to your emotions and your deeper needs. Your life becomes richer."

She wanted that for him, too. Not so much to prove anything, but to help him. The man was twisted into mental knots. Right now he looked like he couldn't wait to escape. "It won't hurt, Dan. I promise."

He sighed. "And after the whirlpool and the shampoo? Then are you finished with me?"

"You make it sound like torture. After the bath, you'll take a rejuvenating nap—in your own room, of course. Naps are not a luxury. They're a requirement of health. Then we're done, you poor, long-suffering man."

"So let's get to it," he said dutifully.

"Sheesh. There are people all over the world who

would kill for a chance to be ministered to by Kathleen Valentine and you can't wait to get away from me."

Before Dan could respond, the phone rang.

It was annoying news. Her masseuse had called in sick today, the spa receptionist told her, and the other therapist was booked, so could Ms. Valentine possibly reschedule?

She declined and hung up, pondering options.

"What is it?" Dan said.

She looked at him. He definitely needed a massage to force some physical release. She'd just have to do it herself, she decided. She'd had training, too. Dan would freak, but she'd be perfectly professional and he'd be fine.

"What is it?" he asked.

In answer, she yanked the cover, blanket and top sheet off one bed, baring the mattress, then freed the top sheet, which she began to fold to a narrow width.

"What are you doing?" Dan asked.

"Take off your clothes, lie on your stomach and use this to cover the danger zone." She laid the folded length of sheet on the mattress."

"Where's the masseuse?"

"You're looking at her."

"You're going to give me a massage?" Reflexively, he locked his hands in front of his groin.

"The masseuse called in sick. Don't worry. I've had enough training to almost have a license. Get ready and I'll change into something more comfortable."

"More comfortable than that?" He nodded at her bared midriff.

"A Spandex top and jersey shorts, okay? Stretchy? For mobility? Don't be so jumpy."

"You're sure you know what you're doing?"

"This isn't brain surgery, Dan. It's a little Shiatsu with a dollop of Swedish. You'll love it."

Mollified by her jargon, he started on his shirt buttons with an efficient strength that gave her a rush. She used to love to watch him strip.

What was she doing? After the building pressure of all the dancing and touching and talking and imagining, she would be rubbing and stroking and…oh, Lord…

She could handle it…so to speak.

She swept to her CD player and popped in some Andean pipe music for atmosphere, then retreated to the bathroom to change and stabilize.

It took so many deep breaths she practically hyperventilated, but eventually she emerged with a squeeze bottle of cinnamon massage oil—meant for sex, but what the hell—and two damp cotton balls to place on Dan's eyelids for the face-up portion of the rubdown.

She found Dan lying on his stomach as instructed, head to the side, his handsome profile dramatic against the white bottom sheet, the top sheet in place over his delicious butt. Above the cover, his spine was a graceful curve in his broad muscular back. Below it stretched long, strong legs. Hell, even his feet were sexy. He could be waiting for a lover. Of course she'd been that very lover many glorious times. Tingles of desire made her legs wobble and her fingers lose strength. The oil bottle hit the floor with a thud.

At the sound, Dan lifted his head and turned toward her.

"Just clumsy me," she said, dropping to grab the bottle and hide the pink in her cheeks. "Pay no attention to the woman behind the curtain."

She set the cotton balls on the nightstand for later, then squeezed oil into trembling palms she briskly rubbed together to warm the oil. She started on his shoulders, rubbing deeply into the deltoids and trapezia with her fingers and the heels of her hands, feeling every ligament and tendon of proof that over the past decade Dan had grown more solid and strong and yummy...

"So what do you do for physical activity?" she asked to distract herself.

"I run...lift weights...nothing special. What about you?"

"I only exercise if there's a fun component. I dance, play volleyball, ride a mountain bike."

"Wow, that feels good." He nestled into the pillow with a luscious moan that sent a thrill through her.

She bit her lip and bore down on her work. "Massage has therapeutic properties." And arousing ones. She focused on Dan's physiology, picturing the massage diagram of twining muscle groups, the net of ligaments, the bands of tendons, feeling her way along the ropy muscles beneath his gorgeous flesh, loosening the knots of tension where she found them.

The bed was neither the right height nor width for a non-sexual massage. For the proper leverage, she had to change position. She sighed, closed her eyes for a moment of courage, then said, "Now don't panic, Dan, but I'm going to have to sit on your butt."

"You what?"

"I need better leverage."

He tensed, which meant his gluteus maximus were fabulously tight as she straddled him, her heart kicking up like a *Chorus Line* audition.

"Mmm," he groaned.

You can say that again. She ignored the tightening

in her sex. This was therapy. This was purposeful and professional. Never mind how easy it would be to roll him over, all slippery with oil, and go for it. Instead, she gritted her teeth and, while Dan moaned in pleasure, she worked her knuckles up and down his spine.

"You're good," he said huskily. Muffled against the mattress, his words were as intimate as pillow talk.

"Why, thank you." She managed to sound calm. She moved down to his tightly muscled hamstrings and on to his soles, earning more thrilling moans and groans. He was a sensualist, no question.

Wait until she got him into the whirlpool bath. He'd be a convert for sure. She held that thought for courage as she kneaded and stroked and slid along the incredible length of him.

Finally finished with the back side of him, she gave him a soft pat. "Turn over for me."

"Um, that was great," he said, stilling. "I'm all relaxed."

"You'll be more relaxed when I'm through with your front."

"That's just it. My front isn't…uh…relaxed."

"Oh, I see," she said, sounding casual, even though every inch of her was alive to the news. "So you got an erection. It's a natural bodily reaction." She was having an uncomfortable reaction of her own. It just didn't show.

"Okay, I guess." He sighed and turned over and his eyes met hers over the tent he'd made in the sheet. "Oh, my," she said softly. "I think a family of four could sleep under there."

He smiled. There was a darling crease on his cheek and his mouth looked soft. His eyes wore a soft glaze. He wanted her.

And she wanted him. She itched to toss away the

sheet and fall onto his cinnamon-scented body, slip him inside, quick as a heartbeat, fast as desire.

Battling the urge, she whispered, "Close your eyes," knowing that would help her resistance. When he did, she practically flung the water-soaked cotton balls onto his lids. Now he looked goofy, thank God. Except for his gorgeous body and that promising erection, still poking proudly upward.

"We'll be finished soon, don't worry."

"Take your time. You were right…this is great."

If you're into torture. She locked her jaw and focused with all her might, digging into his muscles, rubbing his pectorals, then down his biceps and forearms to his strong hands and those wonderful fingers.

"Ouch," he said.

"Sorry," she said, realizing she was working him over like a meat tenderizer. She moved to his shins, a muscle group with limited sex appeal. "So, are you feeling more comfortable in your body, Dan?"

"I feel…very…good." Each word was a moan of pleasure. He was physically looser, at least. Now to see what effect the experience was having on the Ace bandage he'd wrapped around his mind.

"What else are you feeling?" She rubbed the muscles around his knee cap. "What comes up for you?" An unfortunate choice of words, she realized, glancing at his bulge. "I mean what feelings…what thoughts arise…?" Her hands moved to the thick muscles at the tops of his thighs, along with the sartorius muscle gliding diagonally across his leg—the longest muscle in the body and prone to overwork.

Her fingers slid higher, a little under the sheet and felt a little jolt of desire to move just a bit closer, closer…

She began to pant. His chest rose and fell with a ragged breath.

She could do this, finish this, but Dan relieved her of the strain, sitting up abruptly so that the cotton balls tumbled to his sheet-covered lap. "I think I've had enough massage."

"Yes, I believe you have." Whew. "As I said, massage offers relaxation, releases toxins, stimulates circulation and, um, organ function."

"Organ function?" He grinned. Both sets of eyes darted to his lap, then up to meet in a lock, like a ball bounced and caught.

"I'll, uh, go fill the tub. You just rest a bit. When you're ready, join me in the bathroom."

"Sure. Got it." He flopped back on the bed.

What a relief to be away from Dan, stretched out on the white sheet, body smooth and warmly oiled, so accessible, so delicious, so, um, ready.

She knelt and turned on the bath tap. But instead of pouring from the faucet, ice water rushed down from the showerhead onto her head and arms, making her gasp. She pounded the faucet off, then struggled to push in the knob that would turn the shower back into a bath.

"Is there a problem?" Dan asked, entering the bathroom behind her.

"The…knob…is…jammed." She wiggled, then banged it.

"Let me try." He crouched beside her, the sheet tied at his waist, and she made room for him. With a quick jerk, he forced the button into place, then rose to his feet.

Kathleen plugged the drain, turned on the water and adjusted the temperature before she stood to face a half-naked, oiled and shiny Dan. She kept her eyes high on his face, fighting the urge to check out his sheet. Had he put on underwear or was he naked under there? Behind her, the water roared into the tub.

"Why don't you go ahead and climb in?" She turned away, as she'd promised, and when she turned back he was lowering his Jockey-covered butt into the water, his arm muscles flexing as he sagged against the back of the tub. "Ahh," he said, the sound buzzing through her like a coin-operated vibro-bed.

She turned off the water and pushed the button that started the whirlpool jets going. Streams of bubbles zoomed around the roomy tub.

"This feels so good," he said. Exactly what he used to say whenever he entered her. Dear God.

"That's the general idea. The pulsing jets increase blood flow to the capillaries and enhance brain function." *And turn me on. How about you?*

She wished she hadn't promised a scalp massage, but she would give him the full treatment if it killed her. She fetched her rosemary-mint shampoo, filled her palm, knelt by the tub and began rubbing it into his thick hair, the fresh scent rising to her nose.

"Wow. You were right about the scalp," he said, putty in her hands, which she vowed to keep above his neck. "It *is* sensitive. I feel like pasta too long in the pot."

"That's good." Maybe his special noodle had softened, too. The water was draining away, she saw, so she turned on the faucet to add some. "Rinse, please," she told him.

He plunged underwater, then rose, his hair sleek and dark, water sluicing down his torso. He blinked, rubbed water out of his eyes. God, he looked inviting. She longed just to tumble in there with him.

"How's your head? Physical experience is indulgent, yes, but it's also soul-illuminating. Try to focus on your inner dynamic, Dan. What's happening inside?"

His gaze shot to hers and the daze cleared to a sharp blue heat. "Kathleen," he said softly. "I'm inches from you, nearly naked in a tub. If I pay more attention to my inner dynamic, I'll drag you in here."

"Oh," she said. Her heart jumped into her throat and she began to tremble. "I see what you mean."

"I remember every bath we took together."

"You do?" She was shaking in earnest now.

"I remember the vanilla and the soap and your slick body…and…everything."

"Oh, me, too." It was such a relief not to struggle alone. She felt as though she was levitating off the floor with lust.

"This is killing me," he said.

"Oh, yeah."

"Ah, hell." He cupped her cheeks, pulled her close and kissed her.

She kissed back, madly shifting to get more of his lips and tongue. Her elbow dipped into the bubbling water. Water was still rushing in from the tap she'd turned on, but she didn't care a bit. The roar drowned out her good sense.

Dan's, too, evidently, because he pulled her up and into the tub, clothes and all. She landed with a splash on his lap, still kissing him, inhaling him, absorbing every iota of sensation from his sweet lips and tongue, while the hot tub rushed and vibrated around her, and her internal whirlpool pulled her down and down into Dan and what she wanted—his naked body, his mouth, his cock filling her. She wanted it all.

And Dan seemed to feel the same. He reached under her Spandex top with both hands, pushing it up under her chin so he could get at her breasts. "You're so beautiful," he said, pausing to look at her breasts, the nipples tight with desire.

She pushed into his hands, wanting his fingers to tease and torture her. And more.

Dan's tongue reached into her mouth and she took it, offering hers to him. He sucked it inside, as if to sample every tiny bud on its surface. The water steamed and swirled around them and his hands were hot and tight on her breasts, his lips and tongue searching, hungry, as desperate as she was.

She reached under the water and found his thickness through his Jockeys. He was long and full and ready for her. He groaned and pushed against her, slipping lower into the tub. She wanted to stretch out over his body, rub against him.

"I want you so much," he said, barely catching his breath, pressing his face against her cheek, then kissing her again.

What were they doing? They were hot and wet and slippery and it had been so long, so long, and she wanted this so badly.

The water was still pouring in and their movements sent waves sloshing over the edge of the tub. She shifted to make enough space to get out of her shorts, slipped, and caught her balance against the tub, pushing, as she did so, the shower button. There was a hesitation, a hiss, and then freezing water poured down in a brutal waterfall.

Kathleen shrieked and pounded the wretched button, which just *had* to be stuck again.

Dan lunged forward and turned off the faucet—the

obvious solution—and they fell to opposite sides of the tub, gasping in counterpoint from the cold and the shock of what they'd been about to do. Kathleen pulled down her shirt.

"Interesting timing," Dan said, his hair over his brow, looking so sexy—naked and chagrined like that—a bad boy caught in the act. "Freud says there are no accidents."

"Freud was full of it."

"Maybe this is an intervention by the patron saint of the tempted." He pushed to his feet and out of the tub, still half-erect. She took the hand he offered to help her out.

They stood together dripping for a moment—Dan making his underwear bulge, her own nipples jutting from the top that clung to her like skin—until Dan grabbed two towels off the rack and handed her one.

They dried themselves, studiously avoiding eye contact. That had been insane. Hadn't it? She didn't know what she thought. She felt frustrated and a little freaked about how fast they'd zoomed into action. At least it had been Dan who'd started it this time. She wrapped the towel around her body, chest-high. Dan had tied his at the waist.

"So, I guess we'd better call it a session," she said.

"Yeah," he said. "I'd better get out of here. I'm sorry, Kathleen, that I…did that."

"Don't apologize, Dan. Just don't let it detract from the rest of the day…the sensual discoveries…and all."

"Sure," he said, but she had the disturbing awareness that the best sensual moment of the day for both of them had been in that swirling water in each other's arms.

As soon as Dan had dressed and left, Kathleen collapsed on the mattress where she'd massaged him. Tempting cinnamon filled her head, along with the scent of hotel soap and Dan. *Oh, Dan.*

She pushed open her towel and laid her hand over herself. But she wanted his fingers, not her own on her body, so she let her hand drop to the mattress.

She couldn't nap, that was certain. Her mind was spinning and her body was alive with energy. She had to do something to keep from running down the hall naked and banging on Dan's door.

She couldn't get over how intense it had been. They'd practically consumed each other. When was the last time she'd felt that hot? It was like that Victorian romance—denial tied you into incredible sexual knots.

Which was an interesting concept. She should write that down. She sat up, delighted to realize she wanted to work on her book. This very instant.

The memories of sex with Dan, the tension, the focus on sensation seemed to have awakened her muse like No-Doz washed down by espresso.

She wanted to write about the session with Dan—the luscious lunch, the swaying dance, "Ruby, My Dear" in her ears, cinnamon in the bed, mint in the bathroom, straddling Dan's body, looking at him over the tent he'd made in the sheet, and that desperate embrace in the roaring whirlpool.

This was what she'd needed all along. An intense focus on sensation spiked by sexual tension. Rethinking her theories, tempting herself with Dr. Moderate, had reawakened her creative energy, given her the same burning need to share her ideas she'd had with her first book.

Forget roots and rhetoric—her proposed new book.

She had to start from scratch, see her ideas through Dan's eyes and his resistance. Just thinking about how she'd felt when he dragged her into the tub gave her the pre-orgasmic prickles.

Tomorrow, on Moderation Day, there would be more temptation. Temptation was her friend, resistance her ally, the fuel for her next blockbuster.

She was so happy that while she waited for her laptop to hum to life, she climbed onto the bed and jumped up and down for a few glorious seconds. Her breasts bounced, the air fluffed her hair and she felt weightless with delight.

She couldn't contain her joy. The muse was back.

8

AN INSISTENT tap-tap-tap dragged Kathleen from sleep. She glanced at the clock. Someone was banging on her door at six-thirty? Had to be a mistake. Room service wasn't due with her café au lait and chocolate croissant until nine. She'd written late into the night and needed rest to face Dan's challenge. She rolled over and covered her ears with a pillow.

Every word she'd typed had deepened her conviction that the cold shower had been a gift from the universe. The stimulation of being around Dan and *not* acting on it had dosed her with enough writing fever to burn through her block. She'd literally sweated in the delirium of it. Now she needed rest so she could write more after Dan had his day.

Thud-thud-thud. More-insistent knocking reached her ears through the double-soft pillow. Uttering an oath, she dragged herself from her sweet sheets and went to answer—just in case…by some chance. It couldn't be, though…not so early…not even him…

But it was. Through the peephole, she saw Dan, wearing a big fat grin, shorts and running shoes. Oh, hell. He wanted her to go jogging.

She rested her back on the door for a moment, and took a deep breath, sucking energy up from her toes, as if slurping the last drop of a milk shake from the bottom of the soda-fountain glass. Today was Dan's day and she had to give him her best.

She opened the door, managing a smile that was painful before her facial muscles were awake. "I take it you want us to run?"

"Yep." Dan's grin was broad and alarmingly alert.

"You're so awake it hurts to look at you," she said, pretending to shade her eyes from the glare. "If you had a tail, it would be bushy, Mr. Bright Eyes."

At least her lust impulses didn't fire this early, because he looked great in slithery navy shorts, a gray muscle shirt and fancy athletic shoes. His hair was wet and loose and he smelled of the hotel's soap. She should give him something hydrating. And soon. It would be a shame to ruin such gorgeous skin.

He held a small backpack that looked light and he nearly bounced with excess energy. "Ready to go?"

"Not really. I'm hoping this is all a bad dream."

"Should I pinch you?"

"No thanks. It's painful enough just standing here."

"You're just sluggish from excess."

"Please. I was up late last night."

"Me, too," he said, his voice abruptly low and heavy with meaning. He'd been thinking of her. A dangerous arousal thrilled through her—like running a finger through chocolate frosting while on a diet. Surely, that would provide more writing heat. "Yesterday was…difficult," he continued, swallowing.

"But we got through it, right?" she finished, wanting to reassure him that they were in agreement about sexual restraint.

"More or less." He gave a short, pained laugh.

"And today's your day and we won't get sidetracked, I promise." She crossed her heart.

"Right." He blinked, as if he hadn't expected her to be so cheerful about it.

"I was kind of hoping for mellow stuff like tea and yoga, not running and sweating."

"We'll do mellow things, but first we boost you out of your indulgent lethargy."

"You mean my relaxing rest?"

"It's all perception, I guess." The mischief on his fresh-scrubbed face told her he loved every second of her discomfort. "Remember, I did everything you asked me to do yesterday."

"But I didn't cause you physical pain."

"I don't know about that." Again he bore down on the words and again lust washed through her.

"But that was sweet pain. This will be plain pain."

He ignored her joke, his face filling instead with a longing that made her ache, so she kept it light. "So, what's in the backpack? Thumb screws?"

"A light blanket and my journal. I thought we'd run around Grant Park. It's beautiful there. Bridges and flower gardens and a huge fountain. Then we'll spread the blanket under some trees and do some meditation and reflective writing. Do you have a journal?"

"I'll use a notepad." She wasn't into diaries, but it would be a chance to take notes for her book.

"Great. Throw on some shorts and let's go."

"Do I have time for a quick shower?"

"You don't do anything quick in the shower." He stopped talking abruptly, realizing, no doubt, how that sounded. The bathtub hadn't been the only wet place they'd had sex. "You know what I mean."

"I do. I know exactly what you mean." She sighed and headed for her closet to don comfy shorts and a cozy sweatshirt against the spring chill. She pulled her hair into a ponytail and was smoothing on lotion, when Dan yelled, "Are you doing your nails in there? Come on, let's roll, Kath."

She emerged from the bathroom, rubbing in the last of the cream. She shook her head at him. *You silly man.* "Never get between a woman and her moisturizer, Dan."

"Lord."

"You'll take my lotion away from me when you pry my cold, dead fingers from the squirter."

"Your cold, dead, *chapped* fingers?"

"Excellent. I like when you joke." She slapped the small tube into his palm. "Keep this. Use it night and morning. It's the best on the market."

"You're giving me cold cream? Have you no respect for my masculinity, woman?"

"You can handle it. I seem to recall you looking pretty damn macho in my yellow silk robe that one time."

"We needed food. I was cold. It was close." He grimaced, but he did squirt cream into his hand and rubbed it briskly onto his face. "Happy?"

"Slow, circular, pressured motions stimulate blood flow."

He leveled a look at her.

"Okay, okay. It's a start. I'm happy."

He slipped the tube into a shorts pocket, holding her gaze. "You like taking care of people, don't you?"

She did, very much, but she kept her tone light and ducked his gaze. "Just spreading the gospel of sensory appreciation."

"You have a big heart, Kathleen. There's no need to be embarrassed about it. It's very…endearing."

"I'm not embarrassed," she lied, knowing she glowed pink with mortification. Dan looked at her in a way that made her feel bare naked against her will. "I just don't make a big deal of it."

"Sure." But he wasn't convinced. She hated that he thought he knew her better than she knew herself.

Hated it and liked it, too.

"You took care of me back then, too. I can see that now. At the time, I thought you were trying to change me."

"I *was,* I guess. I thought I was helping, but that was pretty arrogant of me." She winced.

"You meant well," he said, his handsome face gleaming with lotion, eyes swirling with a warmth as welcome as a space heater on a chilly morning.

Which she had to shut down before she got used to it. "We were young and clueless, remember?" she said briskly. "Gotta get shoes." She bustled off, but felt his eyes on her while she slid on tennies, fumbled the ties, unnaturally nervous.

This will help your writing, she told herself. Being around Dan, whether nervous, aroused, moved or annoyed, was what she needed for her next book. And her next book was the most important thing to her right now.

Finished, she sprang to her feet. "So, what am I in for today, Dr. Moderate? What's the point of all this running and meditating and reflective writing?"

"Balance," Dan said. "It's about balance." He made a scale of his hands, lifting and lowering them in little curls that made his biceps swell and stretch. "Strain and release, inhale and exhale, surge and stillness. Another way to think of it is oscillation."

"Oscillation? Sounds pretty hot."

"When you say it, Kath. You could make an appendectomy sound sexy. Anyway, we'll also work on mental alertness and agility and on psychic centering and mindfulness."

"Deal," she said, promising herself to limit her teasing. "Balance...oscillation...alertness...agility...mindfulness." She counted the concepts off on her fingers. "Got it."

"Balance is about complementary forces coming together...the wholeness of dualities, the yin and yang. What is within us is also without. The Greek sage Herakleitos said, 'To live is to die, to be awake is to sleep, to be young is to be old, for the one flows into the other...'"

"Ouch. It's too early for paradoxes." She pressed her fingers to her temples in pretend pain.

"So, let's run. Once your brain is rich with blood, we can get conceptual."

They warmed up with a peppy walk, stretched out, then set off jogging. Dan hung back, wanting her to set the pace, it seemed, which was unfortunate, because that obliged her to run as hard as she could for as long as she could to impress him.

She trotted madly forward, her body screaming for mercy, hardly able to enjoy the city sights and the park when they reached it, while Dan chatted as easily as if he were standing still. He explained the importance of healthy habits—balance rituals, he called them—and a mantra that reminded her of the old fire-safety ditty, "stop, drop and roll." It was "stop, challenge and decide."

She was about to stop, drop and faint the entire time and could barely choke out an occasional *uh-huh* or *oh, really.*

She staggered on, determined to impress him, until her burning lungs and flaming calves could take no more and she collapsed against a tree, panting for air across a parched throat.

Dan looked at his watch. "That was barely twenty minutes, Kathleen."

"In superhero time maybe. That's the equivalent of four hours for normal humans."

He chuckled. "Check your pulse and we'll see how your heart's doing."

"My heart's dialing 9-1-1." She fumbled with her wrist. "I can't feel anything except screaming pain."

"Really?" He looked honestly worried.

"Not exactly." She did have a tendency to exaggerate.

"Let me check." He took her hand and rested it in his palm so he could search for her pulse with his fingers. Finding it, he pressed down, then glanced at his watch, while he silently counted.

Her pulse throbbed against his fingertips. He was in contact with the beat of her heart. The act seemed so intimate that her knees caved a little.

He released her wrist. "You're barely in the aerobic range for your age, Kathleen," he said, ruining the moment.

"So, I'll do more dancing and play more beach volleyball." She liked that his fingers had left a tiny warm spot on her arm, while the breeze cooled the sweat everywhere else.

"Something regularly, that's what's important."

"I don't do anything regularly, Dan. You should know that. I think we've earned breakfast. How about fresh croissants? I spotted a bakery." She suspected he'd opt for something disgustingly healthy, but she could at least try for something better. "Maybe a blintz with blueberries in liqueur?"

"How about something better?" Which turned out to be forty-ounce cups of gooey green stuff at a juice boutique that stank of farmland. "This will restore your salts and give you energy," he said, handing her hers as if it were gold.

"I hardly need to drink this," she said, accepting it. "The air's so thick with vitamins we're probably overdosing through our skin."

"Just drink it." Dan watched while she held her nose and gulped, happy as a parent who's convinced a child to eat her brussels sprouts because they're nutritious.

"That's nasty," she said, scrunching up her nose. "No wonder cows have three stomachs. I'm making cud right now."

"You should thank me."

"And you should thank me for not puking on your tennies."

Refreshed—more or less—they headed back to the park. "So, how are you feeling?" Dan asked, eager as she had been the previous day to check her impact on him. "Energized and relaxed?

"I survived." She felt a curious calm and liked the fact that her legs felt as though they'd endured something and come out stronger for it. She felt…healthy. But she hesitated to admit that to Dan for fear he'd go smug on her and ruin everything. "It wasn't too bad, except for the blenderized hay and the shin splits."

He looked so disappointed that she slugged him gently on the arm. "I'm kidding. It wasn't bad. I do feel energized and relaxed, okay? I didn't want you to gloat."

"That's good." His entire body seemed to lift with relief. Kind of sweet, really, that he cared so much.

They went first to the Buckingham Fountain, which was huge—one of the largest in the world, Dan told her—its inward-turning spouts making it look like a birthday cake, its wide pool dotted with gorgeous sculptures of sea creatures. They watched the breathtaking water show, in which the top fountain shot more than a hundred feet into the air. The spray sent a cool mist on the breeze, which was pleasantly startling.

After that, they laid out the blanket under trees lining a narrow pebbled path. The breeze carried the metallic hint of water, clean soil and spring things growing. For a park so much a part of a major city, it was remarkably quiet.

Kathleen sat cross-legged on the blanket, palms on her knees in what she thought was the lotus pose. "Okay, Zen Master McAlister. Talk me to my happy place."

"Be serious now."

"Not my best thing."

"I realize that, but make an effort, okay? For me?" He smiled, then arranged himself in the same position she was in, except he looked like he meant it. "I'll take you through a meditation practice that might enhance your concentration and give you some peace."

"You think I need peace?"

He looked at her for a moment, then said, "Do you really want an answer to that from me?"

"Sure." Now that her muse was back she felt confident enough to want his opinion.

"Promise you won't throw something at me?"

"Go ahead. I can take it."

"Okay… You seem edgy, Kathleen. Worried…and a little sad."

He was so right that she got that stripped-naked feeling again. He was looking at her with kind eyes and she got a little pain like an ice-cream headache in the middle of her forehead. "It's probably just my hatred of book tours you're picking up—bad mattresses, hard water, brutal schedule, all that pain-in-the-ass stuff."

His gaze stayed with her, waiting patiently for the real story. He was good.

For just a second, she considered describing the Troy episode, her writer's block and precarious career, the lost feeling that came over her from time to time lately, but she didn't dare put herself on Dan's therapy couch. Too complicated.

"Let's just do this meditation thing," she said instead, wiggling into the blanket and closing her eyes. "All aboard for the peace train."

He remained silent.

She opened her eyes. "Dan…? Hello?"

He sighed. "Okay. Close your eyes and become aware of your breathing. Since you focus on physicality, I thought I'd show you a body-based meditation."

"Great. Let's go."

"Inhale, please, to a slow count of seven, then exhale to the same count."

She did it once. "God, that's slow. I could pass out before the next inhale."

"Take your time, you'll be fine."

"Okay." She managed a few more slooow breaths, distracted by the thought of Dan sitting before her. Was he meditating or watching her? She squinted to peek.

"Eyes closed, please, so you can focus inside."

"Okay, okay." She snapped her eyes shut.

"I take it your mind isn't clear."

"Not really."

"Do this, then. Notice your thoughts as they arise. But view them as clouds floating through the sky of your awareness. Let them come and go, but don't hitch a ride. Your goal is to empty your mind."

She did what he'd suggested, and found her attention hopping from one thought to the next like that old arcade game where the frog tried to zip across the highway without getting mashed by passing trucks and cars. Eventually, though, the cars in her head slowed down and the spaces between them lengthened.

As if he sensed her progress, Dan spoke again. "Now I want you to focus on your body, one part at a time, giving each your full attention. Start with the top of your head. Feel the sun on your hair, heating your scalp. Notice any tension and release it…"

She followed his hypnotic instructions, tensing, then releasing her scalp, followed by her forehead, her nose, her jaw, her neck and her shoulders. His voice seemed to warm each body part as he spoke its name. He led her down her arms to her fingertips, then back to her collarbone and then…

Breasts. Next were her breasts. She stilled, listening for the word, her nipples tingling in anticipation of being named.

But Dan didn't speak.

"My breasts?" she coaxed.

He cleared his throat. "Sorry. Yes…*those.*"

"Those? You're calling them those?"

He took a strangled breath, then burst out laughing. Delighted, she laughed, too, and opened her eyes to find him grinning at her. "Not very Zen-like of you, Master Dan."

"Oh, hell," he said. "The last thing I feel while giving a tour of your body is Zen-like."

"If it helps, I was thinking about your body, too."

"I don't know if that helps," he said, his eyes roving her face.

"I miss the fun Dan," she said. "We used to laugh a lot."

"For a while. Until things got so intense."

"Yeah. I remember." Too bad they'd wrecked it with love.

"Anyway, the idea of meditation is to still your mind and center yourself so as to enhance your mindfulness." His eyes still twinkled with humor. "If you become more mindful, you're better able to direct your energy with purpose."

"And find peace?"

"That's the idea," he said with a sigh that told her he was far from feeling peace at the moment. "There are other exercises in my book you can try on your own, since I'm obviously not setting much of an example. How about we go to a Taoist Center near here for a class in energy release?"

"Energy release, hmm? I thought sex was off the table."

"Not that kind of energy."

"I'm just teasing. You're so cute when you feel guilty." She patted his sun-warmed cheek.

"I'm not trying to be cute. I'm trying to help you."

He looked so earnest, she wanted to make him happy. "You have helped me, actually. After you left last night, all the turmoil got me in the mood to work on my new book. I wrote for hours. It was such a relief."

"A relief? You've had trouble?"

Sitting there in the park, the sun warm on her head, Dan's eyes so kind, she just told him. "Yes. It's been a struggle. You're only as good as your last book, you know, and my last was not my best. I think that's part of why I stalled. I was afraid I'd lost my muse."

Dan put his hand over hers. "Everyone goes through writing lulls. You're a talented writer. You'll figure it out."

"I hate to point out that you haven't read a word I've written, Dan."

"But I know how smart you are and how determined and resilient."

But she wasn't resilient. If he only knew what she'd gone through after he broke up with her. But this minute, he looked at her as if he had all the confidence in the world in her. She felt the sting of grateful tears.

She blinked and let her hair fall over her face to hide them. Why the hell was she crying?

The relief of sharing her awful secret with someone who cared about her probably. JJ was sympathetic, but she was more of a business friend. Kathleen didn't have many close friends. She'd been that way all her life. She enjoyed spending time with people—dancing, debating, joking at parties, playing sports or going on adventures, but then she headed home, happily alone. It seemed like pursuing people too closely, getting too involved, led to disappointment on both sides.

Dan wanted that, he'd said. *Someone to share my life with. A partner.* She wanted to dismiss the idea, but it rattled around inside like a loose bolt in some complicated machine.

"What do you want out of this tour?" Dan asked abruptly.

"What do I want? That's easy. Book sales, more fans, people hot for my backlist and watching for the new book."

"Buzz? That's what my agent kept talking about. It makes me think of getting stung."

"Buzz is good, Dan. Buzz gets you on bestseller lists. You want buzz, don't you?"

"I want my books to sell, all right. My practice is busy and rewarding, but with a book and maybe workshops afterward, I can reach more people. I get a lot of satisfaction out of helping my clients straighten out their lives. Maybe it's corny, but I feel like I make a difference."

"It's not corny. Not when you say it. I feel the same way, except coming from me it does sound corny."

"You don't give yourself enough credit, Kath. You're generous and you have such a big heart. You—" He stopped, lifting one hand. "Sorry. No lectures."

She smiled, grateful that he'd backed off. The shadows of leaves fluttered across his face like emotions. It was nice to feel his concern, warm as the sun on her scalp. "I know what you mean. Wait until you start getting reader letters. It's so great when someone takes the time to tell you how much they appreciate what you've taught them."

"I look forward to that."

"Reader letters inspire me to do more and be better at it. But they're also intimidating. I mean, what if I can't?"

"Maybe that's part of your block. Thinking you've hit the ceiling on what you can offer readers?"

"Could be…" She gave him a speculative look. "Something tells me that except for your bogus theories, you're a damn good therapist."

"Coming from you that means a lot. Can I quote you to reporters?"

"Don't you dare." She laughed. "If anyone on this tour gets the idea we've learned from each other, that we actually respect each other, we're cooked."

"And that would lead to bad buzz?"

"Very bad buzz. Let's pinkie-swear to stay enemies no matter what…at least for the next five days."

They linked fingers and smiled ruefully at each other, coconspirators again. They were quite the team.

"Anyway, whether I was intimidated or burned out, I don't know, but making out with you—and stopping— gave me this frustrated energy that translated into a white-hot urge to write."

"I'm glad the tub episode was good for one of us. I was up late, too, and in more than one sense of the word."

She got a little shiver of desire at the thought of him feverish with lust for her.

He cleared his throat. "Enough about that. I am curious about something. I told you in our media training how I came up with my moderation theory. What about you? Where did your sensory focus come from?"

"I said you were a good shrink, but that doesn't mean I want a session, Dan. It's just how I am. I've told you that before. So, do we have time to write before the class?" She desperately wanted a change of subject.

"That's the plan." He seemed disappointed, but telling him about the accident would be a bad idea. He'd go all analytical: *Ah, so zis childhood trauma caused zis preoccupation wiz za visical body.* It would become an excuse to dismiss her theories as crackpot, the result of the accident, not a legitimate worldview.

Dan took out his journal and she reached into his backpack for her purse and the notepad inside. She intended to compare and contrast the body meditation

Dan had showed her with the body massage she'd given him, except that made her think about what had happened the day before. How close they'd come…how Dan had lain awake wanting to make love to her…

JJ would absolutely flip if she knew how close Dan and I came to having sex, she wrote, glancing up at Dan, who was bent over his journal scribbling away, innocent of her wicked words. *In fact, this trying out each other's theories fits in exactly with the idea of a conversion book. Wow.*

She looked up at Dan to catch him smiling indulgently at her. "What?" she asked.

"Nothing. I'm just glad you're really trying this out."

Not exactly. She closed the notebook and braced her elbows in the grass beyond the blanket. "This moderation stuff wouldn't be so bad if you weren't so deadly serious about it all the time."

"Is that so?" He raised a brow in his sexy way.

"Our theories aren't far apart in some aspects. We both focus in on physical things. We both strive for more satisfaction out of life. We both value the quality of the journey, not just the destination. We both appreciate nature." She looked up at the trees overhead and the bright blue sky. "I just have more fun than you do."

"Who says I don't have fun?"

"Dan."

"I'm just saying fun can be defined more than one way."

"Fun is where you find it. Like this." She pushed away from the blanket, put her head down and did a somersault, then sat up laughing, only to go again and again until she was dizzy. Then she flung out her legs and watched the sky spin for a few seconds while she inhaled the scent of dirt and grass and reveled in the sun-soaked ground solid beneath her.

She lifted her head. "Your turn now. Have fun."

"Okay." With a sigh, he rolled over a couple of times, then fell back beside her to look up at the sky. "I'm dizzy."

She rose on her elbows and looked down into his face. "That's the whole point. You know what would be more fun? Playing tag in the fountain."

He chuckled softly. "You're crazy, you know that?" He pushed a side of her hair behind her ear, his gaze tender.

"Around you, yeah."

"Me, too," Dan said. "Around you."

"Aren't we a pair?" She longed to touch his lips with hers and start the magic again, but neither of them needed that.

"You were right about the antacids, Kath. I never needed them when I was with you."

"I'm glad you said that." She paused, then confessed, "It hurts me that you think we were all wrong together, that it was all bad."

"It wasn't all bad. And you were right. I was there, too, for every insane minute of it."

"I didn't make it easy on you. I pushed too hard."

She looked down at him and he looked up at her, their confessions swirling between them like JJ's cigarette smoke—illicit and impossible to ignore. But they had to.

Fighting new feelings, Kathleen pushed herself to her feet. "We'd better go."

Dan stood, too, and looked at her. He came close to brush grass from her hair, his breath warm mint on her face.

She closed her eyes, felt his fingers shake and linger, heard his breathing slow and go raspy.

She opened her eyes to see an agony of want in his face. She felt it, too. They stood in the grass together, the breeze lifting their hair, brushing Dan's onto his forehead, the smell of water and flowers and life in the air, and the feeling between them so strong she almost felt lifted off the earth.

She focused on one consoling thought: oh, she would get some great writing done tonight.

9

LYING ON the cool wooden floor at the Taoist Energy Center, Dan should have been intent on the teacher's description of release points, but all he could think about was Kathleen lying beside him, breathing softly, her spice overriding the incense in the air, her nearness making his ears buzz so that he could hardly hear the flute music designed to soothe and center the less horny students.

He was a mess. Worse, even, than when he'd dragged Kathleen into the whirlpool bath with him the previous afternoon. It was no small irony that today, while Kathleen innocently performed one nonsexual activity after another, he could only think of getting her naked. What a hypocrite he was.

Today was supposed to be a day of balance. Maybe a dunking in the huge fountain would have cooled him down. At least he'd confirmed what Kathleen wanted out of the book tour—sales and buzz, and to get back her writing drive. He'd helped with that by kissing her, which wasn't exactly ethical or even decent.

She'd opened up to him, but just a little. Kathleen held her emotions on a tight leash. His own feelings were hounds so wild they would jump a six-foot fence, heedless of razor wire or guards.

The class ended and Dan opened his eyes to see Kathleen leaning over him, rosy with energy, her eyes clear and steady and amused. "So, what's next, Master Dan?"

"We go back to the hotel to study and review what we've learned today," he said, rising to sit.

Kathleen merely nodded, not even bothering with a smart remark about him sounding too professorial. She was doing exactly what he'd asked—seriously considering his ideas about balance and moderation. Meanwhile, he plotted naked adventures. He was the same horny bastard he'd been ten years ago.

They headed back to Dan's room and, once inside, his gaze shot straight to the nearest of the two beds, where they could be naked and making love in less than one immoderate minute.

Kathleen flopped onto said bed and braced herself on her elbows, flapping a bare foot against the mattress. Her breasts, a mere button flick away, taunted him. He'd kissed and stroked, licked and sucked every blessed inch of the silky flesh beneath the thin fabric of her shirt. No bra, either, dammit.

Kathleen smiled, sweetly unaware of his lascivious thoughts. "What do I read, Dr. Dan?" She turned her head, spotted the stack of books on his bedside table and lifted the top volume—his own book. Beneath it was hers. She extended that one to him. "I'll read yours and you read mine."

He accepted it and looked down at her, lying there so invitingly. Maybe having sex wasn't so terrible. Maybe this was the kind of tension release they needed. They'd come to terms with the past, so maybe this would be healing and...

"Dan? You look like you want to eat me up."

"Sorry." Was he losing his mind? Even Kathleen knew better than to suggest sleeping together. And if anyone found out, bad buzz would be the least of his problems. He'd lose all credibility. As well he should.

He galloped across the room as far from the bed as he could get. Which put him by the refreshment area. "I'll make us some tea." He filled the decanter with water from the bathroom, emptied it into the coffee machine, then put on a CD he liked to read by. The music filled the room, calming him.

Kathleen groaned. "Not New Age flat-line… Must get real music…brain cells failing…willpower draining…"

"Cut it out," he said, smiling.

"This is the East taking over the West by stripping the life out of our music."

"We don't need Asia for that. Muzak's doing a fine job."

"This is one tubular bell away from Muzak, sweetie."

He enjoyed her teasing. A blessed distraction. He dropped tea bags into two mugs, filled them with steaming water and carried both to where Kathleen lay on her side, legs stretched, chin propped on a palm, flipping through his book. She was so comfortable in her body, so easy in her skin, with a natural sexiness that a man had to be dead not to react to. It wasn't fully his fault that he spent so much time with a hard-on.

He handed her a mug, which she clasped with both palms and sipped. "Mmm. Soothing, mindful, centering."

"You're making fun again."

"Just a little. Even balanced, I have to tilt a little."

"I know." He sighed with everything in him, then put his mug on the night table between the two beds and lay on the far bed, bracing himself against the wrought-iron bars of the headboard, hoping the discomfort would keep him alert. How much trouble could he get in just reading? He opened Kathleen's book to a random page. "Sex...The Sensory Buffet." Good Lord.

At his abrupt inhale, she leaned over. "Where are you?"

He showed her.

"Ah, my best chapter."

"I'm not surprised." He avoided her gaze, afraid his desire was a palpable wave rolling out of him and over her.

Evidently not, since she settled into the pillow on her bed with a sigh. "Enjoy," she said.

Yeah, right.

KATHLEEN WIGGLED deeply into the double-down pillow on Dan's bed and cupped the warm tea he'd given her. This was working out just fine. Dan was reading her best chapter, the tea was rich with calming herbs, the music wasn't too mind-numbing and the day had actually done what it was supposed to do—soothed her jitters and centered her. She felt, well, content. Even better, the sexual tension that bound them was stoking her urge to write like coal in a furnace.

"Are you comfortable?" Dan asked. "Can I get you anything?"

"Nope. I'm perfect. Thank you, Dan."

"My pleasure." And he truly meant it, she could see in his face. She'd been with men who worked at pleasing her, but she'd never had a man look at her as if he wanted nothing more than to ensure her happiness in every ordinary moment.

He hadn't been that way ten years ago. Or maybe she hadn't noticed. Or maybe ten years ago it had felt like being smothered in a pillow.

Looking at Dan now, her heart filled with an emotion from early in her childhood before her parents were at war—before her accident. It was the feeling of being securely loved. Snuggled in the fat of it, like a tummy full of fresh milk and homemade cookies. Cozy, warm and safe.

"Why don't you read here?" She patted the bed beside her.

Dan's face filled with alarm.

"It's okay, Dan. No funny business." She just wanted his solid body and dependable breath beside her. She wasn't going to think very hard about why. She was just going to enjoy it.

Without another word, he settled in beside her, her book on his lap and sipped his tea, the sound of his swallow tickling her ear, his hotel-soap smell sweet in her nose.

"This has been a nice day," she said to make him feel good.

He closed the book on a finger and shifted to face her. "I wanted that for you. I hoped I could—"

"Stop right there," she said, raising a hand. "Don't ruin this with the father-knows-best bit. You'll get further with me if you don't act smug. You don't have all the answers, you know."

"I know." His smile went crooked and sheepish. "I can't seem to help myself around you. I turn into a twelve-year-old showing off for the cutest girl in class."

"You showed off for girls? I can't imagine."

"Oh, yeah. For Sara Simpson. I got detention for making an outrageous joke behind our math teacher's back just to make Sara laugh."

"Was it worth it?"

"Oh, yeah. She kissed me after school. With tongue."

"Oh, I get it. You're not an arrogant ass. You just want me to make out with you."

"And you know where that's gotten us," he said, his eyes glued to her lips, which she found herself nervously licking. He gave her a look she remembered from the old days—absolutely enthralled. Like a boy seeing his first belly-dancer. Mystified and transfixed and adoring.

God, how she'd loved that look. She loved it now. She felt understood. And cared for. Aroused, too, but mostly cozy and safe. If they hadn't had sex all those years ago, they might have made damn good friends.

She watched him force his gaze away.

But she wanted his attention again. Not for sex. For something more important. She wanted to tell him her story. "It was because of the accident," she found herself saying.

"What?" His eyes shot to hers, brows high with surprise.

"Where my focus on sensory experiences came from."

He didn't say anything. Just waited for her to continue.

So she told him about the spinal damage, the numbness, the terror, the endless days of nothingness and finally the joyous beginning of sensation.

He listened closely while she told it all, and when she finished, he remained silent.

"Now don't go all Freudian on me," she said, desperate for him not to ruin the moment. "I was already a physically sensitive person. The accident just made my body more important to me. This in no way negates the solid basis of my theories."

"I'm honored that you trusted me with your story,"

he said, ignoring her accusation completely, honing in on what mattered.

"I do trust you," she said with an intimate warmth that made her want to blurt a joke or a barb, but nothing would come. Her vulnerability just hung there in the air between them.

"I'm sorry you had to go through that. I don't like to think of you as a little girl suffering that way." He looked at her with a brimming heart and not a speck of pity, thank God.

Again her eyes stung with emotion. And there was more she wanted to talk about now. Because he was so kind, because he knew her so well, because he was Dan. "The accident was bad, but what happened to my parents because of it was worse."

"What happened?"

"My mother was furious that my father had allowed me on the big street with my bike, of course. But it turned out the *client* he was so anxious to be alone with was a woman. He was having an affair. I overheard my mom talking to her friend about it."

She remembered her mother at her bedside, tear-streaked and dramatic, crying as if the accident had happened to her, too. In a way it had. "They were divorced within six months." She gave a hollow laugh. "Bizarre, huh?"

"Your world was overturned."

His matter-of-fact tone comforted her. Damn, her eyes were bothering her. Stinging and filling. She blinked fiercely. "Sure, but I got over it. I saw Dad on summer vacations and occasional trips. Mom and I did fine. She dated and worked. And I did my thing like any kid."

"That's a lot to endure all at once and at your age."

"Yes," she whispered. Her mother's mantra to Kathleen ever after had been to take care of herself, be responsible for herself. But that wasn't a new lesson—her mother tended toward self-involvement—it just had more punch after that. After the divorce, her mother became even more distant and private.

The secure family feeling had gone, too, and Kathleen realized that love faded. It could disappear altogether and there wasn't a damn thing you could do about it.

Dan put his arms around her and hugged her. Not long and not tight. "You're a strong person, but that doesn't mean you don't get hurt. It's all right to talk about it. You won't break or crumble."

She pulled out of his arms, blinked hard and steadied her voice. She had to make a joke to put some space between them. So much emotion zipped around inside her she thought she might burst. "Why, thank you, Dr. McAlister. Do you accept insurance?"

"I'm not your therapist, Kath. But I hope I'm your friend."

"You are." She hoped she didn't look foolishly teary.

"We all have childhood issues. You remember my parents, right?" She knew he'd brought that up so she wouldn't feel embarrassed about her story. "I think the emotional roller coaster we lived on made me want calm in my life."

"How are your parents?" She'd always wanted to meet them—to compare reality with his stories of their passionate fights.

"Good. Mom's had some successful shows and my father's teaching creative writing at the community college."

"Still throwing plates at each other?"

"My mom was the one with the arm. Dad's specialty was jealous accusations. They've mellowed over the years."

"It's hard to imagine you as their child. Did you ever wonder if you were adopted?"

"I'm theirs, no question. I have some of my father's tendencies. You saw that." He looked away, shook his head.

She remembered the grabby possessiveness of their last few weeks together. She must have reminded him of his mother, now that she thought about it, being so passionate and restless.

"It didn't help that I backed away," she said. "I felt like you were smothering me. I couldn't breathe."

His laugh was soft and sad. "We hooked each other at our weakest spots. I needed you near and you needed room."

"Don't forget my attempts to change you."

"I should have understood what was going on. I was a psychology student, for God's sake. I was too in love with you."

"You mean obsessed? Like you accused me of being in your book?" She waved the book at him, keeping her tone light.

He grimaced. "I did slant that a bit."

"It's your book, Dan. You get to tell it how you saw it. And you weren't exactly wrong. I was so thrilled that you wanted me so much that I went a little crazy. Remember that time at the soda machine?"

"I'll never forget it." Remembered heat sparkled in his eyes.

"I dream about it. In the daytime, no less."

"Oh, yeah." He sighed.

She sighed, too, with a strange peace. They'd never

been this easy with each other back in college. "This feels comfortable," she said. "Maybe even healing."

"Yeah, right." He seemed to think she was teasing.

"I'm not joking." She turned to look at him and was startled to see raw desire shining in his eyes.

"The joke's on me, Kath," he said roughly. "You're talking about healing and comfort and all I can think about is tearing off your clothes and taking you."

"Oh, Dan." Lust swept through her with a stupendous thrill and she closed her eyes. Comfort and healing fled, leaving her whole being alive with desire.

Dan groaned her name and found her mouth. His tongue collided with hers, his lips slid everywhere. She scrambled to get it all—lips and tongue and teeth and panting breath.

Dan's fingers made short work of her buttons and he soon had her left breast in his mouth. He sucked so deeply she thought she might come from that sensation alone.

What about the sexual tension that was helping her write? Forget it. If tension was good, release would be better. She gripped him through his pants, but that was too frustratingly padded, so she went for his zipper.

He was helping her with his belt when there was a knock at the door. Not a knock, a heavy thud…repeated…like the giant's tread in *Jack and the Beanstalk*.

"Don't answer it," she said, going in for another kiss.

But he held back. "Whoever it is sounds upset."

DAN STAGGERED to his feet, so hazy with lust he wasn't sure he felt the floor beneath his socks. Even dazed, he managed to zip his zipper and hook his belt, his mind sluggishly begging fate: *Let it be the maid. Let her go away.*

But it was Rhonda, he saw through the peephole,

holding a manila folder and looking upset. Dan looked back at Kathleen, who lay with her blouse open, dazed, her lips swollen and wet.

"Dan?" Rhonda shouted, pounding harder. "I have media clips." She said it in a coaxing singsong.

Kathleen pointed toward the bathroom and dashed there, closing the door behind her with a soft click.

He should welcome this interruption, of course, but he was too far gone. He wanted Kathleen. Now. And he'd have her, dammit. How long could it take to look at a few newspaper blurbs? Minute and a half, tops.

He ran his fingers through his hair and wiped his hand across his mouth to remove what remained of Kathleen's lipstick. Too bad he couldn't clear off his expression as easily. He took a deep breath, then opened the door.

Rhonda fairly burst in. "Clips from the New York event," she said, opening the folder. But instead of clippings, she picked up a palm's worth of tea bags and showed them to him. "I brought us a new tea. Can we talk?"

"I just had tea, as a matter of fact." He realized there were two mugs on the nightstand. "Two mugs of it actually."

"Oh. Well." She blinked, confounded for an instant, then beamed. "I'll just fix myself some, if it's okay." She headed for the beverage space, grabbed the coffee pot and turned toward the bathroom. For water! Damn.

He lunged forward and snatched the pot from her hand. "Allow me." He zipped into the john, shutting the door behind him.

Kathleen had her hand over her mouth, fighting laughter it seemed, looking wicked and beautiful, her hair wild around her face. He flipped on the faucet and filled the pot. When he finished, she kissed him on the nose. He looked in the mirror to make sure she hadn't left a lip print on him. She winked and waved him out. Good Lord. What was he doing?

Outside the bathroom, he poured the water in the coffeemaker, slopping it all over the place. "So what did you want to talk about, Rhonda?"

"You won't like it."

"Did something happen with the tour?" He realized he'd just poured water on his shoe.

"No, no. That's all good. I'll leave the clips for you." She sank into a chair as if she intended to stay for a while. "It's not the tour. It's Dylan. I slept with him."

Before he could respond, he noticed that the bed he and Kathleen had been lying on showed the distinct impression of two bodies, the pillows held twin head prints. He sort of leaped to the bed and slid across it in an attempt to smooth the covers and fluff the pillows.

"Are you okay?" Rhonda asked.

No. He was a complete nutcase. "Fine. Just fine. It's been a long day for me."

"No problem. You just lie there," she said, not taking the hint to leave. "Why can't the therapist lie down? You have to do all the thinking. We patients just spew. Not that I'm a patient or anything. I know you're doing me a favor. Which I really, really appreciate. Like I keep pinching myself."

"Why don't you tell me what happened?" he said, fighting impatience.

"You probably think I have no self-control whatsoever, but it's not that simple. Dylan's not the same dog he used to be. For example, he told me he can't promise me anything. That's new. He's usually full of promises."

"Okay…"

"It was just like old times only better because we've both changed. I'm less needy and he's less of a cheating bastard, like I said." She jumped up, and headed to the coffee pot, now full of hot water, which she poured over a tea bag in a water glass since the mugs had been taken.

He noticed that one mug bore a smear of lipstick.

Rhonda turned toward him just as he jammed it to his mouth and rubbed the waxy spot with his lips.

"Want me to freshen that for you?" she asked, extending the pot.

"No, no. I like it cold."

She looked puzzled, then doctored her tea with sugar and creamer before returning to the table. "We were in his apartment, and it was like old times. There was the sofa where we used to make out and the CD rack we'd bought together. And the shower curtain and tissue holder I'd given him." She bobbed the teabag like a high-speed yo-yo. "I just was flooded with good memories."

"You were in the mental framework of the past," he managed to slip in, very aware that Kathleen had just heard him describe what had probably just happened to them.

"I haven't felt that good in bed with a guy since… Dylan."

"Sometimes our memories alter perceptions."

"There wasn't much foreplay, of course, but I didn't really need any…which I'm sure he could tell. I mean I didn't know which end was up or who had the condom…in fact, the thing flew across the room at one point and—"

"I'm uncomfortable with the intimate details, Rhonda."

"Oh, sure. But you get the idea."

"I think I do."

"So, now I feel bad about Mark. You know, back in New York? This would kill him if he knew. I care about him. But not like I do Dylan. It's a new relationship, though, and these things take time." She paused to drink some tea and he spoke quickly, wanting to help her if he could get a word in edgewise.

"What's really changed about Dylan, Rhonda?"

"Mainly his honesty. He said he can't promise me anything, right?" She blinked, looked up at him, and her eyes welled with sudden tears. "I know. That doesn't mean he'll be faithful. So, do you think I've been swept away by the sex? And because I feel redeemed? I'm not thinking long-term to the possibility of getting hurt? I mean, what if he's still a dog, except now he's just wearing a sheepskin jacket?" Her lip trembled and she grabbed it with her upper teeth.

He waited for her to answer her own question. Clients usually knew what they should do if they listened to themselves.

"But it felt so right," she whispered.

"In the excitement of having a cherished desire fulfilled, we often gloss over details that don't fit our fantasies."

"If I could do an instant replay, you mean, it wouldn't look so perfect? I mean, no matter how hot things get, foreplay is a compulsory, right?"

He remained silent.

Rhonda sagged into gloom, but only for a moment. "Still, he's coming to Manhattan to see me…and to check out the music scene." She sighed. "You think it's really just the music he's interested in?"

"I think—"

"That some people are toxic to each other. I know. Maybe if you met him you could tell me what you think."

"I think that would be—"

"Weird, right. It's not like he's agreed to couples therapy or anything. Forget it." She smiled sadly. "Okay, I want to do this right. I don't want to run my heart through the shredder again. I'm meeting him for dinner. How should I handle it?"

He opened his mouth, then shut it as she rattled on.

"Don't be alone with him, right? Meet at the restaurant. Take a cab back to the hotel. Set a limit for the time we spend together. Evaluate him with my clothes on, not all naked and sweaty and…"

He cleared his throat.

"Sorry." She looked at him. "So, do you, like, practice abstinence? You don't ever really say in your book, but it sounds like it."

He thought he heard a noise from the bathroom. "I think we should focus on you, Rhonda."

"Sure. Okay. Anyway, thanks for the therapy." She blinked a few times, took a long swallow of her tea, then stood. "Tea always goes right through me."

Before he realized what was happening, Rhonda strode straight for his bathroom.

"Ah, wait!" He lunged forward, practically knocking her down in his rush to get in front of her. "Maybe you should use your own bathroom?"

"Mine? But yours is right here…Oh." She gave him a look.

"I just…well, I'm particular about my things," he

said, running his fingers through his hair. Let her think he had some kind of bathroom fixation if it kept her from finding Kathleen huddled behind the door.

As soon as Rhonda left, Kathleen emerged. "You could have let her in. I was behind the shower curtain."

"I couldn't risk it. Lord knows what she thinks I've got in here—lace panties or something."

"That could be arranged." She pretended to unzip her pants.

"Never mind." Dan shook his head at the lunacy of it all.

Kathleen grinned. "So, is that how you treat your clients? Let them talk themselves out of what they want, while you smile and nod and ask them what they think?"

"Rhonda's not a client. And with her it's impossible to get a word in edgewise. She knows what's best for her, though, like most people."

"What about us, Dan?" Do we know what's best for us?"

"When we're thinking straight," he said, grateful that she stood more than arm's length away, or he'd have yanked her into his arms already.

"So Rhonda was our cold shower for today?"

He nodded, frustrated that he was too rational at the moment to pretend otherwise.

"Sometimes our memories alter perceptions?" She'd repeated his words, but not as a joke. And he agreed.

"And some people are toxic to each other," he finished, even while his whole body ached to hold her.

"You're right, I think," Kathleen said. "I've got this drive to write going and I don't want to foul it up by starting something…pointless."

"Ten years ago you wouldn't have hesitated," he said, more wistfully than he'd intended.

"I've changed, I guess."

"Right." For just one hopeless moment, he was sorry she had.

She approached him and studied his face, lust sparkling like broken glass in her sad eyes. "Thank you, Dan. For today. For everything." She put her arms around him and hugged.

It wasn't the impersonal, bodies-apart embrace she'd delivered the first night of the tour. It was tight and close and he was washed in her scent and swept away by the glory of her body against his, curved in all the right places. It felt so right to hold her.

She broke off the hug. "I'm still glad we did the experiment. I learned a few things from you."

"You did? Like what?"

"Oh, that if you plug your nose you can choke down a pastureland smoothie without retching." She seemed to want to keep the moment light.

"Useful knowledge, I guess." He felt as though a tight band squeezed his lungs so he couldn't draw a clear breath.

"And how to play Frogger with my thoughts."

"Excuse me?"

"Turning my worries into clouds rolling by. That's a good technique. And I learned that my out-of-shape heart needs more dancing. How about you? Did you learn anything from me, Dan?"

"Let's see…I learned that *haole* means *breathless*." Which he was around Kathleen. "And that chocolate was Moctezuma's Viagra." And that he still wanted her with an intensity that scared him.

"Sounds like we have a draw here."

"A draw? Were we competing?"

"Absolutely. The battle of the books, remember?"

More like the battle for his soul…his good sense…
his integrity. And he had the feeling he'd started to lose.

10

DAN'S HEAD rested on Kathleen's shoulder and his breath brushed her neck in warm, sleep-heavy waves. Though she loved the simple comfort of it, she realized that Rhonda, sitting across the plane aisle from them on the flight to Phoenix, might get the wrong idea, so, with a sigh, she shifted Dan so his head lay on a pillow braced against the window.

Kathleen was damned proud of herself. She'd conquered her unhealthy obsession with Dan and become his friend. Or at least was getting there.

Oh, there were sexual twinges. Aches. Waves. Floods. But they had a sexual history, so that was to be expected. Plus, she'd been lonely lately. There, she'd admitted it. All that meditating and reading and lying in bed with Dan had made her realize that. Maybe getting close to one particular person and staying there wasn't as deadly dull as she'd thought.

So maybe, later on, she could settle down with one particularly vibrant, wildly surprising man. The main thing was that she'd channeled her sexual frustration into her writing and that was very, very good.

Of course she'd been sorry when Rhonda had interrupted them, but not desperate to get back to it. She'd been relieved, in a way, since she'd shared some intimate secrets with Dan and the sexual stuff on top of it would have made everything more…well, intimate. She and Dan were toxic to each other and they both knew it. The intensity came from nostalgia—they were looking for an emotional do-over, maybe, without the agony?

She perused his long, sexy length in the plane seat and felt the fleeting desire to cover them both with an airline blanket and wake him up with her hand. A mere vestige of their long-ago heat. Useless as an appendix. An aimless fantasy she would be sure to incorporate into her next writing session.

There were annoyances, too. JJ had left a message asking her how her seduction of Dr. Moderate was going. She hadn't called her back, fearing her hypersensitive agent would pick up the vibe and interpret it all wrong. Instead, she'd left an after-hours voice mail explaining how well the work was going.

She wouldn't mention she'd dropped *Roots and Rhetoric* in favor of her new approach until she had a decent outline and sample chapters to wow JJ with. Kathleen feared that talking about it too much too early might scare away the muse. And if JJ started picking apart the idea…Kathleen just wasn't confident enough for that particular assault. In the meantime, her message should hold JJ. For a while at least.

She glanced at Rhonda, who looked upset. Something must have gone wrong with Dylan last night. "You okay?"

"I'm just preoccupied. And tired." She leaned back.

Kathleen had to be careful what she said so Rhonda wouldn't realize she'd eavesdropped on her tea-and-therapy session with Dan the day before. "If you want to talk, I'm available."

Rhonda turned sad eyes on her. "I'm afraid I'll just

cry. I did firm up your appearance on the top morning show in Phoenix. There's some talk radio and some regional radio feeds for tomorrow afternoon. Then the speech at the university." She sighed, her sorrow weighing her down like cement shoes on a swimmer.

"You're doing a great job with media for us, Rhonda."

"I intend to. I got distracted in Chicago, but I'm turning over a new leaf. If I focus on my job, I can keep balanced." Her lip quivered.

"Balance isn't everything. Not if you go around numb. Cut off the highs and lows and you become a zombie. Life is risk."

Rhonda's smile didn't reach her eyes. "I admire you so much, Kathleen. You put yourself out there. I wish I could enjoy sex for its beauty, like you do, instead of always wanting to turn it into a big hairy deal. You're so self-sufficient."

And where had that gotten her exactly? Weary at the prospect of sex with a fabulous man like Troy. The real risk was sex with her heart engaged and she hadn't been willing to try that since Dan.

And why exactly was she so glad they'd declared sex a bad idea? "Things aren't always as easy for me as they seem."

"Really? You struggle?"

"I cut myself off, maybe. Focus so much on experiences that I brush off people and feelings."

Rhonda blinked at her, shocked, but not nearly as much as Kathleen. What was she saying? And was it true?

And if it was, what should she do about it?

DAN'S HEART seemed to be pounding a bruise into his ribcage as he stood with Rhonda and Kathleen in front of the soda machine where he and Kathleen had made love ten years before. He caught Kathleen's eyes over Rhonda's head. They'd done that so many times the woman's hair should be standing on end from the electric current passing through her.

"Diet or regular?" Rhonda asked.

In her effort to make up for "neglecting" them in Chicago, she'd been a buzz saw of entertainment from the moment they set down at Phoenix's Sky Harbor Airport, bustling them through media interviews, whipping them onto a tour of the Desert Botanical Garden, then out to an outdoor festival at the Scottsdale Center for the Arts, and now they were wandering around the Arizona State campus—his and Kathleen's old stomping ground—before their speaking engagement.

"Diet or regular?" Rhonda repeated, looking from one to the other. They were both staring at the machine—different model from that one they'd made love beside, but still…

They both answered incoherently at once. "Oh, um, well…"

"Either one."

"Are you guys, like, heat-stroked?" She put money into the machine, which rattled, then dispensed three sodas. "The spring heat's deceptive here because of the breeze, I'm told. You could be walking along and just collapse into a faint."

She handed them each a soda. "So cool down in the shade." She indicated a bench beside the Lyceum Theater, where they'd once kissed each other crazy waiting for a play. "I'm going to the rest room."

She left and Dan and Kathleen sat on the bench,

shaded by a mesquite tree. Nearby bougainvillea were bright with magenta blooms.

"It's hard to pretend this is new, huh?" Kathleen said.

"Yeah." Everywhere they went, memories slammed into him like bumper cars. They were all happy ones. The bad moments had faded and the place wore the overbright glow things took on when you were in love.

They'd walked past Danforth Chapel—they'd made out late one night in its quiet garden—looked at the library where they'd spent countless hours pretending to study, grabbed a snack at the Memorial Union where they'd fed each other spoon-thick milk shakes and licked chicken-wing sauce from between each other's fingers, groaning with sexual need every minute.

No woman before or since had hit him as hard as Kathleen had. He'd had steady relationships since her, but he'd never again felt the world-on-tilt, nothing-else-matters firestorm he'd experienced with her.

"Who was that guy who looked at us like he recognized us when we passed the library?" Kathleen asked.

"My intro-to-psychology professor." Only a shadow of recognition had flickered in the guy's face. Ten years had passed and neither he nor Kathleen had put ASU on their curriculum vitae. They'd concluded that even if someone they'd once known noticed the publicity for the event, Kathleen had a different last name, so their identities were safe.

Which proved to be true through the speech at ASU that followed. The questions were thoughtful, their books sold well, and twenty minutes after the event ended, they were back at their resort, tucked into the Tempe buttes, waiting to be seated for dinner at the cliff-top restaurant.

Rhonda sighed and turned to them. "I hate to do this to you, but I'm completely beat. I'm thinking room service and nighty-night. Do you mind eating without me this once?"

"You've entertained the hell out of us all day," Dan said. "I think we can manage dinner on our own."

"We'll carry on somehow," Kathleen said.

"Good. And I promise total focus from here on out."

They waved her off with cheerful good-nights and the hostess seated them at a table by a panoramic window. From it, they could see city lights below desert foothills, as well as the path away from the lobby that Rhonda now traveled, her gloom evident in her sluggish steps and the sag of her shoulders.

"Poor thing," Kathleen said. "I have to get her to tell me what happened with Dylan so I can console her."

"She'll be happier without him, Kathleen."

"How can you be so sure?" She dangled her water goblet between two fingers and gave him a provocative look. "You're a therapist, but when was the last time someone broke your heart?"

For a few long seconds, Dan sorted out possible answers, then went with the truth. "Just about ten years ago now. And in Tempe, as a matter of fact."

Her eyes widened and color rose to her cheeks. "Oh. I didn't realize…really?" She seemed relieved, but startled, too. Maybe flattered? It was hard to tell with her.

"That shouldn't surprise you. You're a once-in-a-lifetime woman, Kathleen."

"I don't know about that." She blushed brighter and didn't seem to know where to put her eyes or her hands. Her fingers fluttered near her hair, then settled at the base of her water glass, which she turned this way and that. She kept her eyes there when she spoke. "You were my only heartbreak, too." She glanced up with that shy half smile that always surprised him.

"Something else we have in common," he said softly. "Besides good pens."

"Yeah." They looked at each other, trading emotions—tenderness, intimacy, curiosity and, of course, desire—which had hummed steadily between them all day, as they pretended to be mere book-tour mates.

After a full day of that, Dan's nerves were raw, his calm shot to hell. And now he was looking into Kathleen's green eyes. She was beautifully backlit by an orange-and-purple desert sunset and nearly irresistible.

Kathleen opened her mouth to speak, then closed it.

The waiter arrived before Dan said anything more about what they shared. They ordered a bottle of wine and began a rapid-fire conversation, as if they both were afraid that if they stopped talking for a second, they'd fill the silence with things best left unsaid.

They discussed Rhonda and Dylan, the tour, the upcoming conference in San Francisco, his parents and hers, his practice, his house in Vermont and his sailboat, her condominium in San Diego and its nearby beach, her magazine column, her fans, his book and hers.

They talked about everything except the heat that vibrated between them like a third person—the person they'd been in each other's arms.

Dan hardly tasted dinner or the two glasses of wine he downed and before long the waiter was asking if they wanted coffee or dessert. He knew he should beg off, head to his room, escape this growing force pulling him closer to Kathleen, dragging him toward the danger drain.

"I had an idea for an outdoor dessert," Kathleen said, her eyes big with hope. "Are you interested?"

"Why not?" Because they had media events the next day and needed sleep. Because more time meant more yearning.

"It's up the path," she said.

They walked together out of the restaurant and along the winding trail carved into the mountainside. A silver moon lit the way, decorative lights turned the cactus and agave that edged the path to gold and gray.

They were alone in the quiet night, so soft and fresh with spring that they might have been Adam and Eve, if the garden were a carefully tended desert. A gentle breeze sent creosote's medicinal musk to his nose, almost a physical reminder of all the desert picnics Kathleen and he had shared back in college. Hadn't Kathleen said smell was the most primitive sense…a direct path to the brain? In this case, it brought him back fast to those days.

They reached stone steps and climbed upward, where Kathleen showed him a hot tub flush with the ground, secluded and open, with a twinkling carpet of city lights rolled out below.

"What do you say to truffles from the gift shop and some of my champagne up here? Or hot tea, if you'd prefer." She looked so pretty with the moonlight gleaming on her cheeks that he wanted to pull her into his arms and kiss them both mindless.

Instead, he made himself say, "You and me in hot water again? Sounds dangerous."

"We've been having such a nice time."

His chest tightened. "I don't have the willpower, Kathleen." Already he was mentally scrambling for some time-warp permission for one more night together. What was wrong with him?

"Maybe tonight you forget willpower," Kathleen said, her heart still singing at what Dan had told her before the wine arrived—that she'd been his only heartbreak. *You're a once-in-a-lifetime woman.* This changed everything. Balanced it all out. And now they were together and it seemed like the third act of an important play, the period to a sentence, graduation or a lost love letter finally found.

"Maybe tonight we need to be together. Just tonight." Instinctively, she stepped close and slid her fingers up the sleeves of his loose shirt to his chest in their old gesture of connection. His skin was warm and his heart pounded under her fingers the same way hers was thudding against her ribs. "Maybe it will be good for us."

Couldn't they steal a moment? Didn't they owe it to each other? Weren't they strong and smart enough to manage it without ruining anything?

Dan gripped her wrists from outside his shirt. "When you used to touch me that way, I always felt needed."

"I did need you."

He released her wrists and took hold of her waist with his big, firm hands.

"And when you did that, I always felt you'd never let go."

"I never wanted to." A muscle ticked in his jaw and sadness flickered in his face. "And that was the problem. You couldn't breathe, remember? You would have left soon." He let go of her waist and stepped back.

"What happened wrecked me, Kath. I became my jealous father, crazy and out of control, unable to think or work or even be away from you. I don't like to remember that."

"We're different now."

"Not different enough. We have a lot at stake here, both of us. I'm uncomfortable with the risks. Let's leave well enough alone."

Her joints ached with disappointment, even as she knew he was right. She chose to joke. "Damn, I've lost my touch. I can't even tempt you to be wicked anymore."

He laughed harshly, the sound sharp in the quiet night. "Are you kidding? Everything about you tempts me, Kathleen. The way you smile, how you bite your lip when you're nervous, the way your hair flies around your face, the tilt of your chin when you're pissed, how nosy you are…and restless and alive."

"You notice all that?"

"That and more. The way you tuck your legs under you when you sit. And how fragile your collarbone is, the beat of your pulse in your throat, the softness of your skin, the curve of your breasts." The words were tumbling out of him in a way she'd never heard before.

"Your sighs and gasps. Your voice, of course. The way you hum to yourself, that funny little hitch in your walk, the mischief in your eyes. You knock me out. Still."

In the moonlight, Dan's eyes flashed—like lightning over twin blue lakes murky with emotion.

This was why she'd been wild about him. He was as sensual as she was; he just hid it from everyone but her. She got to him. Only her. And she'd loved it, melted with it, gloried in it. And now she wanted him.

He cupped her face in both hands, ran his thumbs down her nose and across her cheekbones, studying her. She touched him the same way. She'd always thought this was what couples should do at the altar. Hold each other's faces, look into each other's eyes and make those vows. This was the circle of connection that could not be broken. Eye to eye, fingers to faces, a straight path to the brain and then the heart, where all the love lived.

She saw in his eyes that he could go either way—kiss her or let her go. She had the power to decide for him.

So, she did. She stepped back. "You're right. We've both worked hard to get here." The night air cooled her cheek so quickly it was as if he'd never touched her at all.

Dan looked surprised, but he gave her a quick, sad nod. "Shall we head up to our rooms?"

"You go ahead. I'll stay for a bit. Settle myself." She looked beyond him at the gorgeous lights of the city, that rolling rug of civilized heat, the romantic twinkle wasted tonight.

She watched Dan walk away from her down the lit pathway, shadows of mesquite and saguaro flickering on his back. She sighed and looked down at the dark water of the hot tub. She could get her champagne and truffles and climb in. Enjoy herself alone. She'd done it many times.

Not tonight. She did not want to be alone tonight. She needed company and color, so she headed to the bar for new drinks, new people, music and laughter.

She made her way to the hotel's lounge, which was elegant, with golden light, romantic music and subtle ambiance. Too bad, because tonight she needed a noisy, trashy bar…and maybe Jell-O shooters to spark some fun.

The bartender had potential. He was a darling twenty-something with close-cropped hair and an easy smile, but he ruined it when he had to get help making her champagne cocktail. What bartender worthy of the name didn't know the delights of a sugar cube sizzling at the bottom of a grenadine sunrise in a golden champagne sky?

The drink came and she took a careful swallow, reveling in the sweet startle of it, the lovely fizz, happy to stop feeling the knot in her stomach, the ache in her throat over Dan.

Now to find some company. She turned on her stool to survey the patrons…and was startled to find Rhonda at the far end of the bar, hunched and miserable over a bubbly, lime-wedged drink.

Okay, here was something to do. Cheer up Rhonda and herself, while she was at it. They were all in this mixed-up life together—joy and misery, gloom and surprise in unpredictable proportions—as if life's bartender was a little tipsy himself.

She picked up her drink, moved down the bar and slid onto the stool next to Rhonda. "So, a horse walks into a bar…"

Rhonda looked up, bleary-eyed, but managed a lopsided grin when she saw who it was. This obviously wasn't her first vodka-tonic of the evening.

"…and the bartender says, 'Why the long face?'"

"Very funny," Rhonda said, her cheerleader pep completely pooped.

"I thought you were headed for bed."

"I was too bummed out to sleep."

"Bummed out about what?"

Rhonda studied Kathleen a moment, as if deciding whether or not to confide in her. "Dylan," she finally said. "Dan told me not to sleep with him last night and now I'm sorry I didn't."

"Hon, Dan McAlister is the last guy you want romantic advice from. You should have talked to me."

Rhonda blinked at her. "But his book really helped me."

"He makes some good points about balance and awareness and avoiding extremes, I guess, but when it comes to love? Trust me, he's as lost as they get."

"Really? You think so?"

Kathleen just looked at Rhonda, afraid she might say too much.

"I did wonder a little... I asked him about how he handles...you know...urges, but he ducked the question. Do you think he's, like, celibate?" She leaned in, as if to get the skinny.

"Let's talk about you. So, you didn't have sex with Dylan last night and now you regret it?"

"Yeah. The first time was amazing. But it wasn't enough to know for sure if we really had something. So I missed my double-check point...or whatever." She drained her drink and waved it at the bartender. Kathleen caught his eye and canceled the order with a head-shake just before Rhonda looked back at her.

"Are you still in love with him?"

"Yeah, but so what? There's a guy in New York..." She explained about Mark, whom Kathleen had heard about through Dan's bathroom door.

"Here's the deal," Kathleen said. "Just because Dan McAlister is afraid of emotion, doesn't mean you should be. You *care* about Mark, but you *love* Dylan. It's obvious."

"You really dislike Dan, don't you?"

Had she sounded angry? She wasn't angry; she was frustrated. "No. I disagree with him, that's all."

"There's a weird vibe between you. He stares at you a lot."

"That's because he can't figure me out."

Rhonda was still watching her face. "Did you ever think about sleeping with him? Wouldn't that be funny?"

"Hilarious." Kathleen sucked down the rest of her drink—breaking her vow to savor every drop—and waved the empty glass for a refill.

"Imagine you two together…"

"Yeah, imagine that."

"But opposites attract, right? And where there's friction, there's fire."

Kathleen felt heat in her face and prayed it was too dark for Rhonda to see her blush. If only she had that poker face most people donned when they needed it.

Luckily, Rhonda was too intoxicated and sad to focus on her for very long. "That's the way it is with me and Dylan. He's a free spirit and I'm a nester. I want to settle down and buy furniture and he wants to cross the country on a Harley. Not to mention all the women in his life."

"Maybe he's changed. People change."

"That's exactly what I told Dan," Rhonda said, blinking at her.

Yes, I know. "What can I say? I'm good."

"Dan said something about memories and how they get…something…I can't remember."

"Mixed up with reality?"

"Exactly." She grinned. "You sure you weren't there?"

Kathleen laughed a tight laugh. "When you're good, you're good."

"And he said that Dylan is toxic to me."

"Do you think he is?"

"I don't know." Rhonda hung her head, poked at her

lime triangle with her straw, splashing liquid up into her eye, which she halfheartedly rubbed. If it stung, she didn't appear to feel it.

"So, talk to Dylan. Tell him how you feel. And when he comes to New York you'll see what happens."

"You think? Just come right out with it? When he comes to New York? Wait, how did you know he was coming to New York?"

She'd heard that from her bathroom hideout. "You must have said so. He's a musician, isn't he, and New York is Mecca for musicians."

"I guess…" She blinked, then brightened. "So, can I use your cell? Mine's upstairs."

Kathleen extracted her phone and was about to hand it over when Rhonda flapped at the bartender with a wobbly hand. "Where's my drink?"

"Maybe you'll call tomorrow. I can't let you drunk-dial."

"I'm not drunk. I'm absolutely fine." Reaching for the phone, she half slipped off her stool.

Kathleen helped her back up. "Tomorrow. After the hangover fades."

"Kath-leen," she whined.

But Kathleen was firm. She kept Rhonda from ordering another drink, gave her two Hangover-B-Gone tablets and walked her to her room.

Once inside, Rhonda threw her arms around Kathleen in a walloping hug. "I'm so, so, sooo honored to be on this trip with you. Getting your advice. And Dan's. I feel so…honored…and priv-*hic*-leged. Pinch me."

"I don't want to pinch you."

"Come on. Do it. So I'll know it's real."

She gave a hunk of Rhonda's upper arm a light squeeze.

"Not like that. Like this." Rhonda pinched herself hard. "Ouch. That's real. Anyway, my friends will not, not believe I got drunk with *the* Kathleen Valentine. This is so wunnerful."

"Do you need help getting into bed?"

"No. I'm great." She flopped onto the bedspread, legs hanging to the floor and kicked off her shoes.

Kathleen ducked to avoid a flying espadrille. Lord. "Now, no calling Dylan until tomorrow."

"Cross my heart," Rhonda said, making a clumsy approximation of that gesture. "God, the room is spinning."

"Plant one foot on the floor and it'll stop."

She jammed a bare foot onto the carpet. "Yes! You are so, so smart."

"And you are so, so drunk. Good night, Rhonda." Kathleen stood in the doorway long enough to be sure Rhonda wasn't going to be sick, then gently closed the door and headed down the corridor.

Outside Dan's door, she paused. She'd told Rhonda to listen to her heart, but she'd always protected her own. Should she knock? Just a tap maybe. If he was awake, then it was kismet. If not, she'd just go to bed and forget it. And him. Forever.

She tapped and waited, her heart in her throat.

Nothing.

He might think it was next door, so she tapped again a little harder.

Nothing. The air-conditioning units could be noisy, so she banged hard enough to hurt her hand.

Still nothing.

Why did he have to be a sound sleeper? So much for

kismet. She rested her forehead against the door for a moment, then gathered her strength and walked away. What was the point, really? It wouldn't lead anywhere. And it might go badly.

She crossed the resort to her building, took the elevator to her floor and then opened her suite door…to candlelight and music…and Dan, standing in the archway between the living area and her bedroom.

Her heart jumped into her throat. "You're not in your room," were the first words she could choke out.

"The maid was turning down the bed." He crossed the floor to her. "I found myself in the hall—for ice, I thought, but I didn't even have the ice bucket. And then I was in the gift shop buying condoms."

"Really?"

"Really." He put his hands on her waist, surveyed her face, heat and pleasure in his eyes. "After that I took the elevator in the wrong building…and there was the maid putting chocolates on your pillow. It was a sign. So here I am."

"I'd say buying the condoms was the sign, Danny." She hadn't called him Danny since the early days of their love.

"It felt right to be here, waiting for you." He pulled her against him, tight, that big Dan blanket she'd loved, a windbreak against the world.

"I just got back from pounding on your door, you know," she said. "I probably woke neighbors on both sides."

"See, another sign."

"My knuckles still sting."

He cupped her fist and kissed her knuckles one by one. "All better?" The tenderness made her feel weak.

"I don't want you to regret this, Danny."

"I won't."

"We're stronger and smarter than we were ten years ago."

"Absolutely. We can have one night together," he said, obviously trying to convince himself, too.

"Of course. One night won't hurt anybody. I mean this is for healing. It's like a time-out, kind of, for old time's sake."

"It could help our work, too, don't you think?"

"Exactly. It will calm us down. Smooth out the tour."

"Absolutely. And we'll sleep better."

"So it's healthy. And, after all, we're adults."

"We're babbling," Dan said.

"I know and I don't care. We've been fighting this so long that it's only natural to—"

He shut her up with a kiss.

11

REMEMBER this kiss, Kathleen told herself before she was completely swept into sensory overload. *You'll never have another like it.* It was as lush and startling as the first one in New York, as intense as the one in the tub and as powerful as the ones from long ago. More powerful, really, because it contained all their history and all their healing.

They both took their time. Dan tugged at her tongue and she tugged at his, creating a delicious push-pull she wanted to go on and on. Dan held her butt in both hands, then hiked her off her feet just enough so he could walk her into the bedroom, holding their lovely kiss the entire way.

She noticed that he'd neatly folded the spread at the foot of her bed, just the way he used to do in his monk's apartment. But he'd lit all her candles, because she liked them, he knew, and their golden glow made the room seem both erotic and dreamlike.

Dan lowered her to the mattress and joined her, pushing her onto her back and kissing her slowly, exploring the soft insides of her mouth with his tongue, taking possession, owning her.

She tangled her legs with his, reaching to hold his backside, tight and firm, thinking ahead to how he would thrust into her body the way his tongue was be-having in her mouth.

He stopped working on her mouth and moved to her throat for a soft, slow kiss before he pressed his tongue at the base of her neck—her pulse, the spot he'd men-tioned out by the spa.

She shivered and squirmed, molten below the waist. Dan was going slowly just the way she loved. He'd re-membered that, too, along with everything else. She could feel his muscles tremble with the effort of hold-ing back and his breath came in hot, damp bursts of air.

He lifted his head and studied her body the way she used to love, as if it were extremely precious to him. He undid her buttons lovingly, so that each one snapped crisply, releasing her breasts inch by delicious inch. She wore no bra under the stretchy shirt, a fact that made her very glad just now.

"Mmm," Dan said, examining her breasts as if he couldn't take his eyes off them. He cupped them in both hands, lifted them to his mouth and squeezed them to-gether so that he could touch each nipple in turn with his hot tongue. Exquisite moist heat suffused the spot, making her nerves dance and her sex tighten and twist. She squirmed beneath him.

Now he served one breast to himself, sucking the nip-ple inside, running his tongue along the bumps and tender flesh. He shifted his attention to the other nipple, treating it with the same care—touching the tip with his tongue, sucking it, tasting its surface, then pulling it in all the way.

His other hand held her other breast and he squeezed and tickled that nipple while his mouth continued its glorious work on the first, resulting in a dry tight sen-sation on one tip and hot wet suction on the other.

"Oh, that's good." Her hips pivoted against him, ready for action, impatient for him to enter her, though she knew delay increased the pleasure. "My clothes," she whimpered.

"One thing at a time."

Maddening, but true. After so much time apart and so much longing, she wanted everything at once. This seemed like a dream. In fact, she'd had this dream many times.

She flopped back on the mattress to let him have his way. And what a way it was. He kissed and licked along the underside of her breasts, focusing on the line where they met her rib cage, giving her a delicious tickling throb. He was so good at this. He knew exactly what she needed. She'd noticed this when they were together before, but now that she was more sexually experienced, she realized he was unusually sensitive and skillful.

"You are so beautiful," he said, stopping to admire her body. The candlelight had melted his ice-blue eyes to a shimmering slate. She loved looking into them, seeing the adoration there, loved the bruised softness of his mouth, the intimate angle of his jaw. She felt beautiful and desired.

"It's still there." He smiled and kissed between her breasts, where she had a small beauty mark he used to admire. He pressed her breasts together, licked the place where they met, then sucked each nipple in turn.

She needed some action below, though, and she pushed herself up against his body. He stopped kissing her and smiled. "Okay, okay," he breathed, then unfastened her belt. Eagerly, she lifted her hips so he could push her pants off, then stretched out, legs wide and welcoming, stilling herself to maintain this slow, lovely pace.

"I've dreamed of your body," he said, running a hand

along her hip, stroking her skin so that she trembled and twitched. "Dreamed of your skin, your breasts—" His fingers brushed her breasts, then her stomach and her pubic hair "—this spot, which makes me want to be inside you."

He pushed a slow finger in her cleft, slid it between the folds of flesh and pushed her hooded clit enough to give her a sharp charge of lust, like a switch turned on. She felt pinned in place and floating above the bed at the same time.

"Now you, Dan," she said, fighting her lust enough to try to undress him. Arousal had made her clumsy, so she fumbled with his buttons until Dan paused his finger-work long enough to remove his clothes with brusque jerks.

At last, they were naked together, bodies sliding, chest and breast meeting, feet and legs twining, genitals pushing and rubbing, hungry for more.

She gripped his penis, so familiar in its smooth, swollen strength, eager in her hand, pushing into her fisted fingers, wanting more. Being with Dan like this made her feel truly present and fully alive for the first time in forever. It was gloriously familiar and startlingly new and it registered deep inside her. Dangerously deep.

But she would not think about that. She would focus on the little window of sensual pleasure they'd granted themselves.

Dan moaned, moving against her palm, his face an agony of emotion. "I love...your hands...on me." He seemed barely able to speak. "I...have...condoms...in my pants."

She stilled her hand to clear up this detail. "Can we skip that? I'm on the pill and my tests are up-to-date. You?"

He took a labored breath, obviously trying to gather a coherent thought. "I haven't been with anyone in a long time."

"Good. Because I want to feel every single inch of you—" she squeezed him with one hand and gripped his balls with her other "—inside every inch of me."

"Kathleen," he murmured. "I…missed this."

The tender yearning in his voice slid into her like syrup and melted something inside. Before she could figure out what, Dan's finger pushed all the way in and she bucked against his hand.

She would come in a few seconds, but she didn't want that yet. She stopped his hand, kissed him softly. "First, I get a taste." She wiggled down to take him in her mouth.

He shuddered and moaned and dug his fingers in her hair. She sucked him in, opening wide to take him deep, loving the salty velvet of his most tender part. She ran her tongue along the delicate tissue just beneath his crown. He quivered and rocked against her.

She squeezed his shaft and licked the salty bead of moisture that appeared on his tip. Then she licked up and down his shaft in long strokes that made him moan and clutch her hair, so that she smiled inside.

She tugged on his sac and squeezed gently the way she remembered he liked. He slid into her mouth, groaning, slow and deliberate, moving as if he were dreaming.

His thrusts soon quickened in response to her mouth and she tightened her lips around him to intensify his climax. But then he stilled himself, stopped her with his hand and pulled out of her mouth with a reluctant sigh.

"Come up here," he whispered, his face sweat-damp and dazed with lust. "I want to see your face when we come."

She smiled and rolled onto her back. His words made her heart squeeze. There was that melting feeling again. She was making love with Dan again. After all these years. It was like before and it was better than before.

Dan rose above her, and she wanted him there—on top and inside her, pumping into her as far as he could. He slid in deep and fast, making her gasp and pant and shove herself up against him, and grab his butt with her fingers. She couldn't get enough of his body, his penis sliding inside, deeper, searching for her pleasure and his, the muscles of his butt straining.

He pushed in. "You feel good."

"You, too. Good. More. Please more." She could only gasp out confused syllables. She locked her ankles around his back, so he couldn't get too far away. He began to pump in earnest, holding her gaze, keeping her with him, giving her exactly what she wanted.

He lowered his mouth to kiss her, thrusting his tongue inside her mouth the way he was thrusting his cock into her body. She was lost—a striving, groaning mass of desire. She needed Dan, his body, his passion, his sounds, his love.

They strove together, two-as-one, at the brink of release. "I'm coming," she said.

"I know." He pumped once more and exploded inside her as if her orgasm had dragged his along for the ride.

Her pulse pounded through her body, her nerves fired and fired and she thought her heart would burst with all the emotion it held. She had to keep this in perspective. This was a lovely intimate moment between two old lovers, not the earth-cracking, sun-spinning-out-oforbit, Milky-Way-crashing-to-Earth act of love it seemed right now. "That was great," she breathed, understating it as best she could.

"Oh, yeah," Dan said. "Great." His eyes held hers, telling her he knew it was a hell of a lot more than that.

They couldn't go there, couldn't say it or even let themselves think it. She had to lighten things up. Her throat ached, but she forced out the words. "You've learned some new moves, I see." Her voice wobbled and her heart pounded against his chest, so she was sure he knew she was more shaken than her words indicated.

Evidently not, because the warmth in his eyes cooled with disappointment. "I just followed your lead."

"I always said you were a natural." She took his penis in her hands. It obediently surged to life.

"What you do to me," he said so sadly her heart ached.

"What we do to each other," she said, stroking him, determined not to let her emotions swell out of control. "Again and again."

"Yeah… We've got just one night. We'd better make it count." He brought a hank of her hair to his nose and breathed in. "I missed your hair."

"I missed you smelling my hair," she said. She began a rhythmic stroking that made him groan. "Out by the hot tub, when you described all the things about me that tempted you, that turned me on a lot."

"It was all true, sorry to say."

"There's nothing wrong with being a sensualist, Dan. Don't apologize."

"Mmm," he said, his eyes closing with pleasure.

"You tempt me, too, you know," she said. "I love when your icy eyes go hot with lust and I love your lips—soft and strong at the same time—and your square jaw, and your face…so serious that when you smile it makes me feel like I've conquered Rome."

She rose on her knees and slid him inside her. He grabbed her hips and gave a deep groan.

"Oh, and that sound. I love that. It feels like I'm making you lose control."

"You are and I am." He reached for her breasts, so she leaned forward and gave them to him. He teased her nipples with his fingers so that she wiggled on him and let out a soft sound.

"That's mine—that noise you make," Dan said, his face tight with emotion. "Like you can't bear what I'm doing."

"I can't. I feel like I should scream or I'll explode, so I hold it down to that squeal."

"It's great. Don't stop making it."

His fingers tickled, teased and plucked at her swollen nipples, sending darts and stings of pleasure everywhere.

"I love how you touch me...so…carefully…like…oh, oh…" It was hard to talk when she was feeling so much, but she wanted to share this glory, help them both remember. "…like you have to get the most out of all of me."

"Mmm-hmm. I do."

She rode him harder now and faster. She was so wet that he slid in and out of her as though he was covered in butter, and she loved the tight fullness of him jamming into her deep and easy. "You fit perfectly in me. I love that stretch…yes, that…that…good pressure… yeah…that feeling…" *Like you own me.* She wouldn't say that. "How do I feel to you?"

"Firm and liquid…like a soft, slick fist wrapped around me tight, but letting me slip through your fingers."

"That's good…so good." She got lost for a second.

"I like…your smell…" Dan was struggling to speak, but he'd joined in with her description. "You smell sweet."

"You…too." She rocked back and forth, side to side, faster and faster, hardly able to hold a thought. "And you taste…great… Fresh and human and like tea or mint."

"I like your taste, too," he said, pushing into her. "I want to bury my face in you." His words came out hoarse and needy. He pulled her firmly onto him, then pushed up hard.

"You will. Next time." His words, so intense, thrilled her. She felt wanton and powerful—all woman—on top and in control, holding him with her internal muscles, leaning forward to let him suck on her nipples, allowing her hair to brush his face, then leaning back to strain the place where they were joined, feeling him thrust up to reach her deep.

Never, never had sex been so rich and satisfying. She'd had good lovers before. But there was more to this. Dan was deeply in tune with her. Not because he wanted to be a good lover, as some men did, but because he truly wanted her to feel good.

She felt the hitch in her sex that told her an orgasm was seconds away, so she quickened her pace.

In response, Dan placed his thumb on her clitoris, matching the rhythm she was employing on him.

"Oh, yes," she cried out. "You are so… This is so… Oh, yes." She lunged into her orgasm, riding it, riding him, rocking wildly, making incoherent sounds. He called out her name like a hope, then burst inside her with so much force she felt the splash deep inside.

She collapsed onto his chest and to her surprise and embarrassment, tears slid from the corners of her eyes.

What was that about? All the strain and struggle? The frustration of the trip? Of her life of late?

It was all of it and more. It was this man, who had meant so much to her, caring for her the way he did.

"It's okay," Dan said, stroking her hair.

Lord, he hadn't seen her crying, had he? Somehow, he knew.

She kissed his neck, damp with sweat, and nuzzled the soft skin there, a few beard bristles rough against her lips. She was so happy to be with him now. Learning he'd felt the same pain about their breakup made everything seem right again. It had come full circle. Become balanced—a concept Dan would love.

He ran his hand down her hair to her back, to cup her bottom and begin a gentle massage. *Oh, yeah.* She'd forgotten this. After an orgasm, most men wanted to roll away and recover, but Dan could never get enough of her body. He would hold her on top of him and rub her shoulder muscles, her back, her bottom, her thighs, in a delicious post-orgasmic rubdown.

She'd loved this—she'd loved him. So much it had scared her. Did she love him still? How could she? It was impossible. She slid to the side, not wanting him to see her confusion.

"You okay?"

"Sure," she said. "I'm great."

"You seem sad."

"How could I be sad? That was amazing. And we have the rest of the night for more."

He stopped stroking her. "That's not very long."

Did he want more time? She did, but that would be insane. She needed to remind them both what they risked. "Can you imagine what Rhonda would say if she saw us like this?"

His body tensed. "She'd be shocked." He laughed, but sounded worried. Her reality check had hit him like an ice bath.

She hadn't intended to start him worrying. "Relax. She'll never suspect. She thinks you're a monk."

"You talked with her about my sex life?"

"She was in the bar drowning her sorrows over Dylan and she asked me whether I thought you were celibate."

"How long ago did you leave her? Her room is near mine, you know. If she's wandering the halls…"

"She's out cold. I walked her to her room to sleep off too many vodka tonics. You can sneak back to your room later." She lifted her head and kissed him. "Much later."

He didn't kiss back. "Maybe I should get back."

"But the night's young, Dan." Damn, damn, damn.

"It's 1:00 a.m., Kath. Don't we have an early talk show?"

"Yes, but—"

He sat up. "I need a clear head to argue with you on live TV." He patted her. "I'd better go."

Her reality check had worked too well. "We've got time."

He didn't answer, just headed for his clothes, all naked glory, his erection proud and high. How could he ignore that? He could, though. He seemed to climb into emotional withdrawal along with his golf shirt and slacks.

Dressed, shoes on, he returned to the bed and sat beside her. He stroked her hair, untangling it with his fingers, and looked down at her, his eyes unreadable.

"Regrets?" she asked him, her throat tight.

"No. This might have been wrong, but I'm not sorry."

"Me, either." *Don't go.* She bit her tongue to keep from saying it.

"This was good for us, I think." He paused, as if he wanted to say more, then he closed his mouth. A muscle flickered in his cheek. "Good night, Kath. Sleep well." And he kissed her on the forehead. The *forehead,* for God's sake.

"Good night," she said, wishing she could think of a reason to call him back.

Which meant it was a damn good thing he'd had the sense to leave. She'd felt a wave of the intensity that had turned Dan into her world, made her forget that she was responsible for her own happiness, that she couldn't count on him—or anyone—to be there for her for long.

They'd had a few lovely hours together. That should be enough.

With her heart pattering like hail on a window and her mind playing hyper-speed Frogger, Kathleen knew she wouldn't drift to sleep any time soon. She turned on her computer to work on her book—record some thoughts about intensifying sensuality—a lesson she'd learned well tonight.

But she didn't want to write her book just now. She wanted to write about Dan. She forced herself to work just long enough to ensure that the sex they'd had hadn't killed her muse, then she let herself fish out her notepad journal.

She read over what she'd written about what JJ would say about almost having sex with Dan. Ha! Now she'd actually done the deed. JJ would snort smoke out the top of her head with that little bit of news.

She started a new paragraph.

Well, JJ, we did it after all. Slept together. I don't know if I converted Dan to anything except how good we are in bed. It was…amazing. Now that would make a book.

What kind of book? How to repair a ragged breakup? Making the best of reunion sex? Or was there more to the story? There couldn't be. If Dan could walk away so sensibly, so could she.

THE NEXT AFTERNOON, Dan watched Kathleen type away on her laptop at the table where they sat near the resort's huge pool. She wore a barely-there bikini and now and then delivered a dreamy smile his way. How could she concentrate after the night they'd spent together?

"Come on in, the water's like warm silk," Rhonda called to them from the pool. "How's that for sensory detail, Kathleen?"

"In a bit," Kathleen called, then spoke softly to him. "Looks like that call to Dylan wiped out Rhonda's hangover."

It seemed that Rhonda had called Dylan first thing this morning and now he planned to meet her when the tour got to L.A. He'd made appointments at a record company, which suggested to Dan that he was less motivated by love than ambition, but Rhonda had confided this information to Kathleen, so he didn't dare venture an opinion. Not that she'd asked.

His gaze fell on Kathleen's nearly nude body, pale

under the umbrella's shade. She was clicking away, humming to herself. How could she concentrate?

He'd barely managed a restless doze after their love-making. A hangover-subdued Rhonda had led them through television and radio appearances and several print interviews, during which he'd been sluggish, Kathleen self-possessed and serene. Maybe a little muted. He was a space case.

Of course she was comfortable with nights of wild sex—ouch. The thought of her with other men torpedoed his lust. But then he looked at her and desire sluiced through him in endless waves.

One night. Right. He felt the same hunger to be inside her as he had years ago. The few hours they'd spent together had been a nibble of shrimp cocktail, stimulating his appetite, not quenching it. Lord, now he was sounding like Kathleen with her food metaphors.

He knew better than to sleep with her, dammit. Had known it even as he bought condoms and headed to her room. He'd done it anyway, crashed headfirst into feelings he'd banished a decade ago.

Why hadn't he gotten seriously involved with another woman since Kathleen? He'd been busy, sure, but *that* busy? He'd deliberately avoided women with the kind of passion that was Kathleen's lifeblood. Holding her in his arms again had made him feel so alive, so grateful and so eager for more.

But it was over. They had a closure of sorts.

So, why did he feel so raw?

Kathleen tapped away and his gaze slid to her sleek legs—freshly shaved, he saw—and her delicate toes with bright red polish. The laptop covered her belly so his restless eyes moved to her bikini top. Three beads of sweat, round as tiny buttons, nestled between her breasts, lucky things. He longed to lick them away, rip off those triangles of fabric and...

As if she'd read his mind, Kathleen raised her eyes to him. Heat snapped between them like a towel in a locker room. "You're doing it again," she said in a voice husky with emotion.

"Doing what?"

"Looking at me like you want to eat me up."

"I do. I didn't get a chance to last night."

He watched a shiver pass through her. Under his gaze, her nipples tightened, becoming more visible through the thin fabric. *Come and get us,* they taunted him.

"If only we weren't in public," he growled.

"What would you do, Dan?"

"I'd pull you onto my lap, get rid of that excuse for a swimsuit and lick you dry. Everywhere."

She quivered again, closed her eyes and leaned her head back as if to absorb the blow of his words. After a few shaky breaths, she leveled hot eyes at him. "There's a rest room over there." She tilted her head toward the dressing rooms.

"The doors don't lock."

"So we prop something against them."

"Like our bodies?"

"Absolutely."

"The fact that I'm even considering that shows how low I've sunk. I'd better hit the water. Hope it's cold." He pushed out of his chair. Maybe a dip would settle his hard-on and clear the fog from his mind.

"I'll come with you," she said.

He let her walk ahead of him—it was tough going with an erection aching in his trunks. She glided across the decking and dove smoothly in, making barely a ripple, and broke the surface sleek as a seal. She never tiptoed into anything, his Kathleen. Just jumped right in. He slid off the side of the pool, sorry the water was too warm to shrink his erection. Besides, Kathleen was mere inches away and soaking wet. Ouch.

"Isn't this great?" Rhonda said, standing three feet away. She extended her arms to indicate the pool. Part lap-pool, part lounging lagoon, it was surrounded by artificial sandstone so it looked like a river in a mountain canyon.

"It's wonderful," Kathleen said, nabbing an empty air mattress and climbing aboard.

Dan averted his eyes, not willing to watch Kathleen's body surge and wiggle into place.

"I wanted to talk to you both about the media interviews," Rhonda said. "How did you think they went?"

"I thought they were fine," Dan said, "except—"

Rhonda cut him off. "A little canned, right? In Chicago and even at ASU, there was more, I don't know, dueling. You know, where you say she's indulgent, Dan, and you say he's repressed, Kathleen. This morning you were…agreeable. Slow and flat."

"We'll be nastier to each other in L.A., I promise," Kathleen said, winking at Dan. "We're saving it up."

"Okay." Appeased, Rhonda smiled. "I guess I'll do laps—tighten up this travel-food flab before I see Dylan again." She set off, splashing wildly, sending children in water wings and inner tubes sloshing to either side.

Kathleen squinted up at Dan from her float. "Feeling any better?"

"How could I, looking at you like this, knowing that all I have to do is untie that little string and I can have your breasts in my hands?"

"I see what you mean." She squirmed on the raft.

He scooped up water and let it drizzle from her breasts to the edge of her bikini bottom.

She sucked in a breath, then shaded her eyes to look at him. "Keep that up and I'll have to see how long I can hold my breath underwater with you in my mouth."

That sent a charge through him. "Close your eyes," he said, remembering what she'd said about blindfolds and surprise.

She settled back down and closed her eyes, the waves making her raft shimmy.

"Is your skin hot?" he asked.

"Getting that way."

"Would you like me to cool you down?"

"Yes, please." Her husky voice made him ache.

"How bad do you want it?"

"Very bad. Please, Dan. I need it." She was deliberately trying to arouse him, but he also felt the edge of need in her voice.

He was hard as a rock. The only satisfaction he had was that no one could possibly know what was going on. He was just standing beside the float calmly talking to her, running his fingers through the water.

"You have to really want it," he said.

"I do. I have to have it." She wiggled, spreading her legs. He wanted to climb on board, slip her bikini out of the way and ram himself into her as far as he could go.

"Where do you want it? Tell me."

"On my arms…my legs…my belly…"

"How about here?" He let a few drops fall between her legs, right on her sweet spot.

"There. Yes." She looked up at him, the heat in her

gaze brighter than the spring sun bearing down on them. "Give me more. Now."

"This is a dangerous game we're playing," he said.

"I know and I don't care. I want you inside me. Now."

"Oh, yeah." He glanced toward the dressing room, ready to go there, slam the door shut with Kathleen's naked body and go at it. He was just about to say so when he noticed their peppy chaperone flailing toward them, raising a frothy wake. "Looks like Rhonda to the rescue again."

"Damn," Kathleen said, sounding as desperate as he felt.

"Time to cool down with some laps," he said and dove toward that side of the water. He'd be at it for hours.

12

KATHLEEN LAY naked on freshly laundered sheets that were exactly the way she liked them—smooth and crisp and lavender-scented—but they felt scratchy and sweaty and irritating.

She couldn't sleep. Why had she said just one night? Why not two? Why not the rest of the tour? What was wrong with turning a miserable book tour into a joy?

That one night had supercharged her desire for Dan. It didn't help that Dan was getting the hang of acting sensually. She'd practically climaxed right there in the pool when he dripped water on her spot. And now she was cranky with frustration.

She'd begged off dinner, claiming she'd have room service so she could write. The only good thing about the tension between them was that her muse was dancing in her head, itching for the keyboard all the time…well, except when she was itching for Dan.

She'd written about how the contrast between restraint and indulgence made indulgence all the more delicious. She tied the idea into her recent interest in Victorian-era romances and the way that repression sexualized everything—even drops of chlorinated water in a pool. And how, with the right person, with the right tension, you experienced sensory impact squared. Or tripled maybe.

But now she was too wired to sleep. She'd have to take another bath. And then a sleeping pill. She turned on the water and buried her hand in its hot rush, focusing on the pleasure of it. If only Dan were here. She squeezed her eyes shut and pictured her big bar of vanilla soap in his broad palm, his long, strong fingers thick with foam…

Then she heard a knock. Or had she? She shut off the water. Sure enough, there was a measured, careful rap, pause, rap, that could only be…please, let it be…

It was, she saw through the peephole, so glad she was naked, She opened the door and Dan eased in fast, sneaky as a cat burglar on a heist. The visit was illicit, after all.

"You're naked," he said, pure delight in his voice. He grabbed her into his arms and kissed her hard, forcing her backward a few steps. He broke away from her mouth long enough to say, "I remembered that I didn't get to taste you."

"I see," she said, grinning at him while he tossed off his T-shirt and shoved off his jeans. Nothing underneath. He'd wanted to come so badly he'd come commando. That made her so happy. A distant warning bell sounded in her head. This was reckless behavior from Dan.

Too bad. She wanted him, ached for him, her arms and legs and sex all clamoring at once for his attention.

Which he seemed happy to give. He lifted her up and found his way inside her fast. She wrapped her legs around his body and he thrust again, hard, then again and again, as if every ounce of his being was in each thrust. They came together with a tremendous noise— a groan from him, a cry from her.

"Kathleen," Dan said, burying his face between her

breasts. "I just wanted you…so much." He kissed her neck, under her chin, pressing her breasts into his palms.

That was how it had been at the end. Her slow, careful seducer had become a ferocious lover—forceful, insistent and fast. And she'd liked that at first. Dan McAlister unchained. She'd felt powerful and important to him. Except that hadn't been the real Dan. That had been frantic Dan, fighting to hang on to her. And she'd pulled away. Making it worse.

This was different, though. She was as fierce and eager and needy as he was. And everything was more intense because they'd denied themselves. This was definitely different.

"I was just fixing a bath," she said.

"Great. I love you in the bath…and in the bed. On the couch…"

"Against the wall…in the hall," she added in a sexy purr Dr. Seuss never intended. "And in a box and with a fox."

Ten minutes later they were together in the tub, soapy bodies sliding over each other, tongues exploring while their fingers found each other beneath the vanilla-scented bubbles and they rubbed and teased each other to overwhelming orgasms.

And then Dan insisted on drying her off, covering her with moisturizer, and carrying her to the bed, where he kissed down her belly, heading slowly and deliciously toward his target.

Her sex taut with anticipation, the rest of her swamped with pleasure, she tried to memorize the moment. She took in the golden light and how it played on Dan's wet hair, the scent of vanilla soap and white-tea-and-ginger lotion, the sound of his mouth on her skin, his muscles sliding down her lotion-slick body, the crisp sheets under her damp back, cool air brushing where his mouth had been on her breasts and her stomach. And then he found her with his lips and tongue.

Oh, man. Oh, man. Oh, man. Did it get any better than this?

She wished she could shift and get his cock into her mouth, too, to give him the same pleasure she felt, but she was too swept away by what he was doing to her.

He licked and sucked softly, his tongue and lips moving exactly the right way, for exactly the right length of time, with the perfect pressure and suction and stroke. Her climax went off like a skyrocket.

Dan pressed his tongue against her, lapping up her pleasure until the last twitch had faded and she lay gasping for air.

She reached down for him and he kissed his way up her body to her chin and cheek and mouth. And then she took him inside as far as she could, lost in the extra something that came from caring for someone so much that pleasure passed effortlessly between the two of you as if you were one person.

The climax washed over them both, long and slow and lovely.

"I can't get enough of you," Dan said.

"Mmm," she said, kissing him again.

"I love how you taste. And everything else." He seemed drunk with it all.

She leaned back and smiled at him, feeling very happy.

"You've got me," he said softly, kissing her below her earlobe. "You win. Sex is a sensory buffet. And I want to eat all day and all night."

"For the whole trip, you think?"

He nodded into her neck.

She put her arms around his broad back, stroked his skin, gloried in having him all to herself for the next five days…well, between book-signings and conference appearances. "We'll have to be careful. If Dylan is meeting Rhonda in L.A., I'm sure she won't mind if we entertain ourselves a bit."

"Sounds good." He lifted his face from her neck. Something feverish in his eyes made her stomach twist. Was this a mistake? Should they declare it finished? Were they pushing it?

But then he kissed her softly and laughed a big, happy laugh. "God, this feels good."

He looked better, too. Gone was the gaunt look she'd noticed when she first saw him. He was engaged and aware, not distant and indifferent. And that made her just plain happy—not because she'd proved herself right, but because she'd helped him. And, despite everything, she cared about him still.

This was good for him. For her, too. Her jitters were gone, as was her edginess. And learning that he still cared for her was rejuvenating. It had reaffirmed her mission, too. It was all good. Surely it was.

No MATTER what else happened, he'd been good for Kathleen, Dan thought as the plane lifted into the air from Sky Harbor Airport on its way to LAX. He watched her talk to Rhonda, smiling and calm, fully inhabiting her body. All that frantic irritation and brittle tension he'd noticed when he first saw her was gone. Her radiance had returned.

It was partly due to sexual release, of course. But he hoped there was more to it. He'd seen her scribbling

away in the hotel notepad that was serving as her journal, so maybe she'd picked up that habit. He'd caught
her lost in contemplation once and she'd claimed she
was "playing mental Frogger"—her joke about meditation. These were small things, sure, but at least he
hadn't been a bad influence on her.

Now her eyes shone with pleasure and her glance no
longer skittered away. She looked him straight in the eye.

And when she did, he felt alive.

She'd been good for him, too.

"More tea, Dan?" Rhonda asked. She was frantic
with excitement. Over Dylan, which was a mistake, he
knew, but Rhonda sought Kathleen's advice now, not
his. It might be because of the weird bathroom incident
when he'd blocked her way, but he suspected he'd come
to represent her conscience, her higher self, who knew
that Dylan was dangerous to her. That was the problem
with people bent on unhealthy practices. They searched
out supportive voices, books and magazines, instead of
the truth.

Was he doing that with Kathleen?

No. He still believed in self-control and goal-directed
behavior. Informed action and mindfulness represented
a higher way of being to him. That hadn't changed.

But being with Kathleen these few days had made
him wonder if maybe he hadn't stripped his life of passion. Had balance and moderation insulated him against
deep feelings? Maybe Kathleen was right and he'd
"boiled the sweet peas of life to mush."

What if he shook off the checklists and rules? What
if he just opened his heart, let loose and danced in the
streets, licked the bottom of the ice-cream bowl?

Would he be happy?

Kathleen had him thinking that way. It wasn't comfortable and there was a low rumble of warning inside, but he chose to ignore it. For now. After all, even having wild sex, they'd established parameters. They had just five more days together—two in L.A., three in San Francisco for the conference—and then it would be over. So why not enjoy the time that remained without a lot of soul-searching? Why not use the guest towels, the best silver, the antique teapot, as Kathleen recommended?

Tomorrow they had media events and signings, but most of the evening was their own. He had a great idea that he knew Kathleen would love. He couldn't wait. He was a fool in love. Just like Rhonda.

THE DAY had worn Kathleen out. They'd arrived in L.A. two hours ago and she was exhausted. But that had nothing to do with the plane flight or book tour. Yearning for Dan was what had worn her thin. Every glance, each accidental brush of arm or thigh ratcheted up the tension.

It had gotten so bad that they'd made out in an elevator between floors during their only alone time. *It's happening again.* She felt the pressure of Dan's desire heavy as a lead blanket and her own passion for him consumed her every thought.

She should take some time to write, but she only wanted to plan her next chance to go to bed with Dan again. Worse, the more she went to bed with him, the less she wanted to work on her book. That was a scary trend.

On the other hand, it was no wonder they couldn't leave each other alone. They had so few days and not much time then, since they had book-tour obligations to fulfill.

Remember the book tour? The sales? The fans? The buzz? That was supposedly what was most important to her. *Get a grip.*

She grabbed her journal notepad and wrote herself some advice:

> Use the affair to build your book. Let the connection enrich your understanding of your work. What did Dan say? *You win.* Yes. How ironic. JJ was right again. The Pied Piper of Hedonism has converted Dr. Moderate to her religion of the senses. You've won the battle of the books. Be happy.

But she didn't care about a battle or winning. She stopped writing. She wasn't sure Dan's conversion was an entirely good thing. He'd needed to loosen up, not let go of the reins altogether. That seemed reckless and wrong.

Before she could write that down, Dan tapped at the door and all analytical thoughts or worries flew from her mind. Dan was here. They would make love. Hooray! She tossed her notepad into a drawer of her nightstand and went to let Dan in.

He entered, dropped the backpack he carried, pulled her into his arms and kissed her until she went liquid.

"Let's go to bed," she said, weak with desire.

"First close your eyes."

"What?"

"You heard me," he said, his eyes filled with mischief.

She shut her eyes and felt him untie her robe. "What are you doing?"

"Showing you what a good student I am."

Her robe fell open and she held out her arms, thinking he'd strip her, but instead cool silk crossed her eyes…twice…and he tied her sash behind her head.

"You're blindfolding me?"

"Mmm."

The idea was a good one, but her stomach jumped with nerves. She preferred to be the person in charge of the mask. Then Dan pushed her robe from her shoulders. It dropped into a warm heap on her insteps. The next instant, she felt a hot, squirming dot of wet pressure on her nipple—Dan's tongue, and oh, was he outdoing himself!

"Oh, that feels amazing." she managed to say as he moved to the second nipple. Now both were tight, aching beads. Goose bumps chased themselves down her body. Her knees gave, but Dan caught her and swung her into his arms. She grabbed his neck, unsettled to be off her feet and blinded.

"It's me, Kathleen. I won't do anything you won't like."

"I know," she said. Reassured, she tucked her head under his chin and tried to relax. The air changed temperature and scent as they moved from the sitting room to the bedroom and she caught the lavender of her sheets just before Dan lowered her to the bed.

"I'll be right back," he whispered. "Don't move. Unless I need to tie you down?"

"No, no. I'll stay." The last thing she wanted was to lose total power. She heard him walk away and then a zipping sound. He was getting something from his backpack. She heard him cross the room away from her.

She couldn't stand not knowing what was coming, so she lifted the sash a little and saw that he was filling the coffeepot at the wet bar. He was making them coffee?

He turned toward her, so she dropped the sash in

place so he wouldn't know she'd cheated. In a second, the bed sank as he sat beside her.

"It'll be a moment," he whispered.

She felt the barest brush of his fingertip along her jawline, then down her neck. "Can you guess where I'll touch you next?"

"I have a suggestion."

"That's not how this is going to go."

She sighed, fighting impatience. "Somehow, I figured that."

"The moment in the pool gave me this idea. I liked how you squirmed when I wouldn't cool you with the water."

"I couldn't help it."

"I know. It's the combination of trust and fear and desire and restraint, I think." As he talked, his fingers traced a line down her belly, tightening her desire like a spring. She stretched out her legs and turned her body toward him.

His finger went away. "Also the idea of who has control. That's an erotic concept, don't you think?"

"Yes. Please keep going." She didn't care about theory right now. She wanted action.

"Oh, but if I do what you tell me, that will ruin everything, won't it?"

She growled in frustration. He was right. The whole point of this experience was turning yourself over to the other person. Knowing the delicious torture of wanting, being denied, then the surprise of finally getting what you so desperately craved. Dan was too good a student.

She thought of him looking down at her nakedness, her knotted nipples, quivering belly, her blond hair, her now-damp cleft and felt simultaneously powerfully sexual and very vulnerable.

"I'll be right back." He left and returned before she had time to peek, bringing with him the scent of lemon and orange and nutmeg. Steam heated her face.

"Tea? You brought me tea?" How sexy could that be—ahhhhh. Something warm and wet landed in the middle of her chest. Had to be the tea bag. "That's so good," she said. "Very good."

He dragged the tiny tea sack to her navel and then back up. "Now taste," he said, and he placed it to her lips.

Warm liquid slid into her mouth, tasting sweet and tart.

"You like?"

"Yes. Citrus and spices."

"Let me try." He shifted his body and then his tongue moved on her belly, following the path of the tea, licking, digging in, as if to get every drop. She squirmed under him, spread her legs, desperate for him to go lower, to put his hot tongue right on her spot and not move until she came. She knew better than to ask for that, but she couldn't help bucking up at him.

"Uh-uh, not so fast." He shifted his position, reached across her body, then returned and slid the tea bag— he'd warmed it up—along her thigh. She trembled in reaction. The sensation of warm liquid sliding down her leg, teasing her skin, turned out to be surprisingly erotic.

Dan pushed her thighs wide so that cool air washed where she was so eager for his touch, then pressed the warm, wet bag against her most tender flesh. It was like a hot washcloth on an anxious brow. She dissolved inside.

"How's that?" But he sounded as though he already knew.

"What do you think?"

He surprised her with a soft finger stroke, and she

gave a startled squeak. "You liked that, too, huh? You're swollen for me. I can't wait to get inside."

"I want you inside." Now they were getting somewhere. She squirmed on the bed, wanting to push off the blindfold, see the heat in Dan's face. But she also enjoyed this private arousal, the way the blindfold forced her to focus in on the scent of tea, the taste of it on her tongue, the sounds of her own harsh breathing in her ears and the anticipation of where Dan would touch her next.

"I like knowing that." He slid his fingertip the tiniest distance inside her, teasing her, she could tell.

"Please," she couldn't help saying, writhing a little.

"So, this is exciting?" His finger moved on her and then maddeningly disappeared, waiting for her to answer, no doubt.

"Very. I don't know what you'll do next…taste me, put your finger all the way inside me…or put your cock in as far as you can…" She was hinting like crazy, hoping she could arouse him so much he'd have to take action.

"That's the idea," he said shakily, but she felt his determination to hold back. Oh, he'd figured out this sensuality thing, all right. He was a quick learner. "So, are you going to do something *soon?* Please?"

And then, of all things and of all times, there was a knock on the door. She froze. Rhonda again? Damn.

But Dan chuckled. "It's okay. That's room service. I think you'll like what I ordered. And the way I plan to use it."

"Oh. Wow." She positively vibrated with arousal. He'd just zoomed to the principal's list, class president, valedictorian. Whatever he wanted to be.

She listened to him walk to the door, dizzy with anticipation. What had he ordered? Whipped cream?

Strawberries? Something chocolate to drizzle on her nipples and lick off? She couldn't wait.

"Damn!" Dan whispered. "It's Rhonda!"

"For God's sake, don't answer. She'll go away."

"Too late. The room-service waiter is right behind her."

"Double damn," Kathleen said, brushing her sash from her eyes and sitting up. This was her room, so she'd have to answer the door. "Hit the bathroom, Dan. I'll make it quick."

"With Rhonda, nothing's quick."

What the hell did she want? Kathleen grabbed her puddled robe, threw it on and tied it with her former blindfold, while Dan dashed for the bathroom.

"Hide in the tub in case she has to take another pee."

He paused in the doorway and gave her a crazed look. "What are we doing, Kathleen?"

"We're having an adventure. We'll laugh about this later."

He didn't look so sure.

Kathleen checked the room for evidence of Dan. Nothing except an innocent mug of tea on the nightstand.

Her hand was on the door when she noticed Dan's backpack and shoes on the floor. "Just a sec!" she called through the door, then grabbed the stuff and tossed it under her bed, kicking a dangling shoestring out of sight.

Trying to look normal for someone who'd just had a wet tea bag between her legs, Kathleen opened the door to Rhonda and room service. "Rhonda, hi. I was just having hot tea." She hoped Dan heard that little joke.

"I can smell it. Lemon…spice. It smells like the tea I gave Dan."

"He let me try some." Another joke.

They both watched the room-service guy trundle the

table into place at the end of one bed. Kathleen signed the bill fast and the waiter left.

"What did you order?" Rhonda asked, sitting at the table.

She had no idea. "Just a little…" She whipped the metal cover from the dish. "Ice cream." Two round scoops of mint chocolate chip were circled by small bowls of whipped cream, butterscotch, fudge—was it warm?—and maraschino cherries. Oh, Lord. Dan's plan made her shiver with anticipation.

"Dylan missed his flight," Rhonda said, looking up at her with troubled eyes. "He says he got caught in traffic, but what if he's blowing me off? What should I do?" Her gaze dropped to the dessert spread before her.

"So, he's catching another flight then?"

"That's what he says." Her eyes stayed glued on the food.

"Help yourself," Kathleen said with a sigh.

"Just a taste. Do you mind? I get hungry when I'm nervous." She rubbed her palms together, unrolled the napkin, shook it onto her lap, then lifted up the chocolate bowl. "Can I? For the whole effect?"

"By all means."

Kathleen watched in dismay as Rhonda drizzled the toppings, one by one over the ice cream, then piled on the cherries. She was serious about the whole effect.

"So you'll wait for his flight and see if he arrives," she said, to move things along. "A simple test, right?"

"Mmmph-hmm," Rhonda said over a mouthful. "This is the perfect combination of tastes, Kathleen. No surprise, since you're such an expert on food."

"And if he comes, you'll know he's sincere and has really changed," she said, sticking to the point.

"You *have* to try this." Rhonda held out a spoonful. "Especially the fudge. It's so warm and thick and liquid."

She took the bite. "Mmm." Yeah. That would have been nice—warm, drippy chocolate on her body, followed by Dan's stupendous tongue. And the cherries—Rhonda forked one and plopped it in her mouth—what might he have done with those? She swallowed hard and watched the best of her body-licking adventure disappear down Rhonda's throat.

Rhonda looked at her watch. "Oops, I'd better scoot for the airport," she said, as if Kathleen had begged her to stay. "Mind if I touch up my makeup in your bathroom?"

"Uh, my bathroom? Sure," she said, hoping Dan had hidden in the tub. Just to be sure, she practically yelled, "Go ahead and freshen up *in my bathroom.*"

Rhonda shot her a strange look. "Okay…I will."

Kathleen froze in place, braced for the shriek when Rhonda spotted Dan, but all was quiet except for the click of a lipstick tube, the snick of a mascara wand and a swoosh of hairspray.

After long minutes, Rhonda emerged. "I love your hairspray. It's not sticky and it holds like iron. I sampled your moisturizer. You're right about it being rich, not oily. Thanks so much. You're helping me with Dylan and skin care all at the same time. Plus, you fed me." She gave Kathleen a bruising hug.

"Thanks for everything. I'll let you know how it goes." And she was gone, trailing Kathleen's French perfume in her wake.

Kathleen rushed to the bathroom to release Dan from his hiding place.

"Thank God." Dan shoved open the shower curtain

and pushed himself to his feet. "I'm choking on the fumes in here." His eyes were indeed feathered with red.

"Rhonda ate up a good chunk of the ice cream."

"The fudge?"

"Gone. Most of the cherries, too."

"So, we'll reorder if we run out. Come here." He pulled her into his arms and kissed her.

They were just getting into it when the phone rang.

"Ignore it," he said, kissing her again.

But she couldn't. "It could be Rhonda changing her mind." Reluctantly, she slipped away from Dan's arms and went to the phone. Dan followed. Just as she said, "Hello?" he slid his hands under her arms to cup her breasts through her robe and nibbled her neck.

She was shivering when her caller spoke. "How's the writing coming?" *Suck, whoosh.*

It was JJ the smokestack.

Kathleen tried to pull away to focus, but Dan held tight.

"Fine. Just fine." She twisted her head and saw that Dan wore a stubborn, hungry look that said he wasn't going anywhere. "Can I call you back?"

"Just update me on the tempting Dr. Moderate front. Herman's very interested in the book idea."

"This isn't a good time, JJ. I have, um, company." Dan had pushed off her robe and was tracing her nipples with the most delicate of touches. She was shaking so hard it was difficult to hold the phone to her ear and she bit her tongue to hold in the moan.

"A guest? Oh, God. He's there! You're doing it!"

No, Dan was doing it. She was trying to hold a thought besides *oh, oh, don't stop.* "It's not what you think. But the first draft is coming along fine, as I indicated to you."

"Great," JJ said. "Herman will be thrilled."

"I hope so, but I'm taking a different angle than you envisioned." She could hardly speak with Dan doing what he was doing.

"You sound funny. Oh, I get it. He's right there."

Dan's hand slipped to her sex.

"Bingo," she said into the phone but it came out breathy as a gasp. She sagged back against Dan. "I'll get back with you."

"Sure. You keep working on your *draft*. Keep working, working and working…" She gave a smoke-raspy chuckle. "Bye now."

Kathleen put down the receiver and turned to Dan, sorry to break his connection with her sex.

"Your agent?"

She nodded.

"No more interruptions," he said, placing his finger directly on her clit.

She gasped.

"I'm not stopping for anything short of a bomb threat. And maybe not for that." He kissed her and she mindlessly kissed back. Somewhere inside, she knew this was not a good sign. Rhonda and JJ had just reminded them what was at stake and they were deliberately ignoring both warnings.

"What if Rhonda comes back?" she said to test Dan's good sense.

"Then I'll bring a blanket into the bathtub and wait her out." Dan lowered his mouth to her nipple just as his finger slid into her, the knuckle doing something wonderful to her entrance. If only she weren't naked and he weren't so good, she might be able to think clearly for one blessed moment.

"Forget the blindfold," Dan murmured. "I want to see your eyes when you come. Give yourself to me, Kathleen."

And so she did. She let him sweep her away with strokes and kisses, with lips and tongue and fingers. Her whole body ached for the release that only he could give.

They forgot about ice cream and blindfolds and even maraschino cherries. They fell to the bed and made hungry love to each other. And it was so good.

And so scary. It was happening again.

13

KATHLEEN TOOK a comforting sip of her creamy latte and leaned back in the double-down pillow to worry. She wasn't herself and neither was Dan. She was never up at the crack of dawn and she despised worrying. Now she was doing both. At least she had quality refreshments and a superb pillow to do them with.

She'd had to practically push Dan out the door at three by reminding him that Rhonda would pound on his door at six for their media morning and he'd better be in his room when she did.

The previous night he'd had the sense to leave so they'd get some sleep. But that bit of discretion had been noticeably absent last night.

She had to do something to snap him back to himself, to keep them both grounded in the limits of the healing fling they'd agreed to.

The idea of ending it, though, made the warm latte in her stomach turn to an iced coffee. She didn't want to stop. Dan made her feel more alive and more beautiful than she had in years. It was something about the way he really saw her, knew her and cared about her.

Of course she knew better than to count on anyone for her well-being and happiness. Especially Dan, after what had happened before. But maybe they'd both changed.

The thought surged like an illicit drug through her system. Had she changed? She still believed in her theories, still craved new experiences, was still restless and curious and on the move. But she was weary, too. The constant need to look and try and move could be as tyrannical and limiting as Dan's withdrawal and restraint.

And she did get lonely, dammit. What if she just rested, trusted in Dan, strove for quiet and calm? Would she feel renewed? Would she feel peace? Would her weariness leave?

That sounded so weird. Like trying on some oversize costume—foolish and awkward and scratchy against her skin. All wrong for her. She needed to get a grip as much as Dan.

But what they were doing was far worse for Dan, who'd staked his reputation on restraint. If they were discovered, he'd be in trouble. He'd completely tipped to her side, even announced she'd won. Ironically, she needed good old Dr. Moderate about now, with his wry distance and amused indifference.

Ten years ago, she'd gloried in how smitten Dan had been by her. But he'd been swept away, in a frenzy, not himself. More than anything now, she needed to remember the real Dan. The man who was as wrong for her as a man could be.

"I CAN'T BELIEVE you winked at that guy when you took his card," Dan said to Kathleen as they exited Radio KBUZ, hating himself for being irritated. "You'd seriously go out with him? What kind of guy calls himself 'The Blaze'?"

"That's radio, Dan. And flirtation is currency. It means zip."

"He thinks he's going to get somewhere with you." He felt an echo of the old possessiveness and quelled it. She was right. The Blaze had engaged in mere social posturing. But still. She'd flirted back pretty well.

"If it gets him talking us up on the air, let him think I want to have his love child." She stopped and looked at his face and her words were low and serious. "I'm kidding. What are you doing, Dan?"

He couldn't meet her gaze. "Nothing. I just didn't like the way he looked at you. Like you were breasts on legs."

"How about if you let me handle how people look at me?" She was trying to jolly him up, but he'd seen that frantic look fly across her face like the shadow of a fast-moving cloud. He'd alarmed her.

He was acting irrationally. Feeling that way, too. All he wanted was to get Kathleen alone and all this damn media crap was getting in his way.

He was doing it again. Getting too intense, holding too tightly. There were reasons this time, though—lack of sleep, frustration, the exhaustion of the book tour, the limited time they had to be alone together. He opened his mouth to explain it to Kathleen, when he saw Rhonda heading their way.

She looked suddenly defeated—shoulders slumped, head down, a cheerleader after her team lost the title. She'd been bouncy with joy all morning. Something had sunk her spirits while he and Kathleen were inside KBUZ.

Dylan had flown in, it seemed, after all. He was a new man, according to Rhonda. Kathleen had played her ecstatic voice-mail message for Dan's benefit.

"What's wrong? What happened?" Kathleen asked her.

"Mark called me," Rhonda said, her voice trembling.

"So, I told him about Dylan and now he wants me to choose."

"Why didn't you wait until you got home and talk to him face-to-face? Or at least wait until you were sure?"

"I couldn't stand it. I blurted. He was devastated. He says he loves me and he wants my whole heart."

"If he loves you, he'll wait until you figure it out."

"What do you think, Dan?" Rhonda asked, turning on him abruptly.

He opened and closed his mouth twice. Of all the times for Rhonda to actually want his opinion, when he was in a complete haze. He struggled into his counselor role. "I'd say you need to determine what's in your best interest. Make a pro-con list for each man, evaluate what will truly meet your needs and make a long-term decision."

"Lord. Could you *be* any more intellectual?" Kathleen said, her eyes sparking with sudden anger. "The issue here is Mark making a demand. An ultimatum is a sign of immaturity. So is jealousy or clinging. Tell him to get over it."

There was an edge to her voice. She was talking about him, not Mark. Unfairly, too. He'd merely remarked on the slathering DJ and as far as clinging was concerned, she'd dragged *him* into a janitor's closet at the TV station for a quick grope.

"The man was hurt and in shock," he said, defending Mark and himself. "He doesn't want to lose her and he has a right to find out where he stands."

"That's true," Rhonda said, "and besides, he's—"

"He's a big baby, is what he is," Kathleen said, overriding Rhonda, but speaking to him. "If he loves her, he'll be patient. A man who breaks it off at the first complication is a coward."

She was talking about their breakup. A low blow, since they'd agreed the end had been inevitable. "A coward? Really?"

"But he's not running, Kathleen," Rhonda tried. "He's—"

Kathleen ignored her. "If the shoe fits, Dan…"

She *did* blame him. "Maybe he's confused," he said, fighting for calm. "Or hurt. Or tired of mixed messages— come here, go away, come back." Kathleen had done that over and over—yanked him close, then pushed him away.

Kathleen glared at him, then turned her full attention to Rhonda. "If Mark loved you, he'd be on a plane to fight for you, not whining about you having to choose. You just think you should prefer him, Rhonda. Go with your heart, not your head."

"Don't do anything extreme," Dan said. Kathleen should not turn a fight with him into bad advice for Rhonda. "Don't dismiss Mark because he reacted badly. Try to understand his position—"

"She understands fine," Kathleen said. "People show their true colors under pressure. She can't ignore—"

"Stop it, please, you two," Rhonda said, holding up her hands. "You're flipping me out. This is a great debate for the news conference, but not now."

"Sorry," Kathleen said, shooting Dan a guilty look. "I don't know what came over me."

He knew. They were both on edge about what they were doing, questioning each other and themselves. "We're just tired," he said. "Too many bad mattresses." He winked at Kathleen.

"Yeah. Bad mattresses." She shot him a sheepish, grateful smile.

Rhonda's phone rang and she answered. "Dylan,"

she said, covering the phone. "Excuse me." She hurried off, leaving them looking at each other.

"I'll come to your room," Kathleen murmured. "I have an idea that will help us."

"Great." Lust washed through him so fast it almost hurt, erasing any residual irritation. Briefly, he thought of his neglected journal, his missed meditations, his unwillingness to give up a moment with Kathleen for a head-clearing jog. They'd missed meal after meal for sex. If he did one of his checklists, he'd score in the danger zone. Worse, he didn't care.

AFTER THEY RETURNED to the hotel, Kathleen slid into shorts and tennies and headed for Dan's room, confident that Rhonda would be busy with Dylan until the news conference.

They were going for a run. Not something she relished, but it was necessary for perspective. This thing between them had gotten too fierce too fast. Take that stupid quarrel she'd started, supposedly about Mark, but really about Dan. She'd acted as if they were together again and Dan had better not run out.

That was stupid. The truth was that she needed this painful, sweaty activity as much as Dan. Maybe more.

She tapped on his door and when he opened it, hunger blazed across his face at his first glimpse of her. Then he looked her over and his eyes widened. "You're wearing running shoes."

"That's because we're going for a run." She was delighted she'd surprised him. "To restore balance and get centered and mindful and all that jazz."

"But we won't have time for…" Making love. She read that in his eyes.

"Let's see how it goes." This was more important than sex right now. "Let's hit the street and suck in some smog. Use some of your famous moderation, balance and self-discipline."

He scratched his head. "You really want to run?"

"Absolutely. And write in our journals. Plus I have a wild craving for a wheatgrass milk shake." The thought curdled her stomach, but if it helped Dan, she'd suck down a gallon of glop.

"Okay…sure… Good idea."

He headed for his bureau and she watched as he stripped down to his bare and wonderful backside. If she watched much longer, she'd weaken and drag him to bed, so she forced her eyes away and was startled at how jumbled his room looked—clothes, shoes and books were strewn on the floor, the beds, the desk. What had happened to the serene order that was Dan's trademark?

Not a good sign.

They took a cab to Griffith Park, where they ran until Kathleen couldn't take any more. She stopped, gasping in air, leaning against the rough trunk of a sycamore. "I'm done."

"This was smart, Kathleen," Dan said, speaking easily. The man wasn't even breathing hard. But she could see he felt better. His color was better, his eyes were clearer and his face more relaxed. "I got carried away. The thing about the DJ was uncalled for."

Her calves aching, her breath coming in painful gasps, she managed to say. "The fight…over Rhonda… stupid."

He nodded.

"I thought a jog…would…" she gasped for air, "…clear…"

"Our heads?"

She nodded, sweat pouring down her body.

Dan looked at his watch. "You did five more minutes, Kath."

She straightened and stared at him. "You timed me?"

"And you're making progress." How could he be so energized?

"I'm almost dead."

"It gets easier. It takes a month to build a habit. And if you'd change what you eat, you'd find it even easier." He was practically bouncing with enthusiasm.

"I don't want a jogging habit, Dan. And my diet is fine."

"I know. I just…" He paused, then seemed to accept what she'd said.

She held his gaze. "You'll never like champagne or dessert first, either. We can't change each other. Or for each other."

"True." His mouth twitched into a sad line.

She felt sad, too. And that wasn't good. "What are we doing, Dan? Are we in trouble here?"

"Maybe a little."

"Should we stop sleeping together? Is it too complicated?"

"Do you want to stop?" he asked. He clearly didn't.

"It's only three more days."

"Three and a half."

"Okay. Can we handle three-and-a-half more days?"

"We can try." He smiled, but it didn't quite reach his eyes.

"Okay then. Why don't you check my pulse?" She wanted to stop thinking about why this was wrong. She held out her arm and he pressed her wrist. She felt the welcome intimacy of her pulse fluttering against his fingertips. His chest expanded and released in time with her own. He focused on his watch and his lips moved as he counted. A trickle of perspiration slid down his temple.

On impulse, she leaned in to taste it.

He sucked in a breath and looked at her. "You made me lose count." He released her wrist and pulled her into his arms.

"Sex burns calories, if you do it right."

"And we sure do it right, don't we?" He gripped her cheeks in his exercise-hot hands and she melted again. There was something perfect about being here in the tree-filled park, traffic swishing like an ocean in the distance, mariachi music playing nearby, the smell of barbecue filling the air while they kissed until everything slipped away but the two of them.

"Know what I want right now?" she breathed in his ear.

"Me inside you?"

"A big frosty glass of weeds!" She pulled away, impressed with her willpower. It was worth it to keep him guessing.

"You're joking, right?"

"Hell, no. We're in the spirulina-date-shake capital of the world. Where they invented coffee colonics, spin classes and prosthetic butt cheeks. I'll race you to a designer-water bar."

In the end, they settled for ice cream in waffle cones at a small plaza not far from their hotel—strawberry for the vitamin C, at least.

"It's good we can be sensible," she said. "Sticking to our rules at least."

"What rules?"

"Like ending this when the trip ends, for one

thing." The idea of more time with Dan made her heart race.

"I guess."

She stopped moving and turned to look at him. "What are you saying. We'd be terrible together, Dan."

"Terrible," he echoed, not sounding so sure.

"We're in a haze of lust, so we're ignoring reality."

"Sure," he said, starting to walk again.

"Just think about how differently we spend our time," she said, keeping up with him. "You sitting around in a canoe on a lake just thinking? That would kill me."

"You might surprise yourself. And it's a sailboat, not a canoe."

"Whatever. The only sailing I like is with a crew and an on-board masseuse. You'd hate my life, Dan. I'm always traveling—scuba in Aruba, skiing in Switzerland, lazing in Bali, bar-hopping in Paris. You'd be meditating in the woods and I'd want to dance at a rave until three."

"People compromise."

She moved in front of him again. "Other people, Dan. Not us. We've staked our reputations on how differently we live."

"We share some things."

"Sex. We share that, all right."

"We both want to enhance people's lives—me as a therapist, you as a self-help author. We're both writers. You said there's self-discipline to being a sensuist, so there's that we have in common. We both like nature—you noted that."

"You're stretching the point, Dan."

"I could probably stand more adventure in my life. Maybe not all-night raves, but a trip to Bali wouldn't kill me. You've converted me to the massage thing—with the right masseuse, of course." He shot her his wry smile. "You said yourself you enjoyed the day we spent my way. You said it was 'comfortable.'"

"I was being nice," she said softly. "You're making too much out of not enough. I thought you were the pragmatist."

"People change."

"Not enough. And you don't really believe that." She couldn't afford to give the thought free rein or it would gallop them over a cliff. "Doesn't what's happening scare you?"

"Sure, but we can't ignore it. There's more than sex between us, Kathleen. Maybe we should do something about it."

But it couldn't last. It was a trick they played on each other just being who they were.

She noticed that pink cream had slid down the remnants of Dan's cone and would soon reach his hand, so she licked it, letting her tongue brush his finger.

His breath hissed in and she sucked the finger fully into her mouth. "Sex is our best thing, Dan. Let's not waste what little time we have left."

She watched as lust and stubbornness warred on his face. To tip the scale, she ran her tongue into the space between his fingers and he shuddered and closed his eyes.

"You win again," he breathed. "You put that tongue on me and all I want is to get inside you."

"Sounds good to me," she said. She grabbed the last of their cones and napkins and headed for a trashcan. When she returned, she found Dan standing before the blue-tiled water fountain in the center of the plaza.

"Tiny compared to the one in Chicago, huh?" she said.

He just smiled, reached into his pocket, and pulled out a dime. "Make a wish," he said, handing her the coin.

"Make a wish?"

"Yeah. Don't say I'm never spontaneous. Make a wish and toss the dime in the fountain."

She smiled, then considered the fountain, which consisted of three bowls, smaller as they went higher, in a thirty-foot pool. "All right," she said. "I have to get it in the top bowl."

"The top one? It's pretty small and very high."

"It can't be easy if the wish is going to come true."

"Then get closer at least." He walked her nearer the fountain, acting like a golf pro lining up a crucial shot. Even playing, Dan had to be serious.

She closed her eyes and made a wish that startled her: *Please don't let us hurt each other.* She held her breath, aimed, and tossed the coin. It spun, catching the light, twirled on the very edge of her target bowl, then dropped to the rim of the bottom bowl, pinged away and sank into the far side of the pool.

"You were robbed," Dan said. Then, to her amazement, he bent, pushed off his shoes and socks, climbed into the fountain and waded to where her dime had landed.

"Are you crazy?" she called to him.

"Maybe," he called back as water poured over his head. "But you like me that way, remember?"

"Yeah." She'd joked about jumping into the fountain in Chicago. It seemed an impossible thing he'd never do and here he was doing it right before her eyes. Without a word from her.

He bent down, searched the water and finally rose up, the dime extended triumphantly in the air. While she watched, he climbed onto the lip of the base bowl, then slid the dime into the top bowl, where she'd aimed.

"Wish accomplished." He stepped down, shaking diamonds of water from his hair, then grinned at her, looking just as he must have looked showing off for the pretty girl in math class.

In that moment, her heart aching with tenderness, Kathleen realized the terrible truth: She was in love with Dan. Still in love or newly in love? It hardly mattered. It was impossible and it meant trouble, but it was absolutely true.

So, what could she do but kick off her shoes, leap into the fountain and go to him? She threw her arms around his neck and kissed him. The water was icy, a crowd watched, but she didn't care. "Whatever possessed you?" she asked him.

"You. You possess me. You make me feel alive. You make me want to do crazy things just to see how they feel. I love you."

He pulled her into his arms, holding her tight, making the fountain their private waterfall, and for just that moment, she thought love was all that mattered.

"Hey, can I get your names?"

They broke apart at the voice. A man with a big camera wearing an ID badge was looking at them.

"Our names?" Dan repeated, wading with Kathleen to the edge of the pool.

"Yeah. For the paper. I took your photo."

"You photographed us?" Dan said. "We can't be in the paper."

"It was a great shot. Very spring. They'll run it in color." The guy was coaxing now. "Come on. Give me a caption."

"Thanks, anyway," Kathleen said. "We'll pass."

"Okay." The photographer shrugged and walked away.

"He won't use that, will he?" Dan asked.

"If he does, we'll be 'anonymous frolicking couple.' We're wet, there were shadows. Who could recognize us?" She hadn't given a thought to being seen together. In a place as huge as L.A., Rhonda had seemed the only person they had to watch for.

"Oh, who cares?" Dan said, smiling a loopy smile. "Maybe we should announce it at the press conference…tell everyone we're in love. Maybe it'll sell more books. Hell, I don't care about that anymore."

"Yes, you do," she said, shocked. "You care a lot." Had he flipped out completely? "You're not thinking clearly right now." Neither was she, obviously, because her heart had lifted with joy at his words.

"Maybe I'm thinking more clearly than I ever have in my life. I love you. You love me. That's as clear as it gets."

"Slow down, Dan. Think about your book, your career. We've got a lot to talk about. We can't tell anyone we're together just yet."

"Are we together, Kathleen? Can we be?"

"I don't know." The world seemed to tilt, then spin backward. Mercury must be retrograde or hypergrade or some kind of grade.

"What happened to being spontaneous?" Dan grinned drunkenly. "You love it when I'm spontaneous."

"At the right place and time."

"You sound like me, Kathleen. And I sound like you." He kissed her. "Poetic justice, I guess. But we can work it out. We're older and wiser and we love each other."

"God, Dan, you're giddy." The man and his emotions were barely on speaking terms and he was babbling about love and spontaneity? Dan wasn't a giddy guy. Except when he was in a toxic relationship. Like ten years ago.

She caught sight of a security guard headed their way. "Let's get going before we get arrested." She needed time to think. They gathered their shoes and took off, the sun not quite warm enough to kill the chill that went to her bones.

They went to her room, so she could blow her hair dry and dress. She urged Dan to go change, but he cheerfully stretched out on one of her beds, soggy and shivering and giddy.

Dan wanted them to be together. Wasn't that what she wanted? She thought about his face gleaming wet and brimming with love. What a glorious sight that was. She loved him, too. So why was her stomach tight with tension and her heart closed into a fist that barely moved the blood through her body?

She turned on the blow-dryer and tried to whistle something soothing. What was she afraid of? All the love she wanted was right outside that door. Why couldn't she just take it?

DAN SMILED, listening to Kathleen dry her hair. He would spend many future hours like this—waiting for her to primp and moisturize and overdo her beauty. Worth every minute.

He lay back on the bed and listened to her tuneless whistle and sniffed her complex smells—the creams and potions and mists she applied. He hoped he could convince her she was sweet-smelling enough without all that extra junk.

Except for moisturizers. He'd have to pry those from

her cold, dead, chapped fingers. He smiled, his teeth chattering from the cold. It was true that their lifestyles were opposite and their careers would be a problem—especially his. But a moderate life did not preclude love. He would just be sensible about it.

Sensible and *Kathleen* didn't belong in the same sentence, let alone the same life.

But maybe he needed some craziness mixed in with his serenity. He sure as hell felt more alive the last three days than he had in years. Extremely alive.

Too alive. Feverish with life. The thought edged under his defenses, a knife blade of reality. Look at him, trembling from cold and excitement. He was shaky, buzzed, high, as if he'd mainlined caffeine. He'd felt like this last time and it had distorted everything.

They were more mature, more settled now. They knew what they wanted. Except until two days ago the last thing he'd wanted had been Kathleen. She was too mercurial, too unpredictable and so restless. What made him think she'd stick around this time?

He wasn't quite himself, as Kathleen had said. Was this temporary? Lust-inspired? No. He loved her. They would work it out. Just as he'd said they would. He'd said it and he'd stick to it.

He turned his head and noticed the message light on Kathleen's phone was flashing. "You've got a message," he called to her.

"See if it's Rhonda," she yelled over the buzzing dryer.

He clicked into the message center, grabbing up the notepad on her nightstand to take notes.

"JJ here, Kath. Great news," the voice said. "Marketing is jazzed about the tell-all. Herman green-lighted it. He's checking with legal about possible libel issues, but he'll finesse it. Converting Dr. Moderate is just too juicy to resist. This is exactly what you need. I hate to say I told you so, but…that's why I get the big bucks… for you."

Dan took a deep breath and blew it out, his mind reeling. A tell-all? Tell-all about what? Converting Dr. Moderate, evidently. He couldn't believe what he'd just heard.

He searched the room for some anchor of normalcy to counteract the dizzy unreality that had seized him. He'd been falling in love with Kathleen and she'd been planning a book about their affair? Was this how he'd "helped" with her writing? It was too terrible to believe.

He became aware of the mechanical voice telling him to press numbers to delete or save, so he hung up. Why the hell had he picked up the phone? And, then again, thank God he had.

He looked down at the pad he'd grabbed to take a message and realized it was the one Kathleen had been using as a journal. What had she been writing, after all? Emboldened by her betrayal, he scanned the first page.

JJ would absolutely flip if she knew how close Dan and I came to having sex. In fact, this trying out each other's theories fits exactly with the idea of a conversion book. Wow.

Wow, indeed. He sat there stunned, holding her notepad. He'd been led by the nose—no, led by his lust—into her trap.

But this wasn't like Kathleen. She wasn't capable of faking this. She'd been as resistant to the affair and as relieved when they'd succumbed as he had. But maybe she'd changed from ten years ago. Maybe she wasn't so transparent anymore. *Sometimes our memories alter perceptions.* Right. He should start listening to his own advice.

He was still reeling when Kathleen emerged from the bathroom a few seconds later. "Was it Rhonda?" When she saw his face, her smile turned to alarm. "What's wrong? What happened?"

"It was JJ. Herman green-lighted your tell-all. It's too juicy to pass up."

"Oh, no." She paled, then reddened. "I can explain."

"This was all a setup for a book? Why, Kathleen? To punish me for what happened?"

"Stop it, Dan. That was JJ. I never agreed to it. I—"

"'Use the affair to build your book,'" he read from her notepad. "'The Pied Piper of Hedonism has converted Dr. Moderate to her religion of the senses.'"

"You read my journal?"

"I had to know the truth."

"You could have asked me, Dan." Anger flared in her eyes. "You think I would trick you? Not that I should have to explain, but in the journal I was being ironic and self-mocking. And, anyway, I got interrupted before I finished my thought."

"That wasn't irony in your agent's voice. That was triumph."

"My agent is a bulldog when she gets an idea in her head."

"When she called the other day, you said the book was going well…" That wasn't quite what she'd said, but he was floundering around, trying to put the puzzle together.

"I told her I was going in a different direction."

He looked at her, blinking, sorting it out. He'd been

distracted by her breasts at the time, but yeah, she had said something like that. "You're right."

"You sound disappointed."

"I'm not. I'm confused."

"You were ready to believe the worst, Dan." Her voice sounded dead. "You expected it. You had 'gotcha' all over your face when you accused me."

"The message was a shock. And I'd picked up the notepad to take a message, then noticed it was your journal. I was upset, so I read it. Anyone would be confused."

"Not someone who trusted me."

"Kathleen…" Except she was right. Hearing the message and reading the confirmation in her journal had been an ah-ha. *Here is how it will go bad. This is the way she'll wreck you.* As if the other shoe had finally dropped. "We have a difficult history," he said, trying to explain.

"Difficult? You don't know the half of it." Her eyes reddened, and she blinked rapidly, fighting tears. Her cheeks were pale with angry splashes of red. "I'm not brave or resilient like you think I am. When you left me, I lost it. I went numb like after my accident. I fell apart."

"So did I, Kathleen. We're both scared. Maybe we just need more time." But her words had registered and his faltered.

"More time will only make it worse. This can't last. You're not yourself and neither am I. Maybe I'm tougher and braver and smarter than I was ten years ago, but I don't want to have to prove it."

"We're different now."

"Not different enough. We shouldn't have been together in the first place. You said it yourself—we brought out the worst in each other. You needed me close and I needed to breathe. Why would that change?"

"For one thing, we're talking about it now instead of running away."

"You ran away, Dan. And we're talking now, but that's a phase. Face it, we don't trust each other. We *want* each other, Dan. That's it. Why do you have to make it bigger? Sex is a perfectly respectable thing to share. You have to make it a noble cause so you won't feel guilty about feeling ordinary human lust."

That stung. So he struck back. "Tell yourself whatever you want, but don't blame this on me. For all your talk about being open and free, you're locked up tight as a safe, Kathleen. The minute I said I wanted us to be together you started backing away. 'We have to talk, don't tell anyone,' and all that."

"I can't go through that again." Her voice shook and her eyes shone with tears and anger and fear. He'd never seen her so upset. "You reach me in places no one else does, Dan," she said softly, "but whether that's love or need or nostalgia, I don't know. All I know is that seeing the anger on your face, hearing you accuse me, tells me we're worlds apart. We've had a great time. But that's all we get. We'd just make each other miserable."

He wanted to argue, but her words rang with truth. He wasn't himself—jumping into fountains, ready to announce he was in love to reporters when his book had barely reached the shelves. And he *had* been braced for it to fall apart. How would he feel in a few weeks? He had no way to tell.

"Some relationships carry too much weight," he said finally. The words felt as true as his love for her had seemed just a short hour before.

"Too much weight…yeah. Like cement shoes." Her voice sounded dead. "Better to know now. Before we try for a swim and drown." She snatched her lip between her teeth, looking so vulnerable and sad that he wanted to pull her into his arms and tell her it would be all right.

It wouldn't, though. Not with their history, not with their differences, not with their confused emotions.

The phone rang and they both jumped. Kathleen half stumbled to the bed to accept the receiver from him. "Hello?... Hi, Rhonda.... No problem. We'll meet you... I'm sure. Really. Work things out with Dylan. I'll tell Dan... I'm fine. I understand. We both do... What...? I'm just tired. Bad mattresses." She handed him the receiver and he saw that tears had spilled down her cheeks.

His own eyes burned with emotion. But this was for the best. He'd likely lose himself again with Kathleen, a woman who could change her heart...on a dime.

"What did you wish?" he asked abruptly. "At the fountain."

"It's bad luck to tell." She tried a shaky smile. "But it didn't come true, so why not? I wished that we wouldn't hurt each other."

"Interesting. Because I made a wish, too. I wished that we could find a way to be together."

"Looks like neither one came true," she said, her voice rough. "You moved my dime for nothing. But I guess you can't make a wish come true. It has to happen on its own."

You can try, though, his stubborn heart told him. *You can always try.* Except neither of them was brave enough for that, so he kept the thought to himself.

14

KATHLEEN WAS GRATEFUL for the back-to-back media interviews that kept her and Dan busy for the next few hours. They managed decently, Dan speaking about the magic of moderation, she praising the power of pleasure, though the words were mush in her mouth and she felt fuzzy and sad.

For his part, Dan looked rumpled and puzzled. He kept running his fingers through his hair and asking reporters to repeat their questions. So much for her wish that they wouldn't hurt each other. They were both wrecked.

Tomorrow they'd head for San Francisco. The three-day conference would be the last they'd see of each other. It would be a relief to be away from him and the constant reminder of all the glorious love they'd made. Every time she looked into his blue eyes, stormy with pain, she felt worse.

Dan was right. There was too much weight, too much hurt, too much history between them. They'd been living on infatuation and adrenaline for the past few days.

At least they'd stopped themselves before they did something crazy like announce their relationship to the world. She shuddered to think about the crisis that would have caused.

And even if they could get beyond their history and their careers could sustain the blow, there were her own doubts about staying with one man for the rest of her life. Even if she could do that, she'd never choose a man so obstinate, so smug, so…

…sweet and challenging and tender. Who knew her so well.

Stop it. Stop it, right now. She couldn't think too long or she got that bruised and lonely feeling again. She wanted to curl up in a hot, hot bath with the best champagne and nibble a truffle so slowly her bathwater would be cold before she finished it.

She wanted to slow-dance to Aaron Neville and put glitter on her eyelids and cherry gloss on her lips and get one of those giant plastic rings that made soap bubbles the size of your head and let the shimmering globes pop on her face.

She wanted to wrap herself in her plushest robe inside out—why did they put the softest part on the outside?—and cry her eyes out.

On the cab ride back to the hotel, Rhonda leaned over the back seat. "You guys were kinda subdued," she said, looking at them each in turn. "Halfhearted…maybe bored? What happened to the energy you had this morning at KBUZ?"

"We're tired." Kathleen said. "It's been a long, long death march of a book tour."

"Not to mention all the—"

"Bad mattresses," Kathleen and Dan said together. The smile they exchanged was bittersweet.

"No. It's my fault," Rhonda said, not even smiling at their joke. She sighed as if guilty of a crime. "I've been too preoccupied with Dylan and I've neglected you."

"We've been fine," Dan said. "Really."

"We encouraged you to see him," Kathleen added. "It's us, not you, believe me."

"No. It's my job and I let you down." Her cell phone trilled. "Just a sec," she said to them, then fished out her phone. "Hello? Dylan? Oh, hi… No, I can't—" she glanced at them "—I'm in the middle of something."

"Talk to him," Kathleen whispered. "Please."

"Thank you," she mouthed, then plopped back into the front seat to talk with Dylan.

Kathleen and Dan released separate sighs of relief and turned to look out their respective windows.

Back in her hotel room, Kathleen left a firm message at JJ's office about not, repeat, *not* doing a tell-all book. Then she tried to work on her book, but it was a struggle. *Do what you want,* she wanted to write. *Enjoy or withdraw, indulge your passions or deny them, I don't know what works anymore.*

What if she'd killed her book…even lost her mission? And all because she'd jumped into something with Dan she had no business doing.

Then she felt what she'd dreaded—numbness, seeping up like frostbite. Just like ten years ago, just like after the accident.

She would not go through that again, dammit. She couldn't afford to. She had to do something to reverse it, but what? Her desperate gaze fell on her notepad journal, which lay on the floor near the wall, where she'd tossed it in disgust after Dan left.

She'd enjoyed writing in it, despite the trouble it had just caused. She'd used it for personal worries and speculation and irony. Maybe writing in it would help. She picked it up, opened it to a fresh page and opened her heart to whatever feelings rose.

She started writing about the days with Dan, the words coming slowly at first, then faster, then furiously until her fingers burned from the strain. She wrote about dancing to Thelonius Monk, the ice-cold shower in the whirlpool bath, somersaulting in the grass, the sash around her eyes, Dan hiding in her bathtub while Rhonda ate the ice cream he'd ordered to lick off her body, Dan climbing the fountain to place that dime in the top bowl, and, of course, the hours and hours of lovemaking.

And it worked. The writing pushed back the numbness. Of course it drew tears, too, but she swept them off her cheeks and kept at it. Memories could alter reality, as Dan had said, but they could also save you.

AT LEAST the flight to San Francisco was short, Dan noted, as Kathleen's head lolled on his shoulders. She'd fallen asleep right after takeoff and her head had drifted toward him. Now her hair brushed his chin, her soft breath warmed his neck and her scent filled his head.

He should move her, but he wanted these few innocent moments. He was a wreck, so messed up that he'd actually gone through his clothes until he found a shirt that smelled of her perfume, then turned the room's radio to jazz and flopped onto his bed to sniff the shirt and mope.

This was far worse than last time. So much for his years of self-control and moderation. Kathleen had blown through his barriers like so much smoke.

"You guys look cute together." Rhonda's voice came to him across the aisle.

"Huh?" He realized she meant Kathleen lying on his shoulder. "I didn't want to wake her."

"I can't believe the tour's almost over. It's been so fun working with you. Dylan's coming, too, did I tell you?" Which explained her dreamy happiness. "He'll be there in time for your opening remarks. I want you to meet him. He's got an appointment at a record company this morning, or he'd be flying up with us."

The poor woman was in a daze. He wanted to warn her to watch out, take it slow, not to jump to conclusions, but he was in no position to give advice. "I hope things work out for you."

He had new appreciation for patients who struggled with love. Never again would he sound paternal or smug or above it all. He was right in there with them, stumbling around in the emotional muck, trying to make sense of it all.

Let Rhonda enjoy her moment of joy. He sure as hell intended to enjoy every second of Kathleen on his shoulder, every breath against his neck, every hair tickling his chin. No longer would he deny himself things he really wanted. No matter what else had happened, Kathleen had taught him that.

THE HOTEL was jammed, noisy and chaotic with conferees when they arrived, a welcome distraction from Kathleen's own troubles. She was in okay shape, though, she noted with pride. She'd fought off her misery by writing about it. Sure, she felt sad and lonely and hurt, but she wasn't numb or empty. She'd become more solid over the years, more sure of who she was. And that was important—the silver lining to the black cloud of the breakup.

The three of them checked in, then Rhonda set off to

meet Dylan's plane. She had details about their speeches that she promised to go over when she returned.

Once in her room, Kathleen unpacked, then settled in to look over her notes. She and Dan would be speaking to an audience of two thousand therapists, counselors and self-help gurus. This was the culmination of their tour, the big moment, and she intended to make the best of it. The work was what counted, after all. They'd agreed about that from the beginning.

She called Dan's room to compare notes about their shared portion of the agenda. She preferred talking on the phone to meeting in person. Sitting close and looking into his eyes hurt too much. She'd pretended to fall asleep on the plane just for a few stolen moments of resting on his solid body. Silly, but, dammit, where was the harm?

They talked at length about their debate and she felt proud of the team they'd become. When they focused on work, they were fine. Too bad they hadn't had the sense to stick with that.

Finished, they breathed at each other for a few seconds. She didn't want to hang up. Neither did he, it seemed, so they engaged in small talk about their last bad mattresses and other ridiculously petty subjects. It was stupid, but, again, where was the harm? Time flew by and when she glanced at her watch, she realized they were soon due to speak.

Where was Rhonda with the changes?

When there was no answer in her room, Kathleen and Dan headed for the conference center to at least connect with the coordinator. They were fighting their way through the crowd milling in the lobby, when Kathleen spotted Rhonda in a booth in the lobby bar, staring into a coffee mug.

She led Dan to the spot. "Rhonda?"

Rhonda lifted a sad face and shiny eyes. "Oh. Hi. I was just coming to get you." She sniffed and fumbled with a cocktail napkin she'd shredded.

Kathleen slid into the bench beside her. "What happened?"

"It's nothing." Her lip wobbled. "Dylan missed his plane." She tried to smile.

"So he'll get the next flight like last time, right?" Kathleen looked up at Dan, who slid into the opposite banquette.

"That's just it. He changed his mind. He's heading back to Chicago for a gig. He sounds different. Nervous. I just know he's flaking out on me again." She gulped down some coffee, then offered the cup to Kathleen, who shook her head no.

"Did you talk to him?" Kathleen asked.

"You warned me, Dan," she said, lifting miserable eyes to him. "He's toxic to me. Pure strychnine. I should have listened to you, but I went with my heart."

"Like I told you to do," Kathleen said, feeling punched in the gut. She'd basically ordered poor Rhonda into a romantic head-on collision. How could she have been so arrogant, so glib?

"Mark left me a message, though," she said, twining the ratty napkin like a washrag, still talking to Dan. "I think he'll take me back." She looked as shrunken and miserable as a cat in the rain, her big eyes brimming with moisture.

"Mark sounds like a good guy," Kathleen said, wanting to make up for her crime. "Passion can be overrated. Compatibility is what really counts, right, Dan?"

"Mark is not what you want," Dan said, making

Kathleen drop her jaw. "He's a consolation prize. Dylan's the man you love."

Rhonda's gaze shot to his. She blinked. "But you said Dylan was emotionally dangerous to me...and memories change reality...and that I should set limits."

"Maybe I don't know what the hell I'm talking about. You shouldn't let someone go because you're afraid it won't work. You might not get a second chance. Or it might come too late."

He was talking about them, too, she could tell. "But you have to be careful," Kathleen said, her heart aching. "Dylan and you have a bad history."

"But maybe Dylan does have work in Chicago," Dan insisted. "Maybe he was clumsy and stupid about explaining it. Maybe he's nervous. This is new for him. Give him a chance to prove he's changed."

"But people don't really change," Rhonda said.

"But they can grow up a little, see other points of view, accept people for who they are, not who they want them to be."

"Or maybe they see themselves more clearly," Kathleen said, feeling a warmth ease through her body from her toes upward. "Maybe love gives them the courage to be honest with themselves."

"Maybe they need to be both careful and reckless," Dan said, smiling a little. His eyes met hers.

"Careful when it's dangerous and reckless when it's safe?" Kathleen added.

"Really?" Rhonda asked in a wobbly voice.

"Of course that's not easy to do when everything in you wants to retreat to a comfortable corner," Dan said. "But life is supposed to be lived, not observed. A harbor is safe, but that's not what boats are for."

"Talk to Dylan," Kathleen chimed in. "Ask him to level with you about how he feels. If he knows that you really want the truth, he'll tell you. And you're sturdy enough to take it."

Rhonda twisted to look Kathleen straight on. "You're different." She turned back to Dan. "You, too. What's going on?"

They looked at each other, then away. Kathleen didn't know what to say. She wasn't even sure what she felt. The hope was too new, the lifting joy too fragile.

"Kathleen Dubinofsky?!"

She looked up to see a woman she remembered from journalism school at ASU. "Janie?" Janie Laramie. One of the most persistent reporters on staff at the ASU student paper. Fear rippled through Kathleen. What if Janie remembered her with Dan?

"How are you doing?" Janie asked.

"I'm great. You?"

"I'm good. So, what are you doing here? You live in San Francisco?"

"No. San Diego. I'm here for the psychology conference," she said, hoping she wouldn't have to elaborate.

"Me, too. I'm covering it for the *L.A. Times*. You?"

"I'm not a reporter. I'm actually, um, speaking." Janie would find out soon enough.

"Really? You're speaking?" Janie's reporter antennae went on full alert.

"Yes, and don't we need to head over there now?" she asked Rhonda, longing for one of her peppy rescues.

"Huh?" Rhonda said.

"We have to go, right?" She gestured with her eyes.

"Oh, uh, yeah. That's right."

"Nice to see you," Kathleen said, whipping out of the bench and backing away from Janie.

"I'll call your room. We can catch up," Janie called out.

"Sure. Great idea." Except she wasn't registered under Dubinofsky, so that would slow Janie down. All for the best.

As they ran for the conference hall, Rhonda told them about the change in format—tonight would be a brief speech; the debate would occur during the morning's opening session. And, before long, she and Dan had been hustled backstage and up to chairs behind two lecterns on opposite sides of the stage.

As they sat, Dan smiled a smile like a warm hand of comfort on her back. Could they get beyond their history? Their differences? Count on each other? Compromise?

Her mind fogged, her thoughts blurred. She looked out at the audience and felt panic rise. She had to find a way to stay focused and clear-headed. Dan's meditation advice rose in her mind, so she tried the little game of Frogger, closing her eyes and taking deep slow breaths. *Notice your thoughts, but don't hitch a ride.*

She was amazed that it worked and she calmed right down. *Five minutes faster,* she could almost hear Dan say to cheer her on. *Thirty days to build a new habit.*

She smiled. Her peace restored, she set aside her heartbreak, her confusion and her new hope and listened while the conference chair read their introductions.

After the applause, she and Dan approached their separate podiums. They usually stood elbow to elbow, so this felt lonely, but she smiled and spoke a little about the Pleasure Principle, the DNA lattice of endorphins, the puritanical bent of those who opposed her.

Then Dan took over. This time Kathleen found herself really listening. And his theories didn't sound so awful to her just now. Maybe he'd mellowed over the tour...or maybe there was a place for restraint in every life—even hers.

Hadn't she been rushing from experience to experience, avoiding people and their feelings, just as she'd blurted to Rhonda?

Dan's stability wasn't so terrible, really. In fact, his calm dispassion when problems arose was reassuring.

And he would be there for her. She knew that now as surely as she knew gravity ruled. Yes, his eyes held cool distance, but she could reach the passionate man behind those icy blues. What about his possessiveness? She'd contributed to that by being elusive.

She'd been scared. She still was. Was she closed off emotionally, as Dan said? Perhaps she hadn't quite healed from her childhood accident. She'd certainly stayed clear of close relationships all her life.

And each time her heart had swelled with love for Dan, she'd stuffed the feeling down, like a sleeping bag in a stuff sack, kept it small and safe, told herself how impossible he was. She'd been afraid to get hurt, to depend too much on love.

But who would be more dependable than Dan? She watched his strong face as he spoke and thought of its softness when they made love. He was afraid to be vulnerable around her. And no wonder, considering how quickly she backed away.

Ten years ago, he'd run. This time he'd stay. She could feel it deep inside her, in the same solid place that told her there was one man she could stay interested in for the rest of her life. Dan.

"I believe we can take a few questions...?" Dan turned to the emcee, who nodded.

"Here!" The bright lights kept the audience dark, but by shading her eyes Kathleen could make out a woman with her arm held high. "Janie Laramie, *L.A. Times*."

Janie? Lord. And with a definite "gotcha" in her voice. Kathleen froze.

"Yes?" Dan said, shooting a look at Kathleen.

"I understand you two have been debating your theories across the country, correct?"

"Yes," Dan said.

"You are, in effect, opponents?"

"That's true," Kathleen answered.

"So, how do you explain this photo?" Janie waved a newspaper in the air. "It shows you two standing together in a fountain. Kissing."

Surprised murmurs washed the room.

"How can we explain it?" Dan said, looking at Kathleen, asking her what to say.

The truth would reflect worse on Dan, she knew, so she tried to fix it. "I dropped something in the fountain and Dr. McAlister gallantly got it for me." This much was true. "And, in my grateful enthusiasm, I...embraced him." Her voice wavered, her words went weak. It hurt to lie about that.

"So, you're saying this is a kiss of gratitude?" Jane said sharply. She had walked closer to the stage until she stood equidistant between Kathleen and Dan. She extended the paper.

Dan and Kathleen met at the edge of the stage and Kathleen lifted the newspaper so they could both look at it.

In the photo, they were soaked, hair and clothes clinging to their bodies. She stood on tiptoe, her arms around Dan's neck while he held her tight. The kiss looked like pure bliss. She looked from the photo to Dan, whose ice-blue eyes were now a warm summer lake.

"Not at all," Dan said firmly, not even looking at the paper. He looked straight at her and said, "This is the kiss of two people who are madly in love with each other."

She looked at him, at his dear face, serious and somber and lit with love. Love could free you and love could make you safe. But she wasn't sure Dan knew what he was saying. There was still so much confusion. Even if they were in love, even if they could be together, they were still in a haze. "Dan, don't say…too much."

"It's okay. Come on." He took the paper in one hand, put his arm around her waist and led her to his lectern. "We have been opponents, Ms. Laramie," he said. "In fact, we've tried to convince each other to change our theories, adopt each other's views. In the course of that effort, I changed my mind about some things. Kathleen has shown me that life must be enjoyed, not boiled to mush."

The crowd erupted in noise.

She couldn't believe it. Dan was practically throwing his career away in front of two thousand people. But he didn't look crazed or possessed. He looked calm and happy.

If he could be that open, that brave, then she could, too. She leaned into the microphone to open her heart for the first time since her childhood.

"And Dan changed me, too. He showed me I've been shut down. I've spent my life focusing on experiences, not people. On sex, not love. On getting a man to want me, not letting him love me."

"Kathleen," Dan said, clearly amazed at the words coming out of her mouth. She'd admitted she was wrong to an auditorium of strangers. So not like her. And also exactly her.

"It's true. You taught me that a pleasure shared with someone you love is pleasure multiplied beyond measure."

She watched his whole face light up. "You're good for me, Dan. Every kite needs a string or it flies off forever." She turned into his arms and cupped his face.

Dan placed his palms on each of her cheeks, in her at-the-altar pose and she could imagine their private vows: *To love, honor and cherish. For better, for worse. In wildness and restraint. In meditation and abandon. In wheatgrass smoothie and butterscotch shake. 'Til death us do part.* It was all there in his blue, blue eyes.

"I love you, Kathleen," Dan said and they kissed, gentle and sweet, with forever in every second. Her heart pounded so hard with happiness that she barely heard the roar of applause.

She let herself really feel their embrace—not just the glory of muscle and pressure and warmth, but the love beneath—the tenderness, the concern, the enchantment, the support…its real power.

She looked into the face of the man she loved and realized she'd been wrong as a child. Sometimes love endured.

"What does this mean about your careers? Your books?" Janie called up. She had to be loving this scoop.

"We'll see," Dan answered, not taking his eyes from Kathleen's face. "We'll work it out."

There was a flurry of questions and even more once they left the podium. Their agents were soon on the line, demanding to know exactly what they thought they were doing.

There was irritation, puzzlement, a little anger, then the gradual conclusion that this could be good. They could write a book together. A split-down-the-middle book, using their life together as the living model of compromise and completion.

Somehow in the madness, they became separated, but Kathleen made her way to her room, knowing Dan would find her. She turned on the water for a very hot bath. She wouldn't need glitter or soap bubbles the size of her head. She only needed Dan.

She'd been soaking for a few minutes when someone banged on the door. The knock was too noisy and uneven for Dan, so she threw on a robe to answer.

But it was him. And his arms were loaded with a big bottle of ginger ale, some bedraggled flowers and a giant bag of M&Ms.

"No champagne or truffles in the gift shop and the flowers were left over from a wedding, but you get the idea."

He put his offerings on the table and took her into his arms. "We can do whatever crazy thing you want. Blindfolds or chocolate-covered strawberries or run naked down the street… Well, maybe not run naked down the street…"

"It's okay," she said, sliding her fingers into his hair, looking in his eyes. "We don't have to do crazy stuff…all the time, any way." She grinned.

"I'm a little scared, you know."

"Me, too. But when two people love each other, being vulnerable is a sign of strength, not weakness."

"Yeah. I see that, I guess. I'll try not to smother you."

"You won't have to because I won't push you away. I think I'll like a few quiet evenings of reading and meditation, as long as we end them making love. Of course you running naked down the street, that could be delicious."

"Would you settle for the ice-machine alcove? I think there's room for two bodies." His voice was husky with heat.

"Not this time. I want a bed where we can be naked and noisy."

"Mmm, perfect." He kissed her, then broke off. "Where will we live? New England's gorgeous in the fall."

"My condo's two minutes from the beach."

"So we trade off until we decide?"

"Deal." She was surprised at how little their differences mattered to her. They would work it out. When you loved each other, you did that.

And then they kissed and it was sensual and tender and Kathleen's heart tipped up and spilled over. The book tour from hell had given her insane pace, toxic airplane food and far too many bad mattresses.

But it had also given her true love. Which made it, hands down, the best book tour ever.

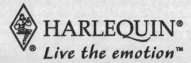

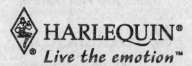

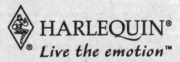